CRITICAL PRAISE FOR *SLIGHTLY SINGLE* BY

# Wendy Markham

"...an undeniably fun journey for the reader."
—*Booklist*

"Bridget Jonesy...Tracey Spadolini smokes, drinks
and eats too much, and frets about her romantic life."
—*Publishers Weekly*

"This is a delightfully humorous read,
full of belly laughs and groans... It is almost scary
how honest and true to life this book is. It is a fun read
for a beach day, or a steamy evening in one's own
un-air-conditioned abode like Tracey's."
—*The Best Reviews*

D017Ø4Ø7

## WENDY MARKHAM

is a pseudonym for *USA TODAY* bestselling, award-winning novelist Wendy Corsi Staub, who has written more than fifty fiction and nonfiction books for adults and teenagers in various genres—among them contemporary and historical romance, suspense, mystery, television and movie tie-in and biography. She has coauthored a hardcover mystery series with former New York City mayor Ed Koch and has ghostwritten books for various well-known personalities. A small-town girl at heart, she was born and raised in western New York on the shores of Lake Erie and in the heart of the notorious snowbelt. By third grade, she was set on becoming a published author; a few years later, a school trip to Manhattan convinced her that she had to live there someday. At twenty-one, she moved alone to New York City and worked as an office temp, freelance copywriter, advertising account coordinator and book editor before selling her first novel, which went on to win a Romance Writers of America RITA® Award. She has since received numerous positive reviews and achieved bestseller status, most notably for the psychological suspense novels she writes under her own name. She was a finalist in the 2002 *Romantic Times* Reviewer's Choice Awards single-title suspense category, and her previous Red Dress Ink title, *Slightly Single,* was honored as one of Waldenbooks' Best Books of 2002. Very happily married with two children, Wendy writes full-time and lives in a cozy old house in suburban New York, proving that childhood dreams really can come true.

# Slightly Settled

Wendy Markham

RED
DRESS
INK™

If you purchased this book without a cover you should be aware
that this book is stolen property. It was reported as "unsold and
destroyed" to the publisher, and neither the author nor the
publisher has received any payment for this "stripped book."

First edition February 2004

SLIGHTLY SETTLED

A Red Dress Ink novel

ISBN 0-373-25047-9

© 2004 by Wendy Corsi Staub.

All rights reserved. The reproduction, transmission or utilization
of this work in whole or in part in any form by any electronic, mechanical
or other means, now known or hereafter invented, including xerography,
photocopying and recording, or in any information storage or retrieval
system, is forbidden without written permission. For permission please
contact Red Dress Ink, Editorial Office, 225 Duncan Mill Road,
Don Mills, Ontario, Canada M3B 3K9.

This book is a work of fiction. The names, characters, incidents and places
are the products of the author's imaginaton, and are not to be construed
as real. While the author was inspired in part by actual events, none of the
characters in the book is based on an actual person. Any resemblance to
persons living or dead is entirely coincidental and unintentional.

® and TM are trademarks. Trademarks indicated with ® are registered in
the United States Patent and Trademark Office, the Canadian Trade Marks
Office and/or other countries.

Visit Red Dress Ink at www.reddressink.com

**Printed in U.S.A.**

For both of my beloved Jens:

Jennie King Eldridge, who was by my side
at the fateful office party, where the story began...
And Jennifer Hill, who has been there for Chapter Two:
Married Life in Suburbia.

And, as always, for Mark, Morgan and Brody, with love.

1

Size eight.

That would be me, Tracey Spadolini. A size *eight*.

Can you believe it?

No, not my shoe size. My size, *size*.

I'm actually wearing a size eight dress—*without* one of those stretchy tourniquet tummy bulge compressors I used to live in—and I'm not even holding my breath.

When I started my summer diet, I figured I had about forty pounds to lose. But I'm down at least fifty, melted off with good old-fashioned diet and exercise, and kept off thanks to the little pink pills I take daily.

No, not the kind of little pink pills in a plastic baggie that you buy in a dark alley.

We're talking a prescribed drug here.

Officially, I'm taking it to stave off panic attacks.

According to the pharmacy's insert, potential side effects

included diarrhea, constipation and severe flatulence. Not pretty, right? So I spent the first few medicated days close to home, not wanting to find myself on the crowded subway with a severe case of the runs—or, worse, uncontrollable gas.

But I've had nary a disgraceful rumble or abdominal cramp. In fact, aside from banishing my anxiety, the pink pills have brought on only one glorious side effect: a diminished appetite.

Happy Pills, my friend Buckley calls them.

He's the one who referred me to the shrink in the first place, after the whole anxiety thing started this past summer. I thought I was just freaking out because my boyfriend, Will, had abandoned me. Technically, Will was away doing summer stock, but, essentially, he abandoned me.

Anyway, after a few sessions Dr. Schwartzenbaum suggested that although Will's leaving probably triggered the panic attacks, I might have an underlying chemical imbalance. That must be true, because I've been on the medication for almost two months now, and haven't had a single panic attack. Factor in that I'm rarely hungry and *voilà*—Happy Pills.

Back to the dress: scarlet and snug; a slinky cocktail dress with a high hem and a low bodice that, last June, would have revealed alpine cleavage. But I certainly don't mind that my boobs shrank along with the rest of me. In fact, I barely notice. I'm too busy admiring my protruding collarbones—the protruding collarbones I've coveted on many an award-show red-carpet walker.

"Tracey?" Kate Delacroix taps on the dressing room door.

"It fits!" I squeal, turning away from the trio of full-length mirrors only for the second it takes to open the door and allow Kate to poke her blond head in.

"Wow. Tracey, you look ravishing in that."

*Ravishing.* There are very few people who can get away with using a word like that and come across as genuine. Kate is one of them, Southern drawl and all.

Embarrassed that she might have caught my admiring gaze at my own reflection, I make an attempt to portray uncertainty.

I shrug. Tilt my head. Pretend to ponder. "Oh…I don't know. I mean, I look okay, but…"

My jutting collarbones might be red-carpet-worthy, but an actress, I'm not. My brown eyes are still enraptured by the mirror, and I can't seem to keep an exultant grin from tilting the corners of my—um, chapped lips.

Okay, it's possible that I've been so focused on myself from the neck down that I've neglected the rest of me.

*Mental Note: buy ChapStick at Duane Reade on the way home.*

*P.S. Make appointment for lip wax ASAP.*

*P.P.S. Haircut, too.*

Back to skinny, ravishing below-the-neck *moi.* I look ten times better in this dress than I did in the silky teal shirt I wore into the dressing room. Kate gave the shirt to me for my birthday. It has a designer label and I know it cost her a fortune. But the cut and color are all wrong. Her taste is expensive, but not necessarily good. At least, not when it comes to others.

Kate's big on teal. Aqua, too. Shades that complement her bluish-green colored contact lenses and year-round tanning salon glow. Shades that seem to cast the same sickly tint to my skin that fluorescent lighting does.

Naturally, I told Kate that I love the shirt. Naturally, I feel compelled to wear it. But only to places like the ladies' dress department in Bloomingdale's, where the chances of meeting a potential boyfriend are about the same as finding one strolling along Christopher Street in Greenwich Village on a Saturday night.

"You don't think this dress is too skimpy for a corporate Christmas party?" I ask Kate now, tugging the hem southward.

She dismisses the query with a wave of one French-manicured hand. "Nah."

"Are you sure? Because the last thing I want to do is look cheap."

"Tracey, that dress is almost two hundred bucks on sale. It's not cheap."

"I know, but sometimes expensive things can look— Kate, what the hell are you wearing?"

She shrugs.

I grab her arm and pull her all the way into the dressing room.

"That's a wedding gown!" I accuse.

"Yup."

"Are you and Billy…?" Still clutching her white-satin-encased arm with price tags dangling, I jerk it up to examine her fourth finger for a telltale diamond.

Nothing.

Kate is unfazed. "I'm thinking we'll get engaged at Christmas. He's coming to Mobile with me to meet my parents and…well, he knows I'm not going to keep living with him forever without a commitment."

"Forever? Kate, it's been three months."

Will McCraw and I were together three years. Three *years*, and instead of moving in together, we broke up. To be blunt, he dumped me. No, first he cheated, *then* he dumped me. And when he did, I passed out cold. Literally. I collapsed in an undignified, heartbroken heap on the parquet floor of his twenty-sixth-floor studio apartment.

But that was almost three months ago.

A lot can happen in three months.

Clearly, Kate thinks so. She sways her narrow hips slightly, the long white skirt rustling above her pedicured toes as she undoubtedly imagines herself at her reception in Billy's arms.

I glance down at her feet. Pretty pink polished toenails in the dead of November. Huh. That Kate sure thinks of everything. I don't even shave my legs at this time of year unless I think somebody's going to see them.

Maybe that explains why she's standing there in a wedding gown with a damned good chance of becoming a bride momentarily, while I don't even have a date for the Blaire Barnett Christmas party next weekend.

But I'm not the only one. Brenda isn't bringing her husband and Yvonne isn't bringing her fiancé and Latisha isn't bringing her boyfriend. It's going to be Girls' Night Out— to celebrate my triumphant return to the ad agency.

I quit my job back in September; in fact, on the same day the dumping/fainting incident took place. But Blaire Barnett, unlike Will, wanted me back.

What happened was this: the temp secretary who replaced me filed a sexual harassment suit against my ex-boss, Jake. Long story short, he wound up getting fired, and they offered me my old position back.

I was reluctant to take it, because I was making more money working for Eat Drink Or Be Married, a Manhattan caterer. But waitressing is hard, dirty work, it encompassed my nights and weekends and there were no benefits. Besides, I missed my old friends at Blaire Barnett; I was offered more money, and they promised me the opportunity to interview for the next junior copywriting job that opens up over in the Creative Department. Meaning I won't be a secretary—or broke—forever.

All in all, it's good to be back.

In fact, all in all, there's not much about my life right now that isn't good. My regular life, that is. My love life is a different story. The kind without a happy ending. At least, so far.

Kate—currently a vision in Happy Ending—gathers her long blond hair on her head with one hand while running the other along the row of satin-covered buttons at her back, feeling for gaps.

I step toward her, my legs engulfed in yards of swishy white, and attempt to fasten two buttons near her tailbone. It isn't easy. They're slippery, and the size of those mini M&M's I haven't had since July.

She says, "I swear, Tracey, three months is long enough to live together without a commitment. If Billy doesn't get me a ring for Christmas, I'll be shocked."

"So will I."

"I thought you just said—"

"It's only been three months. That's what I said. I didn't say I don't think you and Billy should get engaged."

Nor did I say that I like Billy about as much as I like the teal silk hanging on the hook above my head. Kate is my friend, and Billy—like that ugly designer blouse—comes with the territory.

Besides, I can't help wondering if maybe I'd be rooting for Kate and Billy if I had somebody, too. It isn't easy to watch your best friend fall madly in love when two complete seasons have turned since you last had sex.

"Raphael doesn't think I should have moved in with Billy," she says, as I triumphantly manage to hook one minibutton into its microscopic loop. "He said something about Billy not wanting to buy the cow when he's getting the latte for free."

I roll my eyes, muttering, "Raphael has given out so much free latte, he should have Starbucks stamped on his, um, *udder.*"

"Tracey!" Kate giggles. "Raphael is the first to admit he's a slut, especially now that he's not with Wade anymore."

"He was a slut even when he was with Wade," I point out.

"Exactly. But he has old-fashioned standards when it comes to me—"

"And me," I interject.

"Right. He wants to marry off both of us, so that we can make him an uncle."

"He said that?"

"He *said* aunt. Auntie, to be specific."

"Oh, Lord. I can see it now. Auntie Raphael." I shake my head. Raphael is one of my best friends, but he's definitely out there. In a good way, of course.

"Whatever you do, Trace, don't tell Billy what Raphael said."

"About the free latte?"

"About being the aunt to our future kids. He'd probably consider that grounds for a vasectomy. You know how he is about gays."

Gays. That's what conservative Billy calls Raphael and his kind.

*His kind* being another charming Billy phrase.

What Kate sees in him, I'll never know. Yes, he's as beautiful as she is, and yes, he's rich as a Trump. But he's shallow, and opinionated and ultraconservative—the latter being his worst crime, as far as I'm concerned.

I was raised in Brookside, New York, a small town so far upstate that it might as well be in the Midwest. The people there—including my own family—are overwhelmingly blue-collar Catholic Republicans.

Billy might be a white-collar Presbyterian Republican, but there's little difference between him and my great-aunt Domenica, who is convinced that homosexuals will burn in hell alongside Bill Clinton and the entire membership of Planned Parenthood.

"Speaking of Raphael," I say, changing the subject as I fasten Kate's last button, "what time did you tell him we'd meet him for the movie later?"

In the midst of studying her bridal reflection, Kate drops her eyes.

Uh-oh.

"I can't go," she says.

"Why not?"

"Billy—"

Of course, Billy.

"—is taking me to see *Hairspray*."

"You already saw *Hairspray*." Raphael got us both comp

tickets when the show first opened, back when he was dating the wardrobe master.

"I know, but Billy has orchestra seats, and we're going
with his boss and his fiancée. It's like a work thing. You know
how it is."

"Yeah, I know how it is."

There's an awkward silence.

She knows how I feel about her blowing me off for Billy.
This isn't the first time it's happened. And Raphael is going
to be pissed when he finds out that she's not coming. These
Saturday-night outings have been a regular thing for the
three of us ever since Will and I broke up. Kate and Raphael
teamed up loyally to make sure I wasn't lonely.

But Kate didn't come last week, either. Billy was sick, and
she didn't want to leave him.

You'd have thought he had pneumonia, the way she went
on about it. Turned out it was just a cold. But she spent Saturday night being Martha Stewart-meets-Clara Barton:
making homemade chicken noodle soup, squeezing fresh
orange juice, hovering with tissues and Ricola.

Raphael and I spent Saturday night drinking apple martinis and bitchily dissecting the Kate-Billy relationship.

"Come on, don't be mad, Tracey," she pleads.

I sigh. "I'm not mad, Kate."

After all, back when I was desperate to keep Will, I'm
ashamed to admit that I'd have dropped my plans with Kate
and Raphael, too.

But I didn't like myself very much back then.

And sometimes, as much as I love Kate, I don't like her
very much when she's with Billy.

I check out our reflections.

Six months ago, I couldn't handle standing next to Kate anywhere, much less in a three-way dressing room mirror. Now, it's not so bad. We're like Snow White and Rose Red—literally, in these outfits. Svelte Kate with long fair hair and big blue eyes. Not-quite-as-svelte-but-no-longer-*zaftig* Tracey with long dark hair and big brown eyes.

She catches my eye in the mirror.

We smile at each other.

"You really do look good in that dress, Tracey."

"And you look beautiful in that. I hope he gives you a ring for Christmas. It would be fun to shop for wedding dresses, wouldn't it?"

She turns a critical eye toward the gown in the mirror. "Yeah, but remind me that I don't like gowns with full skirts, will you? This one makes me look huge."

"Huge? Come on, Kate. You're teeny."

"Not in this. It's too froufrou. When I walk down the aisle, I'm going to go for sleek and sexy." She reaches for the row of buttons. "Help me get out of it, will you?"

I oblige, still wearing the red dress. I've made up my mind to buy it for the Christmas party. Who knows? Maybe I'll meet somebody there. Blaire Barnett is a huge agency that employs plenty of single men. And a corporate Christmas party is as good a place as any to hook up, right?

*Wrong.*

A corporate Christmas party is no place to hook up.

At least, not according to this article in *She* magazine, where Raphael is assistant style editor.

The article is *Ten Office Party Don'ts*, and I stumble across it while I'm sprawled on his couch, leafing through the December issue and waiting for him to get dressed for our Saturday night out.

*1. Don't dress in a revealing manner.*

"Uh-oh, Raphael," I call. "I'm in trouble already."

"Tracey! Trouble? What kind of trouble?" He peeks around the edge of the chartreuse folding screen that separates his "dressing room" from the rest of the loft.

"Are you wearing makeup?" I ask, realizing that his big dark Latin eyes appear bigger and darker than usual.

"No! It's an eyelash perm. I got it yesterday. Do you like it?"

An eyelash perm. Oy.

I say, "It's *ravishing*."

The lunatic grins and flutters the fringe.

I go on. "So this article in *She* says I'm supposed to wear something corporate to the party next Saturday night. Something I'd wear to work. You know the dress I bought this afternoon? Well, I wouldn't wear it to work unless my office was Twelfth Avenue after midnight and my boss was a guy in a long fur coat and a fedora."

"Oh, please, Tracey. You should see the editor who wrote that article. We're talking Talbots."

This, coming from über-fashionista Raphael, is the ultimate insult. Still…

"I don't know…maybe she's right. Maybe it's not a good idea for me to look like a trollop next Saturday."

"It's *always* a good idea to look like a trollop," declared Raphael, who indeed looks like a trollop in a snug black silk shirt and snugger burgundy leather pants.

"I thought we were going to the movies," I say as he steps into a pair of mules that match the pants.

"We are, Tracey. And afterward, we're going dancing."

I look down at my jeans and navy cardigan. "Raphael, I'm not dressed for a club."

He turns to examine me. "You're right. Tracey—" he shakes his head sadly "—that *outfit*—" clearly, he uses the term loosely "—has to go."

Suddenly I feel like a contestant on that TV show *Are You Hot?*

*Buzzzzzzzzzzzzzzzzzzz.You are not hot enough to proceed to the next round. Please exit the stage.*

"Don't worry, Tracey. After the movie, we'll shop."

"I'm broke, Raphael. I used up my weekly—" more like monthly "—shopping budget at Bloomingdale's this afternoon."

"Oh, my treat, Tracey. I'll write it off."

The beauty of Raphael's stylist job is that he can actually do that. I can't tell you how many times he's treated me to a mini-wardrobe spree on the corporate credit card. Not to mention many an expensive sushi splurge.

"Isn't accounts payable starting to get suspicious, Raphael?"

He shrugs, running a comb through his longish black hair. "Tracey, they love me there."

"Raphael…" (I know—but I can't help it. When I'm with him I tend to mimic his frequent name-user conversational style.) "I don't want to get you into trouble at work. We'll go to the movie, and then you'll go dancing and I'll go home."

"*Home?*" Raphael echoes in horror.

"Yup, home."

Home to my lonely studio apartment in the East Village. It's still about the size of the elevator in one of those doorman buildings on Central Park South—and the only reason I know that is because I worked quite a few catered parties in them. The apartments, not the elevators.

My apartment will never be as fancy as a Central Park South elevator, but it's definitely looking a little better since I started using my catering cash to buy "real" furniture, plus curtains, rugs and even a great stereo system.

Still, that doesn't mean I want to spend the better part of a Saturday night there alone.

Looking as though I've just told him I plan to compose a "Farewell, world" note and scale a girder on the Brooklyn Bridge, Raphael declares, "Absolutely not, Tracey! You can't go home. We see the movie, we shop, we dance. In fact—the hell with the movie. Let's just shop and dance."

"I thought you really wanted to see it."

"I can't believe I'm saying this, Tracey, but…" He looks over his shoulder as though expecting to find someone eavesdropping, then lowers his voice to a near-whisper. "I'm starting to think Madonna should stick with singing."

"Raphael. You? I thought you said she should have been nominated for an Oscar for her last film."

"Supporting actress only," he clarifies, pausing to bend over a table and straighten one of his many small glass sculptures. His apartment is filled with outrageously expensive clutter that he and his delusional friends refer to as *objets d'art*. I call them *chotchkes*, and you would, too, if you saw them. I can think of a zillion better ways to spend what little cash I have.

"And anyway," he goes on, "that was two films ago. Let me tell you, Madonna's no Cher. Her acting went downhill in that last romantic comedy, which I said in the first place she should never have done. And I hear this new one isn't very good, either. I might even wait for the DVD. Unless you really wanted to see it, Tracey."

"Me? No! I was just going for you."

"Then it's settled." He gives a single nod and declares with the veneration of a Hells Angel embarking on a nocturnal Harley journey, "Tonight, we shop."

★ ★ ★

Shop we do.

Two hours, three cab rides and a pit stop at my apartment later, I'm sitting across from Raphael in a dimly lit bar. He's traded the burgundy leather for a pair of equally tight retro acid-washed flare jeans he couldn't resist. I'm in a fetching vintage Pucci print minidress. Raphael insisted on buying me a lime-green boa to go with it—*They're all the rage in Paris this season, Tracey*—but it's draped on the back of my stool over my brown suede jacket. Screw Paris.

"I'm just not the boa type," I tell him when he begs me yet again to wrap it around my shoulders.

"Maybe not a few months ago, Tracey, but the new you definitely screams *boa.*"

I glance down, half expecting to see something other than my newly familiar shrunken self.

I shrug and sip the lethal pink concoction Raphael ordered for each of us. He dated a bartender a few weeks ago, and now he's into all the fancy cocktails of yesteryear.

I forget what this one is called. At first it tasted like Windex, but now it's going down easier. "I have to say, I'm just not hearing the screaming, Raphael."

"That's because you're not listening. You're trying to keep the new Tracey hidden behind the old Tracey's insecurities. I say, release her!"

"And deck her out in a lime-green boa? That seems cruel." I drain the last of my drink.

Raphael leans his chin on my shoulder. "What do you think, Tracey? Want another cocktail here, or should we move on to Oh, Boy?"

Oh, Boy is, of course, the club we're headed to.

I glance around the bar. It's getting crowded. And I'm craving a cigarette, but like all bars in Manhattan, the place is full of No Smoking signs.

I'm about to suggest moving on when I lock gazes with a Very Cute Guy standing with a small pack of Very Cute Guys back by the rest-room sign and the jukebox. He flashes one of those flirty, raised-eyebrow smiles that guys are always flashing at Kate. Never at me. Never until now, anyway.

I realize this might be my fleeting last chance at heterosexual contact this evening.

"Another cocktail here," I tell Raphael, hoping Very Cute Guy doesn't think Raphael and I are together. I glance at him, taking in the snug silk shirt, the pink drink, the eyelash perm.

Nah.

"Are you sure you want to stay?" Raphael asks. "Because this place is getting packed, Tracey."

VCG seems to be shouldering his way toward us. Or is he just trying to escape the bathroom fumes or the blaring Bon Jovi? Hard to tell. But just in case…

"Let's stay for one more," I say decisively.

Cute Guy's name is Jeff. Jeff Stanton or Stilton—something like that.

How do I know this?

Because a few minutes after our second drink arrived, he popped up and introduced himself to me.

His name is Jeff, he's a broker—or trader. I don't know, exactly; something boring and Wall Street.

Oh, and he has an unhealthy obsession with *Star Wars*.

How do I know *this*, you might ask?

Because he has *Star Wars sheets*. Sadly, I am so not kidding.

And if you've figured out how I know about his sheets, you also know that I'm not only *dressing* like a trollop these days; I'm conducting myself like one.

Did I get wasted and sleep with Jeff Stanton/Stilton/Something that starts with an *S* and ends with an *N*?

Yes.

Do I regret it now that the morning light is filtering through the slats of his blinds and I can't even recall which freaking borough I'm in?

*Hell,* yes.

It's bad enough that I'm in a borough at all. I had him pegged for Manhattan, Upper West Side. Tribeca, maybe. But a borough?

*At least it's not Jersey,* I tell myself, sitting up in his twin bed—yes, I said *twin* bed—and pulling the *Star Wars* flat sheet up to my chin as I assess the situation and try to remember how I got from Point A—the bar—to Point X-rated.

It's freezing in here, by the way. I'm surprised I can't see my breath. And there's no quilt on the bed.

Oh, wait…there is a quilt. I can see it when I peer over the edge. It's been passionately pitched into a heap on the floor beside my clothes—with the exception of my lime-green boa, which is draped over a dresser knob across the room.

How the hell did it get there?

And while we're on that topic, how the hell did I get *here?* And where *is* here?

I remember asking Jeff S-n, at one point in the night, if he lived in Jersey.

I remember him laughing and saying *of course not,* as though I'd accused him of being a rifle-toting redneck bootlegger from West Virgin-ee.

What I don't remember is when Raphael abandoned me at the bar with Jeff S–n or how it was decided that I would be borough-bound to have sex with a complete stranger.

I only know that much liquor was involved, followed by a long cab ride over a bridge. It could've been the Golden Gate, for all I noticed while I was making out with Jeff S–n in the back seat.

So what happened when we got here, wherever we are?

Searching my mind for reassuring memories of doormen or elevators or quaint parkside brownstones, I vaguely recall a side street crammed with parked cars, apartment buildings and small houses.

An educated guess tells me Jeff lives in one of them. There are major gaps in my recollection of our pre-bed travels.

I do know that it was dark when we came in, and he didn't turn on lights.

Ostensibly so that I wouldn't glimpse Yoda on a pillowcase and flee screaming into the night.

Maybe it's not so bad, I try to tell myself. Maybe it's even kind of, I don't know, sweet that a grown man sleeps in a twin bed with *Star Wars* sheets, you know?

I turn my head and glance at Jeff, wondering if I'll be swept into a wave of post-coital tenderness.

Nope, nothing sweet about it. It's freakish, that's what it is.

His mouth is open, wafting beery morning breath. I can see all his fillings, and a hinge of thick whitish drool connecting his upper lip to his lower.

Oh, ick. I'm outta here.

He doesn't even stir as I slip out of bed and dive into my clothes. Shivering from the cold, I glance around the room as I dress. I half expect to see cheesy posters on the walls: race cars or topless women. To his credit, there are none. The room is messily nondescript. But there is a shelf lined with trophies and another with a bunch of Tolkien and C. S. Lewis titles.

I take another look at Jeff, half expecting to realize, in the broad light of day, that he's actually an adolescent boy. After all, he was pretty vague about what he does for a living— or was it just that I tuned him out when I found out he was in finance?

Hmm. I note a reassuring stubble of beard on his chin, right beneath the drool, and what's visible of his chest is broad and hairy. He certainly *looks* like a grown man. Snores like one, too.

Lord, I just hope I'm not in his boyhood home. When we walked in, he whispered, "Shh! My roommates are sleeping." Still, you never know. What if his roommates are of the parental variety?

Not that I wouldn't consider dating somebody who still lives at home, but…well, I wouldn't dream of conducting a one-night stand with anybody's parents on the other side of the bedroom wall.

Nor would I, in my kinkiest fantasies, have dreamed of conducting a one-night stand while reclining on an Ewok's face.

I look back at the slumbering Jeff S-n. Should I wake him to say goodbye?

He emits a snorting sound, smacks his lips, rolls over.

I wrinkle my nose.

Okay, but should I at least leave a note?

I could write down my phone number, I think, as I put on my suede jacket.

But what if he calls? Then I'll have to see him again.

And what if he doesn't call? Then I'll feel like a real tramp.

Screw it. Like I haven't already descended into the depths of trampdom?

Carrying my shoes, boa and purse, I step into a carpeted hall, half expecting to find a graying man in corduroy slippers and a cardigan padding toward the bathroom.

But all I see is a row of closed doors and one that's ajar, revealing a fraction of a sink and toilet. I glance in longingly as I pass, wishing I had time to spare. I sort of have to pee; I'm dehydrated; my mouth tastes like somebody vomited in it.

But, sniffing the air, I can smell coffee brewing. One of the "roomies" is up. I can't risk hanging out here a second longer.

*So long, Jeff S-n. Thanks for the—uh, memory blanks.*

I head down the stairs and out the front door, stepping out into what I sincerely hope isn't the Bronx. Or Staten Island.

The instant the frigid fresh air hits my face, I wish I had snagged Jeff S-n's quilt to wrap around me for the trip home. It has to be below freezing, and all I have is a thin leather jacket. Oh, and the boa. I wrap it around my low-cut neckline, hoping to stave off pneumonia.

I walk gingerly toward the street, swept first by a wave of nausea, then a wave of panic—until I reassure myself that my meds will keep a full-blown attack at bay—followed by a wave of homesickness for Manhattan, for my little studio, for Will....

Yes, homesick for Will McCraw.

It's been three months, but that doesn't mean I'm completely over him.

It doesn't mean that when I'm out on the street, I don't constantly, subconsciously, look for him on the crowded sidewalks, thinking that I've glimpsed his face on a passerby—but it never turns out to be him.

And it doesn't mean that I'm over longing for the days of waking up next to a warm, familiar body in a warm, familiar place.

But Will has moved on. He and Esme—his summer stock costar, with whom he cheated on me—are a solid couple.

How do I know this?

Will told me.

That's because Will thinks we're friends.

Yes, you heard me. *Friends*.

Is that a cliché, or what? He wants us to stay friends. So he calls me every week or two to "check in." Usually, he does all the talking. I hold up my end of our conversation by trying to sound enthused about his brand-spanking-new life that doesn't include me. Except, of course, in said *friend* capacity.

Pausing on the sidewalk in front of Jeff S-n's brick row house, I survey the block and light a cigarette. No real clues in the ubiquitous three- and four-story brick apartment buildings or small one- and two-family houses fronted by low wrought-iron fences. My gut tells me I'm in Brooklyn, but it could be Queens, for all I know. I can see a street sign, but it means nothing to me. There's probably a Fifteenth Street in every borough. I could start walking until I find a cross street, but unless it's a major, familiar one (even I know that Pelham Parkway is in the Bronx and Astoria Boulevard is in Queens), I'm still going to be lost.

*Mental Note: Start carrying pocket atlas with street map of entire city.*

*Mental Note, alternative to above: Stop sleeping around.*

An old lady trundles in my direction, pushing one of those wire carts full of plastic grocery bags. She's wearing a down coat and sensible shoes, and I'm wearing a minidress and a lime-green boa.

"Excuse me, which way is the subway?" I ask her as she passes.

"Which line?" She doesn't even bat an eye at my getup. Displaced sluts must be a common sight on weekend mornings in this neighborhood.

I shrug. "Any line to Manhattan."

"The F train is two blocks that way." She points and moves on, rattling off down the street with her cart full of groceries.

I look after her, envying her life's simplicity. It occurs to me that I'd trade places with that gnarled grandma in a second....

After which it occurs to me that I'm probably still slightly drunk.

The F train. Okay, that tells me nothing. The F train runs from Brooklyn to Manhattan to Queens.

Then again, who cares what borough I'm in?

I head down the street, passing a couple of teenaged boys dribbling a basketball between them. They do a double take and snicker.

Well, who cares what they think?

I grab the dangling end of my boa and toss it over my shoulder with a flourish.

One of them mutters something as they pass. I don't hear the words, but I know it's about me and his tone is snide.

And suddenly, I care.

I don't want to be this…this *trollop*.

I want to be me again. Tracey Spadolini. The only thing is, I have no idea who she is anymore.

Three years of entanglement with Will, followed by three dazed post-breakup months…

I'm not just lost and alone in some borough.

I'm lost and alone, period.

Brushing away tears, I make my way toward the F train, hoping to God that it'll carry me home.

3

"**Y**ou know, Tracey, you're really lucky that he didn't turn out to be some serial killer."

That's my friend Buckley O'Hanlon, referring, over lunch on Wednesday, to Jeff S-n and my initiation into the sordid world of one-night stands.

We managed to find a table for two in the crowded upstairs dining area of one of those Korean grocer/salad bar/Chinese buffet/deli/florist places that are unique to Manhattan.

Buckley's doing some in-house freelance work in my office building, just as he was when we first met last spring—back in the bad old days when I was fifty pounds heavier and assumed he was gay.

Even though I know Buckley's totally right about the risk I took going off with a complete stranger, I roll my eyes and tell him, "Of *course* he wasn't a serial killer. He's a trader."

Yeah. Or a broker.

"So? Didn't you ever read *American Psycho?*" Buckley sips his Snapple, then takes a bite of his turkey wrap.

"No, I never read it. But I saw the movie." And now that I think of it, why didn't that pop into my horny little head when I decided it was perfectly safe to dart into the night with a good-looking Wall Street guy? Scary, what a few pink cocktails and three celibate months can do to a gal.

"The movie was stupid. The book was better."

As far as Buckley's concerned, the book is *always* better. He likes to refer to himself as a literary geek, but trust me, there's nothing geeky about him. He's a copywriter, and he's been writing a novel in his spare time. Of which, might I add, there isn't much, now that he's in a relationship.

Do I sound catty? Sorry.

It's just that he gained a girlfriend right around the time I lost a boyfriend. Which is a real shame, because something tells me that Buckley and I have the potential to be more than friends. He's cute and smart and funny—totally my type. Except for that pesky he-has-a-girlfriend thing.

"I don't like the idea of you out drinking and getting picked up by strange men, Tracey," Buckley informed me, frowning.

"I'm a big girl, Buckley. Not as big a girl as I used to be, mind you, but big enough to take care of myself. You don't have to worry about me."

"Yes, I do. I can't help it."

I smile. "How sweet are you?"

He smiles back. "I'm the sweetest."

"I'm serious. You are."

"And I'm serious. Stay away from strange men."

When Will dumped me, I cried on Buckley's shoulder, and he promised me that, someday, I'll be grateful to Will. He swore I'd want to thank him for dumping me, because it's the best thing that's ever happened to me.

I'm still waiting for that day to arrive, and I can't help but feel like it might come sooner if I could replace Will with someone new. Someone better. Like, oh, I don't know… *Buckley*.

"So how's Sonja?" I ask, because it seems polite. And because it will change the subject from my one-night stand, which I'm not entirely comfortable discussing with someone as wholesome as Buckley, who has probably never had a one-night stand in his life.

"Sonja's fine," Buckley says.

I peer at him over my blah bundle of sprouts, aka the 200-Calorie Fat-Free Veggie Wrap. Lawn clippings in an envelope would be tastier.

"Are you sure?" I ask him.

"Sure about what?"

"That Sonja's fine?"

"Yup. She's fine." He pokes an errant tomato back into his sandwich.

"Your mouth is saying yup, but your eyes are saying something's wrong, Buckley. Oh, and you have a glob of honey mayonnaise on your cheek."

He reaches for a napkin, then sweeps it across his face. He totally misses.

I take it from him and dab his cheek, asking, "What's up?"

He sighs. "Sonja wants us to move in together."

My heart sinks.

I smile brightly.

"So…that's romantic," I tell him.

He shakes his head.

"It isn't romantic?"

"No. It's stupid. We both have leases. We both have great places. We both live alone. There's no reason to move in together already. We've only been going out a few months."

Gotta love sensible Buckley. Why rush things? After all, you never know when somebody better might come along. Or when you might notice that somebody who came along a while ago just might be better. *Psst,* somebody whose initials are *T.S.* and is sitting right across from you at this very moment.

"So you don't love her?" I ask, trying to sound casual. I've never let on to Buckley that I could be attracted to him.

"I don't know. I mean…I really think I do."

Oh.

He really thinks he does.

There goes any hope for Buckley ever falling for me. Everyone knows that when a man admits aloud to the merest possibility of being in love, it's only a matter of time before he finds himself standing in the bridal registry at Michael C. Fina on a Sunday afternoon when the Giants are playing at home.

"Buckley, if you love her—"

"I *think* I love her," he amends.

"If you think you love her, what's the problem?" *Shut up, Tracey.*

Yet I babble on. Either Sonja's spirit has been astral-projected into my body, or I've taken up the cause for oppressed would-be live-in girlfriends everywhere.

"I mean, Buckley, it's not like you're not dating other people."

Say…for example, *me.*

"And Sonja's great. She's smart, pretty, fun…"

Somebody stop me.

But I can't help myself.

"After all, you're together all the time anyway. Why pay two rents?"

It's as though I'm talking to Will, back when I wanted to move in with him and he wanted to move to another part of the state without leaving a phone number.

"I guess," he says thoughtfully.

"Look, Buckley, if you've got a good thing going, you shouldn't be afraid to take the next step. I mean, look at Billy and Kate. They moved in together less than two months after they met, and now they're looking at engagement rings."

"They are?"

"*She* is," I admit. "But she's thinking they're going to be engaged at Christmas. She said she wants a June wedding."

"A June wedding. I wouldn't expect anything less from our little magnolia," Buckley says, shaking his head.

"Do you think Sonja wants a June wedding?" I can't help asking.

I brace myself for a look of horror, or at least dismay, but there is only resignation.

Buckley sighs. "Do you know a female who doesn't?"

"Well, *I* don't."

"You don't?"

"Uh-uh. I want a fall wedding."

At least, that's what I secretly hoped for when I was with Will. I had the whole thing planned out in my head—what I'd wear, who would stand up, the flowers, the menu, the pumpkin cake with cream-cheese frosting….

"A fall wedding would be nice," Buckley says. He adds hastily, "Not *next* fall."

He's so sweet, I think, watching him pop the last bite of his sandwich into his mouth. So different from Will and Jeff S-n. Buckley's genuine. He's a really good friend. And when he's not brooding over Sonja, he's one of the funniest people I know.

I wonder, not for the first time, what would have happened if Will had dumped me before I met Buckley.

He was attracted to me back then. I mean, he kissed me—which was how I figured out that he definitely isn't gay. And it was a great kiss. So great that I still think about it sometimes.

Okay, all the time.

Maybe that's just because it was the last time somebody kissed me that way.

Or maybe it's because I could easily fall in love with my good friend Buckley.

But even if he were available, it's too soon. I'm still not over Will. According to Kate, *She* magazine and pop psychology 101, any relationship I have right now would be strictly rebound.

Buckley crumples his sandwich wrapper into a ball and drains the last of his Snapple. "Ready to go back to work?"

"Nah. Let's play hooky for the rest of the afternoon."

"Seriously?" He looks intrigued.

"Nope. I was kidding. I'm in the middle of helping Mike with a New Business presentation. And then Brenda and Latisha and I are going to try to meet and figure out if we can organize a bachelorette party for Yvonne sometime in the next few weeks."

"When's she getting married?"

"Over Christmas. She and Thor are eloping to Vegas."

Thor is Yvonne's Swedish pen pal. When she met him a few months ago, they got engaged. She swears this is merely a green-card marriage, but we think she's in love. When she's with him, she's all girly. As girly, that is, as a tough old broad like Yvonne can be.

"Okay, I guess I've got to get back to the office, then," Buckley says reluctantly.

"Same here."

We push back our chairs and carry our garbage to the can as a pair of hovering corporate drones descend on our vacant table. "But wouldn't it be fun to blow off work and go ice-skating or something?" Buckley muses.

"Me on ice skates? Are you kidding?"

"You grew up near Buffalo. You must have learned how to skate."

I shake my head.

"Really? I'll have to teach you."

An image flits into my mind as we make our way through a sea of office workers, down the stairs, through the deli and onto the street.

I see myself in one of those short, cute pleated skating skirts and a fuzzy white sweater. Buckley is in one of those clingy skating jumpsuits they wear at the Olympics, yet he looks incredibly masculine in it.

I know, I know, but it's a fantasy.

So, anyway, we're gliding around the ice in front of 30 Rock. Classical music is playing, a gentle snow is falling—big, lazy flakes—and there's not a soul on the rink but us.

*Fantasy,* people! It's a *fantasy.*

He lifts me in his arms a few times, and we effortlessly do some fancy moves. Complicated stuff. Then he kisses me, and it's totally passionate, and he says...

"Do I have anything stuck between my teeth? Trace?"

*Thud.* I land on Third Avenue, where a jackhammer is rattling and taxis are honking and Buckley's in my face with his teeth bared, revealing a lovely hunk of chewed-up lettuce.

"There's something green between your front teeth," I advise him, sighing inwardly as I reach into my bag for a cigarette.

So much for fantasies.

Mike Middleford, my new boss, is nothing like sexist, philandering, narcissistic Jake.

For one thing, Mike treats me with respect. He asks my advice on PowerPoint presentations—poor guy isn't very literate—and he doesn't mind if I'm a few minutes late in the morning or if I sneak out for a few cigarette breaks.

For another, he's totally in love with his girlfriend, Dianne. Whenever she calls, I'm suppose to hunt him down to come to the phone, unless he's in the men's room or a meeting. It's refreshing to see a guy light up when he hears that his girlfriend is on the phone. Dianne calls a lot, and she sounds really sweet. She always greets me by name and makes an effort to chat before she asks for Mike.

Like today, she says, "Hi, Tracey, how's it going? Are you psyched for the company Christmas party Saturday night?"

"Yeah, it sounds like it'll be fun." Blaire Barnett had rented out Space, an entire three-floor nightclub in Chelsea, for the party. "Are you coming with Mike?"

"Nah. He wants me to, but I wouldn't know anybody."

Wow. She must feel really secure about her relationship. If Will was going to a party and I had the option of going with him, there's no way I'd opt out.

Then again, Mike goes out of his way to make sure he doesn't miss her calls. Will lied and told me that the pay phone in his summer cast house didn't take incoming calls. And, duh, I believed him.

"Are you bringing a date?" Dianne asks.

"Me? Nah. I'm not seeing anyone right now. My boyfriend and I broke up in September."

Why, I wonder, do I feel compelled to tell people about Will? I'm always bringing it up. To elevator men, cabdrivers, dressing-room attendants in clothing stores… it's like no matter who I'm talking to, I manage to find a reason to announce that I'm recovering from a breakup.

"That's too bad," Dianne says.

"Yeah, it's hard. But I'm sure I'll find somebody new sooner or later." Buckley flits into and out of my mind. So does Jeff S-n. How depressing.

"I wish I knew somebody we could fix you up with, but I'm drawing a blank," Dianne says. "Mike has a roommate, but he's a real asshole."

"That's okay." I'm not desperate enough to consider a blind date…yet.

"It stinks being alone around the holidays, though," Dianne comments. "You get cheated out of boyfriend presents, jewelry, baubles…"

Baubles?

"I never thought of it that way." I find myself thinking, wistfully, All those years with Will, and nary a bauble to show for it.

"Then there's New Year's Eve...."

"Right." I hadn't thought of that either. *Gee, thanks, Dianne, for enlightening me.*

She sighs. "Oh, well."

Yeah. Easy for *her* to say.

"So...is Mike there?"

"He's around somewhere." If he's not out shopping for diamond earrings or on the other line booking the presidential suite at the Sherry Netherland for December 31ˢᵗ. "I'll go get him."

I find Mike by the copier, trying to help my friend Brenda clear a jam. He bolts the second I tell him I've got Dianne on hold.

Brenda shakes her head. "Look at him drop everything and run. I hope she knows how lucky she is."

"Look at you. You've got Paulie." It's all I can do not to pronounce her husband's name the way she does—"Po-aw-lie." Sometimes her accent is contagious.

"The honeymoon is over, Trace. I've been married four months, and already Paulie is telling me I've got to stop calling his cell during the day while he's at work."

"Well, Brenda, he's a cop. It's probably distracting when he's chasing some crack fiend down an alley and his phone rings, and it's you asking him to pick up some fresh *mozzarell'* on the way home."

We laugh, and I help her clear the jam—not without cursing the damned machine and whoever invented four freaking places for paper to get wedged. As we work on clearing it, we chat about the bachelorette party we're going to plan for Yvonne, and then about the upcoming Christmas party.

"Paulie's having a bunch of guys over to watch the fight that night," Brenda says, gingerly running one of her raspberry-colored talons along the paper output slot. "So I've got to clear out of there before six-thirty."

"You want to come over to my place before we go to the party? It doesn't start till eight."

"By the time I take the PATH in and get a cab over to the club, it'll be past seven-thirty anyway, so let's just meet there."

I tug on a piece of paper that's stuck between the rollers. "I don't know, Brenda. We probably shouldn't get to the party right when it's starting."

"Why not?"

The paper tears. I curse under my breath, then tell Brenda about the article in *She* magazine while I pick out bits of torn paper.

"So getting to the company Christmas party on time is a major Don't?" she asks, incredulous. She removes her hand from the copy machine and inspects one of her nails for damage. "You'd think being punctual would be a good thing."

"Not in this case. 'Don't—' and I quote '—be the first one to arrive. Don't be the last to leave.' End quote. Hey, hold this compartment open for me, will you, Bren?"

She reluctantly obliges, and I continue to pull scraps of paper from the roller. Brenda's a fanatic about preserving her weekly manicure; my nails are always a mess. I think I'm the only woman in New York with unpolished, unfiled fingertips. But I can think of better ways to spend the weekly fifteen bucks my friends dole out in nail salons.

Then again, glossy scarlet nails would be dazzling with my red trollop dress.

*Mental Note: See if manicurist has available slot after lip-wax appointment at salon tomorrow.*

"So what other Don'ts are there?" Brenda wants to know.

"Let's see... I told you about the 'Don't dress provocatively' one, right? Then there was 'Don't drink too much.' You're supposed to nurse white-wine spritzers and alternate them with plain seltzer throughout the evening."

"Oh, *Madonna*," Brenda says with a Carmella Soprano eye-roll and my grandmother's old-country accent.

The Jersey Italian in Brenda's blood always comes out when she's peeved. One minute, she's a lady, the next, she's flipping someone off with an *Ah, fongool.*

"Spritzers? That's bullshit, Tracey. We should do shots. It's girls' night out. What else did the article say?"

"Don't smoke. Don't gossip. Don't flirt. Don't dance. Don't—"

"Geez, who the hell wrote this article? The president of Bob Jones University?"

I shrug, peering into the copy machine to make sure all the paper has been removed. "Okay, all clear. Press Start."

She does.

The machine whirs.

Lights flash.

Nothing.

We lean over to look at the little screen on top.

*Paper Jam.*

"Forget it," Brenda says, picking up the stack of originals from the tray. "I'm going down to seven to make my copies. And Tracey, forget about that stupid article. Let's just go have a great time."

I head back to my cubicle, still thinking about the article. It's easy for someone like Brenda to blow off the advice. She's content to stay a secretary, and, anyway, she plans to quit to stay home when she has a baby—which is planned for next year. So for her, this isn't a career; it's a job.

But if I'm going to work my way into a copywriting position, I'll have to watch my step. I don't want anyone to get the wrong impression of me at this party. I don't want them to lump me together with the other secretaries.

Okay, I know that sounds snobby. And it's not that I don't adore my friends. But sometimes, it kind of bothers me that I'm—I don't know…one of them.

Back when I had Will—and supposedly a future with him, even if it was all in my deluded head—it didn't seem to matter as much.

Now that I'm on my own, I can't help feeling that I'd feel much better about myself if I had a "real" career.

*Yeah, and you'd probably feel much better about yourself if you hadn't had that one-night stand with a full-grown* Star Wars *fanatic, too.*

Let's face it: I might be skinny, and I might be bringing in a regular paycheck with benefits…but things could definitely be better. Much better.

I find Mike leaning over my chair to check out the proposal I'm typing for him on the computer screen.

He's a smallish, wiry guy, and I don't like to stand next to him because he's a few inches shorter than I am and we probably weigh about the same. I'm not secure enough, despite the weight loss, to feel comfortable around guys who make me feel large and gawky even now.

"How's it coming, Chief?" he asks cheerfully. Mike has this cute thing where he calls everyone "Chief."

"Pretty good. I caught a couple of typos for you."

"Thanks. You're the best."

I smile. They weren't typos, really. He's a crummy speller, but I never want to embarrass him. He's such a sweetie.

"Hey, I like your tie," I tell him. For somebody who seems clueless about some things—like getting his hair cut when it needs it—he's got great taste in ties.

"Thanks. You want some caramel popcorn? I just got a huge barrel of it from some magazine," he says. "It's in my office."

At this time of year, the agency people get loads of corporate Christmas gifts from magazines and television networks. You wouldn't believe the caliber of some of the gifts. Last week Mike got a crystal Tiffany ice bucket and a hundred-dollar bottle of champagne from one place.

Too bad he didn't offer to share that.

I pass on the popcorn. It sounds good, but I've got to be careful. At this time of year, it would be easy to slip up and gain a few—or twenty—pounds back.

"Listen, Chief," Mike asks, "would you mind going down to accounts payable before the end of the day to get me that cash advance for my trip to Philly tomorrow?"

"Not at all."

That's another great thing about Mike. He doesn't give orders. He asks me to do things. Getting his cash from AP is part of my job, but he makes it seem as though I'm going out of my way for him. He really makes being a secretary bearable for somebody who has bigger aspirations.

Someday, I hope, I'll be a copywriter like Buckley. But until I am, working as a secretary at Blaire Barnett is pleasantly painless. I even get to sit in a cubicle instead of in the secretaries' bay, where I was when I worked for Jake.

I head toward the elevator bank. I reach it just as a junior account executive does. Her real name is Susan, but Yvonne calls her Miss Prim, and I have to admit, the shoe fits. She's always buttoned up in a tailored suit with pearls and pumps, her hair pulled severely back in a clip, and I've never seen her smile at anybody who isn't an executive.

"Hi," I say, since we're both going to stand here waiting for the down elevator, which is bound to take a few minutes. The elevators in this building are notoriously slow.

"Hi." She studies her sensible pumps.

You just wouldn't catch *her* picking up a total stranger and having sex with him in some godforsaken borough.

"These elevators take forever, don't they?" I feel compelled to say.

She merely presses the lit Down button again, as though she can't stand another moment trapped here with lowly me.

It irks me that she won't make eye contact, much less conversation, with a mere secretary. I want to tell her that I have an English degree and a future in copywriting. I want to tell her to let her hair down and live a little; or at the very least, unfasten her top button, for God's sake.

I wonder what she's going to wear to the Christmas party. Somehow, I can't quite picture her in anything remotely festive.

Again, my mind flits to that article chock-full of Don'ts.

The hell with the article, and with Miss Prim, too, I think, as I step into the elevator with her.

I'm going to wear my red dress, and I'm going to get there when it starts, and I'm going to have a helluva good time.

Just watch me.

"Hold the elevator!" a voice calls.

I half expect Susan to reach for the Door Close button, but she doesn't. Nor does she hit Door Open as they begin to slide closed, even though the button is like, two inches from her claw.

I wedge my shoulder between the doors to hold them for whoever is rushing toward the elevator, heels tapping hurriedly along the floor, accompanied by an odd jingling sound.

When I see who it is, I almost wish I'd let the doors close.

"Hi, Mary," I say, as she steps on board with a huge, panting sigh of relief.

"Hi, Tracey," she trills. "Hi, Sue."

I get the impression Susan doesn't appreciate being called Sue.

Mary Kohl doesn't seem to get this impression, or any impressions at all. She's too busy plucking an oversized round jingle bell from the crevice between her oversized round boobs. The bell is suspended around her jowly neck on a red cord and festooned with sprigs of plastic holly.

If I were sharing this elevator with anybody but wenchy Susan, I might be inclined to turn and share an eye-roll with them. Mary, who is an administrative assistant in our department, is easily the most annoying human being of all time. In fact, if this elevator happens to get stuck between floors, as elevators in this building have been known to do, I'm going to find myself wishing I carried cyanide capsules in my pockets like the astronauts do.

Mary presses her floor with a chubby forefinger, and the

doors slide closed with the finality of clanking steel bars on death row.

"Did we all sign up for Secret Snowflake?" Mary wants to know.

She wants to know this in the chirpiest voice ever. Think Baby Bop on helium.

I sort of smile and shake my head.

Susan plays deaf and dumb.

"Uh-oh." Mary shakes her head sadly, her jingle bell jangling noisily from boob to boob. "Didn't everyone hear that Secret Snowflake is mandatory this year?"

I murmur something about it being news to me, although I knew damn well. Who could miss the bright red memo Mary sent out on December first? She signed it with her name spelled Merry, and requested that we all use this spelling for the duration of the season.

"You're kidding! Didn't you get the memo?"

"I guess not," I tell Mary, as Helen Keller pointedly ignores both of us.

"Not only is Secret Snowflake mandatory, but I'm matching up the names on Monday," Mary informs us. "So you'll both need to sign up by the end of today. Okay?"

"Okay," I agree, because mandatory is mandatory.

"Great! Sue?"

"What the fuck is a Secret Snowflake?" Susan barks, just before the elevator bumps to a stop.

"Oh, it's really fun. It's where the whole department picks names and we all—"

Too late.

Susan has fled. This wasn't even her floor. A bike messenger steps on board.

"Happy holidays!" Mary chirps at him.

He glares at her, clearly wondering who died and made her Mrs. Claus.

Unfazed, Mary turns to me and breezily resumes her Secret Snowflake monologue. "Anyhoo, we all pick names and then buy a gift for our Secret Snowflake each day for a whole week. The following week, we have the luncheon and find out who our Snowflake was. It's just a blast."

I smile and nod at Mary, thinking she really needs...what? A life? Some serious counseling? To be smacked upside of the head?

Um, how about all of the above?

Okay, maybe I'm just being mean. Maybe the whole New York attitude has gotten to me at last and I'm too jaded. Maybe I could use a little of Mary's childlike Christmas spirit. Maybe we all could.

I look at her, taking in the jingle bell, the mistletoe earrings, the sprig of holly tucked into her graying bun.

The woman is a freak. That's all there is to it.

"Going to the party on Saturday, Tracey?" she asks.

"I wouldn't miss it," I say truthfully. "How about you?"

"Oh, I'll be there with bells on!"

Right.

I find myself picturing her hitched to Santa's sleigh. On, Dasher, On, Dancer, On, Mary. Er, Merry.

The thing is, I might be jaded, but I'll take that any day over terminally cute and festive, and not just at this time of year.

Mary decorates her cubicle—and her person—seasonally. I heard she actually showed up decked out as a leprechaun last Saint Patrick's Day, and in a witch costume on Halloween. Mercifully, I wasn't here for either of those events. I was, however, forced to participate when she organized a Thanksgiving feast last month, where we all had to bring something. I brought canned cranberry sauce. The crummy Key Food store brand kind. Mary brought pies she made from scratch using sugar pumpkins she grew on her fire escape.

It's like she's embraced her inner preschool teacher, corporate decorum be damned. Reportedly, upper management thinks she's fun and boosts morale. The rest of us think she's a pain in the ass, but the rest of us don't count. We just have to make like pilgrims and Secret Snowflakes, and come February, she'll probably have us all making construction paper hearts and tramping through the woods to cut down cherry trees.

The elevator stops at my floor.

"Don't forget to sign up before you leave tonight," Mary calls after me as I step out into the empty corridor.

I suppose I should be looking forward to the whole Secret Snowflake thing. At least *somebody* will be buying me Christmas presents. Not that a shrink-wrapped drugstore coffee mug filled with hard candies in shiny red wrappers can compete with boyfriend *baubles*.

From someone other than Will, that is—he was as stingy with his baubles as he was with his affection.

As I wave my card key in front of the sensor beside the locked glass doors leading to the floor reception area, I find myself wondering what it would be like to be showered with gifts from somebody who is head over heels in love with me.

Will I ever find out?

Wah. I want to find out. I want baubles and happily-ever-after, dammit.

"Hi, Tracey," Lydia, the hugely pregnant receptionist, says from her desk, where she's reading today's *Newsday*. "Going to the office party?"

"Definitely. Are you?"

She laughs. "If I'm not in labor. Are you bringing a date?"

"Nope."

Is it my imagination, or is that pity in her mascara-fringed eyes?

Look, I know I'm not supposed to go through life obsessed with finding Mr. Right. I'm not supposed to feel inadequate because I'm single; I'm not supposed to need a man.

I'm supposed to be an independent woman who can stand on her own; a woman with a promising career and cultural interests and plenty of good friends.

I'm supposed to be like Murphy Brown, Mary Richards, Elaine Benes. I'm suppose to make it after all—a hat-tossing single woman in the city, confident and savvy and solo. Or does that just happen on television sitcoms? Old, outdated television sitcoms?

As I make my way down the hall toward accounts payable, I decide there is a certain irony in the fact that I'm spending my nights watching *Nick at Nite* and TV Land reruns about women who actually *have* lives. Fulfilling lives that are too busy for endless speculation about how and when and where to meet a soul mate.

In real life, I don't know many—okay, *any*—willingly single women. Everyone I know, aside from Raphael's lesbian friends, either has a man or wants a man.

Is that so wrong?

Well, maybe I'll meet somebody any second now. Maybe I'll round the next corner just past the water fountain and

I'll crash into the perfect man. Maybe he'll steady me by holding my arms just above my elbows, and we'll look into each other's eyes, and…

Kismet.

What? It happens.

It happens all the time.

Well, it does.

Okay, it happens all the time in Sandra Bullock movies, and sometimes it happens in real life, too.

I find myself holding my breath as I approach the corner, wondering if this is more than a fantasy—if maybe it's a premonition.

I decide that if I round the corner and crash into a man—any man—that it's fate. As long as he's single and reasonably attractive.

Okay, here I go.

This could be it.

I squeeze my eyes shut and turn the corner.

Open my eyes.

Empty.

The long carpeted hallway stretches ahead, empty as my love life.

Oh, well. Deep down, I knew it would be.

Deep down, I don't believe in kismet after all.

4

"Where is everyone?" Seated beside me on a bar stool, Brenda lifts the hand that's not holding a blood-orange martini to check her watch.

The four of us have been here at Space for a half hour and a round and a half of cocktails. We're sitting at the curved stainless-steel bar beneath a vast black "sky" dotted with tiny white lights that are supposed to be constellations. The bartenders are wearing silver jumpsuits. Mirrors line every surface, making the place look infinitely expansive—and reflecting me in all my slinky red glory.

I'm not looking at my own reflection. Well, not most of the time. The thing is, when I do happen to catch my eye, I can't seem to get over that this is really me. It's enough to banish any lingering doubts about being the only woman in the place baring a little cleavage and a lot of thigh.

"What time is it?" Yvonne asks.

"Eight. And the party starts at eight. Are the four of us the only punctual people in the whole freaking—"

"Nope," Latisha cuts in, pointing across the cavernous room toward the door. "Look who's here."

"Let me guess. Judy Jetson?" My quip strikes me as more amusing than it should, courtesy of the potent second drink I just sucked down.

"Nope, Mary," Latisha says, gesturing.

*"Madonna,"* Brenda murmurs, wide-eyed.

"Oh, so we're talking Mary, Mother of God?" I swear, I'm cracking myself up.

"No, Mary, the office freak. Look."

Still giggling, I set down my empty glass and turn to see that Mary—excuse me, Merry—has just made her entrance. Her roly-poly figure is encased in a bright red dress with white fake fur trim. Incredulous, I gape at the shiny black boots below and the Santa hat perched jauntily on her round head. All that's missing is a sack full of toys slung on her back.

"Now, that's a real shame," Yvonne says dryly, shaking her pink bouffant, an unlit cigarette in one hand and a martini glass in the other.

Mary spots us and makes a beeline for the bar. "Hi, everyone!"

I can't resist. "Mrs. Claus, I presume?"

She titters and warbles, "Oh, Tracey, you're so funny. Um, Yvonne, you're not allowed to smoke in here."

Yvonne rolls her eyes in the direction of the Little Dipper.

"She knows," I say. "She just likes to hold her cigarette. It's a habit."

A habit Little Miss Merry Two-Shoes couldn't possibly understand.

A jumpsuited bartender materializes. "Can I get you something?"

Mary orders a spritzer.

That's enough to make me order my third martini. I rationalize it by deciding that blood-orange martinis aren't as potent as the regular kind, but basically, I'm about to get trashed.

I'm just one big Office Party Don't, but I can't seem to help it. Blood-orange martinis are my new best friend.

I'm not in the mood for spritzers, and I'm sick of being one big *Do* all my life. Maybe it's just my martini fog, but it seems to me that *Don'ts* have far more fun than *Do's* do.

Soon, thank God, Mary disappears and the place fills up. You don't grasp just how huge an agency Blaire Barnett is until the whole company is in one place. I see plenty of faces I don't recognize, and some that I do. The music throbs, and there are a few people out on the dance floor, most of them self-conscious-looking entry-level drones or grooving mailroom staff.

"Who's that guy? He's cute!" Brenda says, nudging me and pointing at someone I've never seen before. He's got blond hair, which is usually not my type. Not Brenda's type, either, but look at her gaping.

"You're married, Bren. Remember?"

She shrugs. "I'm not *dead*. I can look. And *you* should look. Maybe you'll meet someone."

"Maybe I will."

"You should start mingling."

"Maybe I will," I say again, but I'm having a good time just hanging by the bar with my friends.

Then again, it's getting a little warm in here. The music seems to be abnormally loud, and I'm thinking I should switch to a spritzer after I finish this drink. The insert the pharmacy gave me with my happy pills says that I'm not supposed to overindulge in liquor.

I spot a very familiar face approaching as Brenda and I pose for a picture Latisha is about to take with my camera.

Yes, I brought my camera. Is that a Don't? It's not on the list, but it probably isn't considered a Do. Especially when Latisha and I keep cracking ourselves up pretending to be private detectives furtively taking photos of Alec, a married account executive who looks a little too cozy at the bar with Mercedes, the buxom and boozy sixth-floor receptionist. Which is a borderline violation of *She* magazine's *Don't Gossip* rule.

The familiar face stops in front of me, and its mouth says, "Hey, how's it going, Chief?"

"Hi, Mike!" Am I slurring? "Here, get in the picture with us!"

"How about if I take it?" he offers, setting down his bottled Molson Ice and taking the camera from Latisha. She gets into the picture with me and Brenda and we all pose with our arms around each other, flashing big, cheesy smiles.

God only knows where Yvonne is. Last I knew, she was heading outside for a smoke. I decide I'll join her just as soon as I've had a courteous—and hopefully sober-sounding—conversation with my boss.

"Hey, Mike, great tie," I say, admiring the green silk background imprinted with teeny-tiny Santa Claus faces.

"You like it? Thanks."

I do like it. Somehow, what's grotesque overkill on Merry seems pleasantly festive on anybody else.

"Ooh, anybody want to Slide?" Brenda squeals as a familiar refrain of "boogie woogie woogies" erupts from the DJ booth.

Mike and I pass. I'd do it, but I'm afraid my boobs would pop out of my dress every time I did the leaning-over step. Pleased with my foresight, I stand sedately with my boss and watch Brenda and Latisha join the line dance.

"Dianne said if she ever saw me doing the Electric Slide, she'd break up with me," Mike confides.

"You're kidding."

"Nope."

"Well, then, *she's* kidding."

"She's not," he says. "She thinks it's a ridiculous dance."

I glance at the ranks of office workers gliding four steps back, four steps forward in perfect sync—except for Merry, who keeps going the wrong way and crashing into people.

Okay, it might be a ridiculous dance, but it's fun. Suddenly I feel sorry for Mike, banned from the Slide and God only knows what else.

"You know, Dianne's not here," I point out. "You should try the Slide."

"I can't."

"Sure you can. She'd never find out."

He looks around the room nervously, even skyward, as though expecting to spot Dianne in a trenchcoat and dark glasses astride one of the fake shooting stars.

I find myself thinking of Alec the married account exec, flirting madly with Mercedes. And even Brenda, wearing the rock that consumed a few months' worth of Paulie's NYPD salary, yet blatantly checking out other guys. And Buckley, dragging his heels about moving in with Sonja.

Of course, in the back of my mind there's always Will, who cheated on me with Esme Spencer, who played Dot to his George in a summer-stock production of *Sunday in the Park with George.*

Maybe it's good that I'm single. Maybe I don't want to meet someone after all. At least, not for a while.

I look at Mike, who's wistfully watching the dance floor.

"So, are you allowed to Macarena?" I can't resist asking, expecting a big laugh and maybe even applause.

He fails to see the hilarity. In fact, he takes the question seriously and actually looks uncertain. "She never mentioned that, but…"

You know, maybe it's the martinis again, but I'm starting to really dislike that Dianne. She seems so sweet on the phone, but as a girlfriend, she's a little Nazi-ish, don't you think?

"I need a cigarette," I announce to Mike. "And you need a new beer. That one's empty."

"Okay," he says obediently, and once again I'm saddened. Poor, poor Mike. He may be the boss in the office, but clearly his power stops there.

I head for the door and gratefully indulge my craving for menthol out on the litter-strewn sidewalk with a bunch of other banished addicts.

We smokers are an eclectic bunch. There are stressed-out upper-management types and administrative assistants who wear sneakers with their stockings on weekday subway commutes; fresh-out-of-Ivy-League assistant media buyers and well-past-retirement-age grandmotherly career secretaries who seem reassuringly immune to lung cancer.

We puff away and talk about the good old days when you could actually smoke in a bar in New York. One old-timer (not Yvonne, but she might as well be, given the overall blowsy broad persona, complete with raspy voice and borough accent) waxes nostalgic about smoking at her desk.

Then an icy wind gusting off the East River has us hastily stubbing our half-burned butts and scuttling back inside.

I head directly to the bar. Mostly because I don't see any of my friends in the crowd, and the bar is always a safe place to park oneself. But also because I need another drink.

I order yet another blood-orange martini and try to sip it slowly as I watch everyone on the dance floor bopping around to "Love Shack." I spot Latisha out there more or less dirty dancing with Myron the mail-room guy, who's been after her since before she dumped her loser boyfriend Anton last summer. She'd better not screw things up with Derek, her new boyfriend, a single dad who shares her passion for the New York Yankees…and, according to Latisha, her passion for—well, for passion.

I wonder morosely if I'll ever experience passion again. God forbid my sleazy romp between the *Star Wars* sheets was my sexual swan song, but I can't seem to conjure up any situation in which I'll be having sex any time soon. I've sworn off one-night stands, so unless somebody sweeps me off my feet…

"Hi."

I turn around to see a strange guy standing beside me. Not Jeff S-n *strange*; just *strange* as in I've never seen him before in my life.

I look over both shoulders. Huh. Apparently, he was talking to me.

"Hi," I counter, cautiously.

"I'm Jack."

"I'm Tracey."

*And they lived happily ever after.*

Yeah, right. I wish.

This guy is so cute that I find myself wondering why he's
come over to me, having momentarily forgotten that I, too,
am now cute.

"Do you work at Blaire Barnett?" Jack asks.

Well, duh. Everybody in the room works at Blaire Barnett.

"No," I find myself saying, "I'm a nurse at Bellevue. Mental ward."

"You are?"

I laugh at the befuddled expression in his big brown eyes.
"No. I'm just being a wise-ass."

And probably sabotaging my chances of any kind of future
relationship with this guy, but I can't seem to help myself.

"Actually, I work at Blaire Barnett," I confess, and sip my
drink. This one is stronger than the last. Much stronger. So
strong I taste no blood orange; I swear it's all vodka.

"Yeah, I work there, too," Jack says.

Have I mentioned how much I love big brown little-boy
eyes on a grown man? No?

That's probably because I never realized it until this very
moment. He's tall—much taller than I am, and I'm wearing
heels. He's broad-shouldered. His hair is the same melted-
milk-chocolate color as his eyes; kind of wavy and combed
back from his face. He's got a great mouth with a full lower

lip. And the best part of all: dimples. He has two dimples, one on either side of his mouth. They're there even when he's not smiling.

"So what do you do?" Jack is asking.

Okay, so he's not the brightest bulb on the Christmas tree. Or maybe he's just hard of hearing. But who the hell cares about his brain or his ears when he's got eyes like that?

"I work at Blaire Barnett," I repeat patiently, feeling almost like a nurse in Bellevue's mental ward.

"I know.... I mean, what do you do there?"

Oh. Good. He's not stupid or hearing impaired.

"I work in account management." Please don't make me say the *S* word.

"Doing what?"

I feign confusion. "What?"

Okay, he's not stupid or hearing impaired, but now he thinks I'm one or both. Would it be better to just admit that I'm a secretary? I'm afraid he'll think that's all I am. That he won't believe it if I tell him I'm in line for a promotion.

He starts to ask, "What do you—"

"So what department are you in?" I quickly interrupt.

"Media."

Mission accomplished. Line of questioning derailed. Celebratory sip of drink in order.

I take two sips, then ask, "Are you a buyer?"

"I'm a planner."

"Oh." I nod, fascinated. Well, not really. But I hope I look it.

Actually, Media Planning is a fun job. Relatively low-paying, but I'm not a gold digger like Kate, so what do I care?

"I've never seen you around the agency before," Jack tells

me while I check out his clothes. I'm no Raphael, but his suit looks good on him and it's basic black; he's wearing a white starched spread-collar dress shirt and a black tie with a white pattern.

"I've never seen you around either," I tell him, hoping he didn't catch me looking him up and down.

Maybe he did, because I suddenly feel like he's looking me up and down, too.

Now I feel awkward. And drunk. Not to mention confused. Why is this Jack over here talking to me?

*Cut it out, Tracey.* I can almost hear Buckley's voice. *Why wouldn't this guy want to talk to you? What's wrong with you?*

Nothing. Nothing is wrong with me. I just have to remember that.

Lately, Buckley has been trying to point out that Will really did a number on my self-esteem. The whole time I was with him, I felt unworthy. I'm trying, but it's hard to get past that. I might have lost all that extra poundage, but I'm still carrying around a tremendous amount of baggage.

And now, here's this guy coming up to talk to me; the kind of guy I'd normally be wistfully checking out from afar. It seems too good to be true.

Especially since he just appeared out of nowhere. If this were a movie, he'd have stepped into a dazzling pool of light, and a choir would have sung one big loud Hallelujah. But it's not and he didn't and they didn't.

He's just here, and I have no idea why. I mean, even setting all the usual Tracey insecurity aside, I'm still the lone Don't at the party, and he's…

Well, he's so normal. Good-looking normal, with dimples and a real job.

Unlike Will, the actor. Will was good-looking, too, but he didn't have dimples and he wasn't *normal*. Ask Kate. Ask Raphael. Their hobby, when I was dating Will, was pointing out just how abnormal Will is. That he's narcissistic and untrustworthy and selfish.

And closeted—or so they both suspected.

Kate, because she assumes every man who wears black turtlenecks and cologne and dabbles in theater must be secretly gay.

Raphael, because he and his constantly blipping gaydar think every man is secretly gay.

I try to think of something to say to Cute Normal Jack of the warm brown eyes and stable job.

"So…um, Jack…you just saw me standing here alone and decided to come over and talk to me?"

Okay, I agree, awkward silence was better. But I can't seem to help myself. Three martinis and I start to blurt things. Anyway, it could have been worse.

He shifts his weight, doesn't answer right away.

Uh-oh.

Maybe it couldn't have been worse. Maybe he really wasn't talking to me all this time. I look over my shoulders again, half expecting to see some supermodel standing there.

"Yeah, I wanted to meet you," he says, obviously uncomfortable.

"Oh."

Something tells me there's more to it, but who am I to pry? If Cute Normal Jack wants to meet the Queen of the Don'ts, so be it.

From there, the night unfolds in a series of highlights: Jack asking me to dance to an old song by the Cure; Jack meeting my friends; Latisha snapping pictures with my camera; more drinks; more cigarettes in the bitter cold.

Until now, I've felt that there are two breeds of men in New York: men who smoke, and men who think nobody should smoke.

Jack breaks the whole *If you're not with us, you're against us* mold. He's not a smoker, but not only does he not seem to mind that I am, he comes outside with me, gives me his suit jacket to keep me warm, takes my lighter from me and lights my cigarettes.

He makes me laugh harder than I've laughed in a long time, especially when he sings along to a Billy Joel song that's playing, acting like he's doing a nightclub act and using a beer bottle as a microphone. I can't tell if he really can't sing or if he's just pretending for the sake of the act—not that it matters. After all, Will had the voice of a choirboy but the disposition of an asshole.

Unlike Will, who never shared my sense of humor, Jack also laughs at all my jokes, proving that even in my bibulous blur, I'm not just amusing to myself.

He's a good dancer, too. Not many guys are—not at fast dancing, anyway. Some are embarrassingly unable to get the beat; some don't even try. Some try to hold on to you when you're fast dancing with them, like they want you to jitterbug or something. But Jack just dances—not too close to me, and not too far away. He doesn't try to spin me and he doesn't have that goofy, intense, I'm-so-into-the-music look on his face.

Merry has that look, especially when the DJ plays Madonna's "Santa Baby." She pretty much does a spotlight solo for that song, which nobody else considers danceable.

*Mental Note: Never, under any circumstances, dance alone, no matter how much you love the song.*

"Man, I'd hate to be Merry on January second," Brenda comments as my friends and I and Jack stand around watching her from the bar.

"Yeah," I say. "She's probably curled in a fetal position with pine needles in her hair."

"Nah, by then she's booking her flight to Punxsatawney and airing out the groundhog suit," Jack says unexpectedly, and we all laugh.

"He's a keeper," Yvonne rasps as he flags down the bartender to order another round for all of us.

"Yeah, Tracey, how'd you hook up with him?" Brenda asks.

I shrug. "We just started talking."

Another big plus: My friends approve. And he seems to like them, too. He's even a good sport about Latisha, aspiring photographer, who insists on taking a picture of me and Jack together. He puts his arm around my shoulder and smiles, like we're old pals. Or a couple.

He seems to know a lot of people who work at the agency, and he introduces me to them as Tracey from account management.

He's too good to be true.

What's the catch?

There has to be a catch, dammit. There's always a catch. Men like this don't just drop into your lap when you least expect it. Well, they certainly don't drop into mine.

The crowd is starting to thin out. Brenda keeps looking at her watch, saying Paulie is going to kill her.

I don't want to leave yet.

Or ever.

I'm boozy and blissful, leaning against the bar talking to Jack while the DJ plays one of my favorite U2 songs, "With or Without You."

As the song heats up, Jack leans over and kisses me.

I kiss him back.

Everything falls away. Brenda and her watch, the music, the bar. There's just me and Jack, floating in space. At Space. In front of a few hundred co-workers and, for all I know, my boss.

When we come up for air, my friends are gone.

Oops.

In fact, almost everybody's gone, and the DJ is announcing last call.

"Where do you live?" Jack asks, taking my hand and strolling me toward the coat check.

"East Village. How about you?"

"Brooklyn. Let's get a cab."

To where? The East Village? Brooklyn? (Yeah, I know, a borough, but Jack's the exception to the bridge-and-tunnel-people-aren't-cool rule.) His intent isn't clear, but what the hell?

I've got other things to worry about right now. It's all I can do to concentrate on finding my coat-check tag. Jack helps me look. We both crack jokes and laugh hysterically the entire time.

I guess you had to be there. And drunk.

Ultimately, we arrive at the hilarious—at least, to us—conclusion that I've misplaced the tag. I then have to focus on not slurring when I describe my outdated wool coat to the utterly unamused and fashionable coat-check girl.

Outside, the arctic air hits me, along with a big dose of reality. Suddenly nothing seems funny.

I just made out with some guy at the office party. Now I'm leaving with him.

Does he think he's coming to my place? Does he think I'm going to his place?

I should insist on separate cabs to our respective places, just to make sure this doesn't go any further.

For some reason, Buckley's face pops into my head. I hear Buckley's voice warning me to stay away from strange guys.

I promised him. At least, I think I did.

But Buckley doesn't have to know…

*No. Stop it, Tracey.*

Sleeping with some guy you just met and will never see again is one thing. A *bad* thing.

Sleeping with a co-worker you just met is…

Well, it's just out of the question.

It's the ultimate Don't.

I stand on the sidewalk by a garbage can and smoke a cigarette, trying to sober up while Jack stands in the street and tries to hail a cab. They're few and far between, and when he finally gets one, I'm not about to tell him to let me take it alone. I mean, that would make me a Don't *and* a Bitch. A Bitchy Don't.

I giggle. I can't help it.

Jack looks at me. "What's funny?"

I wipe the goofy grin off my face. "What?"

"Didn't you just laugh?"

"Me? Nope. Not me."

Jack looks confused.

I smile pleasantly. At least, I hope I do. For all I know,

another burst of maniacal laughter can escape me at any moment.

Oh, Lord, am I ever trashed. I try to send myself Sober Up vibes as we climb into the back seat, which smells of mildew unsuccessfully masked by fruity air freshener. I immediately tell the driver my address.

"And after that, I need to go to Brooklyn," Jack says through the plastic window.

Instant relief. He's not planning on coming home with me.

Bitter disappointment. He's not planning on coming home with me.

As the cab barrels down Ninth Avenue, I focus on the driver's name on his license fastened to the dashboard. To inebriated *moi* it looks like Ishmael Ishtar, and I vaguely wonder which is his first name and which is his last.

Then Jack puts his arm around me and pulls me closer. Kisses me. I feel weak.

In the front seat, the driver speaks in a foreign language into his two-way radio.

In the back seat, Jack makes me forget everything I promised myself five minutes ago.

All too soon, we're at my building. Jack opens the door, and we both step out onto the sidewalk.

"Can I come up?" he asks, low, in my ear.

"You already told Ishmael you're going to Brooklyn."

"Huh?"

I gesture at the driver.

"Oh." He shrugs. "I'll give him a big tip."

He kisses me, an intensely sweeping kiss.

Life comes down to a few Moments of Truth. This is one of them.

What will happen if I say yes?
What will happen if I say no?
There's no way of knowing.
Nothing to do but take a deep breath—and make a decision.

# 5

Monday morning, I wear a frumpy navy rayon dress that's two sizes too big for me, no makeup and sunglasses.

The sky hangs low and gray over Manhattan, but I don't give a damn. I'm in disguise. At least, in the lobby and in the elevator, where I stand in the back silently facing straight ahead while the crowd chatters about the office party.

Is it my imagination, or are people nudge-nudge, wink-winking about me?

It has to be my imagination. I'm no stranger to paranoia. Just because I flirted—

Oh, all right, *made out with*—

—some guy at the office party, well, that doesn't mean anybody noticed. Or that if they noticed, they care.

Insert Kinks' guitar riff here. *Duh…duh-duh…duh-duh-duh-duh-duh. Paranoia, Self-Destroya…*

I find myself wishing I had called in sick today. Or, um, you know...*quit.*

On my floor, Lydia greets me as usual from beneath a green-and-silver garland of tinsel. She doesn't even do a double take before chirping, "Morning, Tracey" and going back to her *Newsday.*

*Mental Note: Disguise not 100 percent foolproof.*

I have to take off the glasses anyway when I get to my desk. Luckily, it's barely nine o'clock and the place is deserted. It's also got that Monday-morning chill after a weekend with the heat turned down.

I'm shivering as I head for the kitchenette—also deserted—and grab coffee from the community pot. Normally I drink it with skim milk and an Equal, but I hear somebody coming and duck out the opposite door sloshing black coffee all over my hand. Ouch, dammit!

This is ridiculous. I can't go sneaking around all day like I'm starring in *The Mole.*

Why, oh why, was I such an all-out Don't on Saturday night? Why didn't I stop and consider the consequences?

Back at my cubicle, I set my coffee on my desk and take several deep breaths. I can't stop shaking, and it's not just because it's cold in here. I feel a panic attack coming on.

Needing a distraction, I turn on my computer and sip some coffee while it whirs into action, and then I log on to the Internet and see that I've got a bunch of e-mails. One is from Buckley, asking if I want to have lunch today; one is from Kate, asking how the Christmas party was; three are from my sister-in-law Sara, all of them forwarded jokes as old as my screen name. But she and Joey are new to e-mail, so lame forwards are still a novelty to them.

"Hey, what happened to you on Saturday night, girl-friend?" Latisha calls from somewhere behind me, in her loudest yoo-hoo voice.

"Shh!" I wave my arms at her, almost knocking over my coffee.

"Here," she says, handing over my camera. "I figured you were going to lose this at the club, the way you were—"

"Carrying on?" I supply when she hesitates.

"That's one way to put it." She smirks. "Anyway, I brought it home safely for you."

"Thanks." I didn't even realize until now that I didn't have it. "But why didn't you bring *me* home safely? You guys abandoned me."

"We didn't abandon you. We told you we were leaving," Brenda pipes up, materializing behind Latisha. "Three times. You didn't hear us. You were too busy kissing that guy."

I cringe.

The two of them park themselves on my desk, wearing expectant expressions.

"Well?" Latisha asks. "Did you go home with him?"

"No!" I act totally outraged, as though the thought never would have entered my chaste mind. "Do you guys really think I'm that sleazy?"

They look at each other. Obviously, they do.

"You were kind of all over each other," Brenda says with a shrug. "I was a little surprised."

I rub my eyes with my hand, utterly humiliated. "Oh, Lord, do you think anyone else saw?"

Yvonne pops her bubblegum-colored bouffant over a filing cabinet. "It was hard to miss, honey."

Not *honey* as in You Poor Misunderstood Thing. Yvonne

might be my grandmother's age, but there isn't a maternal bone in her weedy former Rockette body; her *honey* is brash and laced with sarcasm.

I bury my face in my hands, fighting off panic, doing my best not to hyperventilate.

Brenda pats my back. "Look on the bright side, Tracey. You met a nice guy. Did you give him your number?"

"No."

"Why the hell not?" Latisha demands.

"He didn't ask." Talk about humiliating. I add hastily, "And anyway, I don't want him to call me. I just want to forget the whole thing."

"Why?" Brenda asks. "I thought he was a good guy."

"Hot, too," Latisha says approvingly.

"He had tight buns," Yvonne puts in.

Eeewww. Tight buns?

Like I said, she's my grandmother's age. That's hip slang for her. But the phrase has me picturing some unappealing loser in snug-fitting beige polyester slacks—which, if nothing else, is enough to take the edge off the panic.

"Morning, Chief." Mike pokes his head around the edge of my cube. "Ladies."

They greet him and disperse, leaving me alone with my boss standing over me. My thoughts whirl back to the party.

"So I heard you met my roommate."

"Hmm?" I reply absently, trying to remember whether Mike left early. I wring my icy hands in my lap. God, I hope so. Or could he have still been around while I was sucking face with Jack at the bar?

"The funny thing is, he didn't realize you worked for me."

"Mmm-hmm."

Wait a minute.

*What?*

I gape at Mike's big grin, searching for words, coming up with only, "Wait a minute. What?"

"My roommate," he says. "Jack."

Shit. Shitshitshitshitshitshitshit.

"Jack's your roommate?"

You have got to be kidding me.

"Yup."

Clearly, nobody is kidding here.

This development sinks my Office Party Don't-dom to a whole new level.

"Jack? Jack, uh—" Okay, I don't even know his last name. "Jack the guy I, um, met—" that's one way to put it "—is your roommate?"

"Uh-huh."

"But...I didn't even know you had a roommate," I say weakly. (Yes, I know, Dianne did mention it on the phone, but I do not remember that conversation at the moment. It will, however, come back to me eventually.)

Here's where Mike says, "Just kidding. I don't."

But he doesn't. Say it, that is.

He does, apparently, have a roommate and his roommate's name is Jack.

*Mental Note: Update résumé during lunch hour.*

"So what'd you think of him?"

"Jack?"

"Jack," he says with an anticipatory quirk of his eyebrows. Christ, I feel like he's shoving a microphone in my face.

*Well, Mike, to be honest, I thought Jack had nice, tight buns.*

"Jack was a good guy."

There. A nice, G-rated reply.

Thank God, thank God, thank *God* I didn't sleep with Jack.

I wanted to. I really did. Standing there on the street in front of my building, with everything hanging in the balance and his big warm arms around me, I desperately wanted to give in and let him come upstairs with me.

But I mustered every ounce of willpower I possessed, and I didn't. I just kissed him one last time and ran inside.

How the hell did I, in my Stoli-soaked, turned-on state, manage to find and embrace my inner Catholic schoolgirl?

It can only have been divine intervention.

Like I said, Thank God, thank God, thank God.

My inner Catholic schoolgirl zaps me with stinging Catholic guilt.

*Mental Note: Unearth rosary beads from bottom of underwear drawer and check Sunday mass schedule.*

"Yeah, Jack's a great guy," Mike is agreeing. "He's the best."

I smile. Nod pleasantly. *Yup. That Jack's the best.*

Mercifully, the phone on my desk rings before the painful conversation drags out any longer.

"That might be Dianne," Mike says hopefully.

No, it might not. Because it isn't his extension that's ringing; it's mine.

Probably Buckley, wanting to know about lunch. Plus, I screened his calls yesterday.

Or it could be Kate. Or Raphael. I screened them, too.

I had a massive hangover and spent the entire day lying on my bed in sweats eating carbs, rehydrating and watching made-for-TV movies on Lifetime. And shivering, because my apartment is so drafty. Oh, and cringing every time I thought about what I'd done the night before.

All in all, I've had better days.

"Tracey Spadolini," I announce into my phone in a brisk, efficient voice—only because Mike is standing here. Calls that come in on my own extension are almost never business-related, but he doesn't have to know that.

"Hi," says a voice.

A male voice.

Not Buckley's. Not Raphael's.

I make it's-for-me motions at Mike, who nods and disappears.

"Hi," I say cautiously into the phone.

"It's Jack. From Saturday night."

Jack. Boss's roommate Jack.

"Hi," I say again. My heart is beating a little faster. Despite my ambivalence, he's got a great voice. It was hard to tell when we were screaming over the music at the party. He sounds low and manly, unlike Will, the tenor, who was sometimes mistaken for a woman back when he did telemarketing.

"Tracey, you work for my roommate."

No shit.

"I just found out," I tell him. "I, um, didn't even know Mike had a roommate."

"Yeah. I was telling him about you yesterday, and we figured it out."

Cringing, I imagine that conversation.

*Say, Mike, I met a liquored-up strumpet in a skimpy red frock last night.*

*Why, Jack, that sounds like my assistant, Tracey.*

"So anyway…I looked you up in the company directory…."

Excellent detective work, Watson.

Part of me—the eagerly expectant, shamelessly aroused part—is flattered that he wanted to find me again. Part of me—the utterly disgraced part—would have been content to slink on into oblivion.

"…and I thought we should go out."

"You did?"

He laughs. "I mean, I do."

"You do?"

With a Don't?

He wants to go out with me after the spectacle we made of ourselves in front of the entire agency? Isn't he the least bit mortified?

Apparently not. He asks cheerfully, "Are you busy Friday night?"

"I'm, uh, not sure. Can I let you know this afternoon?"

He hesitates. "Okay."

"It's just that I was supposed to have these plans with my friends…."

Did I ever mention I'm a terrible liar?

"That's all right."

"I just—"

"I understand. If you're busy—"

Suddenly, I'm Kate Winslet awash in the North Atlantic, clinging to his icy hand as he begins to drift away.

*Noooooooo! Don't leave me, Jack!*

"Actually I think we switched the plans to Saturday," I say quickly. "I'm not sure. I'll just check and let you know this afternoon. I'm probably free."

"That's fine."

I hear ringing in the background.

"That's my other line," he says.

"Okay."

"So I'll talk to you later?"

"Okay," I repeat, quite the sparkling conversationalist.

"Bye."

"Thanks for calling."

"Sure. Bye."

I'm elated.

He asked me out!

I'm suspicious.

Why the hell would he ask me out?

I'm—

Dialing. That's what I'm doing. I'm calling Kate. I need advice.

She's home, of course. She's not working these days—or, probably, ever again. When I met her, she was temping, just like me. But her parents back in Mobile pay her bills, and the only reason she worked at all was to meet rich businessman types. Now that she has Billy, she's basically a housewife without the house. Or the husband. Yet.

"You'll never believe who's on Regis and Kelly this morning," she says by way of a greeting. I can hear the television in the background; sounds of applause and Regis shouting something.

"Kate, listen—"

"Remember the short blond guy who was in that lame movie we saw last summer at the—"

"Kate, I need to talk to you. I'm at work and I've only got a minute. It's important." Sometimes you just have to pluck her out of her insulated little Kate universe.

"What happened? Are you okay? Why are you whispering?"

"Because I'm at work and I don't want anyone to hear."

"Hear what? Oh my God, are you pregnant?"

"No!" I should have called Buckley instead. He's a better listener.

But I can't leave her hanging now, so I quickly tell Kate what happened.

"Did you sleep with him?"

"No! We just kissed," I hiss. "But everyone saw. And he's my boss's roommate," I point out for, like, the third time. "How can I go out with him? I mean...what if I slept over at his house and ran into Mike walking around in his underwear?"

"I don't know...it might be good for you," she says.

"Spinach is good for you. Seeing your boss in his underwear is not good for you. Or maybe it's good for you, but it isn't for me."

I shudder at the mental image of a scantily clad Mike.

Okay, he probably doesn't wear Spider-Man Underoos in real life, but still.

"I don't mean seeing your boss in his underwear would be good. Nobody said you have to sleep with this guy. In fact, whatever you do, don't sleep with him. I'm just saying that it might be good for you to go out on a date with him. After the way Will shit all over you, you deserve to have somebody take you out and treat you well."

*Well gee, thank you so much for that, Kate.* The thought of Mike wearing Underoos has been replaced by the oh-so-graphic image of Will shitting all over me.

"But he's my boss's roommate."

I can just see her rolling her light blue eyes. Even I'm getting sick of me saying it.

"So? It's a date. Just a date. Period. I mean, it's not like you're ready for another relationship yet…."

"What do you mean by that?"

"It would be purely rebound, Tracey. You don't get dumped after spending a few years of your life with somebody and turn around and meet the right person immediately. It takes time. You've got to heal."

"I'm healed."

Really.

These days, when Will calls me, I never think he's going to ask me to get back together. Well, hardly ever.

Okay, I didn't think that the last time he called. At least, not the whole time. Not after he mentioned that he and Esme were going skiing in Vermont over Christmas.

"You're healing, but you're not entirely healed, Tracey. You're not ready to invest wholeheartedly in another relationship," advises Dr. Phil. I mean, Kate.

"Then why bother going out with this guy at all?"

Her prompt, precise answer: "Because you need a Transition Boy."

"A what?"

"Someone to ease you back into the real world," Kate explains. "Someone to help you cross the bridge between your old identity as Will's girlfriend and your new identity. You know, someone to—"

"Wipe off the shit and make me feel all fresh again."

There's a pause. I picture her delicately wrinkling her powdered nose.

"Well, if you really must put it that way, Tracey…"

"Yes, I really must."

"Well, anyway, you should never turn down the opportunity to get to know somebody new," Kate declares. "Even if it obviously can't work out with him, he may have a friend who might interest you, down the road when you're healed."

Concluding that Kate is watching too many daytime talk shows, I thank her and hang up, still not sure what I want to do.

I can't even remember what Jack looks like. Is he really as handsome as I thought the other night? Or did all those drinks cloud my judgment? For all I know, he looks like Dobby the house elf.

Not that it matters.

Of course looks don't matter. I'm not *that* shallow.

Wait, am I?

Am I *shallow*?

I do spend an awful lot of time thinking about looks. My own, and other people's.

But who doesn't?

Okay, my family back home doesn't.

Buckley doesn't.

My friends at work don't.

But just because I've spent a lot of time and effort trying to look good, and just because I want to make sure the guy I might go out with isn't a beast...

Well, that doesn't mean I'm shallow.

Shallow is *Are You Hot?*

Shallow is everybody who works at *She* magazine.

Shallow is...

*Will.*

Shallow is Will; Will is shallow.

He's also beautiful—but only on the outside. He was

cold and cruel on the inside. That should have taught me something.

I ponder.

I reflect.

And then I think, the hell with it.

If I'm going to have a Transition Boy, I might as well make sure he's good-looking. Correct me if I'm wrong, but isn't it better to go for the looks now and the other worthy qualities later, when, according to Kate the Relationship Guru, I'll actually be ready to find Mr. Right?

So the first order of business is to find out whether Jack is really as appealing as he seemed. I honestly doubt that I hallucinated his cuteness factor, but then, I also thought losing a coat-check tag was *Seinfeld* material, so it would be dangerous to rely solely on Saturday night's drunken judgment.

There's only one thing to do.

My gaze falls on the camera on my desk.

*Mental Note: Get party film developed ASAP.*


Manhattan is full of one-hour film developing places.

Those places are full of crap.

At least, the one in my building's lobby, where I drop off my film during my lunch break, is full of crap.

When I stop back exactly an hour later on my way upstairs, the sari-clad woman behind the counter shakes her head.

"When will it be ready?" I ask.

"Never," she says in some inscrutable foreign language.

At least, that's what I later deduce she must have said, because every time I step out of the office for a cigarette and

pop back down into the store to check, she glares and indicates that the pictures aren't ready yet.

I'm starting to hate her.

Maybe it's my imagination, but I think she's doing this to
me on purpose. Maybe she and the guy who develops the
pictures are enjoying my restless anticipation; enjoying the
power they wield over my romantic future.

At one point, late in the afternoon, I find myself waiting—and shivering—in the drafty lobby for the elevator
with Miss Prim aka Susan, the annoyingly buttoned-up account exec from my floor.

She's with an equally buttoned-up account exec, and I
swear I see them nudge each other when I step into the car.

I know you're thinking this was just my imagination, too,
but it wasn't.

I know this because as the elevator doors slide closed, I
hear Susan whisper, "She's the one."

She's the one…what?

The one who got trashed and made out with some
strange guy at the bar in front of the entire company, of
course.

I shrink against the elevator wall as the car jerks and rises,
praying for death.

Why did I leave my sunglasses upstairs on my desk? I stare
at the floor numbers, pretending I don't notice Susan's companion casting curious sidelong glances in my direction, as
if she's never seen a real live hussy before.

I'm never going to live this down. Never. The only way
to live this down would be…

I don't know, I guess maybe if Jack and I eventually get
married, people won't think what we did at the party was

so bad. They'll just think we fell madly in love at first sight. Everybody knows that true love is forgiveable; sottish lust is not.

So all I have to do is get Jack to marry me.

Death, I conclude, as the elevator stops at my floor, would be simpler.

My pictures are ready at noon on Tuesday.

I snatch them out of the enemy's hand—the enemy being the proprietress of the lobby photo kiosk. By now, our relationship has deteriorated to the point of open hostility.

"Twenty-two-fifty," she snaps, after punching keys on the register.

"Twenty-two-fifty?" I echo, as though she's just requested the entire contents of my wallet.

Which, sadly, she has.

"Twenty-two-fifty," she repeats, indicating the sign above her head.

"But that's the one-hour rate."

"Yes, and you check one-hour-rate box." She points to the photo envelope.

"But they weren't back in one hour."

Looking bored, she indicates the fine print below the box.

"'Cannot guarantee photos in one hour,'" I read. "That's ridiculous! If I didn't want them back in one hour, I'd have checked the other box."

The other box being the one where the photos are sent out and returned the next day, with free doubles, for twelve bucks.

"You check this box," she snarls. "Twenty-two-fifty."

"But that's unfair!"

"Fine. I keep pictures," she says with a shrug, reaching for the envelope.

"No!" I shriek, holding them above my head like one of my sister's kids playing Keepaway. *Neener neener neener, you ca-an't have them.*

"Twenty-two-fifty, you lady. Or I call police."

"Here. Fine. Take the twenty-two-fifty." I throw a twenty and some ones on the counter and stalk across the lobby toward the elevator bank for my floor.

Only when I'm inside—sharing the elevator with a couple of chatty maintenance men and the ubiquitous bike messenger—do I exhale and open the envelope.

I flip through countless pictures until I come to the one of me and Jack.

We're smiling, arm-in-arm.

We look like a couple.

And Jack…

Well, Jack looks great.

That settles it.

I'm going out with my boss's roommate.

Too bad, I think wistfully, staring at the photo, he's destined to be my Transition Boy.

# 6

After work on Friday, I duck into the ladies' room and change into a little black spandex dress that hugs every inch of my body—that is, every inch that it doesn't expose.

I'm going to freeze tonight. The wind-chill factor is in the single digits.

I had considered wearing a nice, toasty, boring long skirt and blazer on our date, lest Jack get the impression that I'm a brazen temptress.

But as I headed out the door this morning, something made me grab this sexy dress out of my closet and throw it into my black shoulder bag.

Okay, not something. *Someone.*

Raphael spent the night in my apartment while his is being fumigated.

"Tweed? You can't wear that, Tracey!" he said in horror, staring at my charcoal wool skirt and jacket, opaque hose and sensible shoes. "Not unless he's taking you door-to-door on a Jehovah's Witness canvass."

So here I am, wearing a dress that's so freaking snug I haven't allowed myself to eat a thing all day in order to avoid an unsightly gut bulge. I wasn't even hungry, thanks to nerves and, of course, my little pink pills.

And I'm freaking freezing. I've been cold all day. All week, really. Cold and jittery and all I want to do is go home and crawl under a warm blanket.

But, instead, I have two hours to kill before I'm supposed to meet Jack.

We're meeting at Tequila Murray's, a semikosher Mexican place in the Village. That was my idea. He had originally suggested that we just hook up in the lobby after work.

Yeah, sure. And take the risk that seeing the two of us together might trigger suppressed memories in anyone who managed to forget the spectacle we made of ourselves at the Christmas party? I don't think so.

As you can see, my morning-after paranoia hasn't subsided in the least.

In fact, I can't believe I agreed to this date. But it's too late to back out, so there's nothing to do but take the 6 train down to Bleeker with Raphael.

No, he's not coming on my date with me. He's got his own date later, with some construction worker he met. According to Raphael, they were cruising each other over satin panties at Victoria's Secret.

I know. Don't ask.

It's two-for-one margarita happy hour at Tequila Murray's, where Raphael and I grab a table by the window.

"Hey, Raphael, how's it going?" asks the waitress, depositing a basket of tortilla chips, salsa and guacamole between us.

"Geri! I didn't know you worked here!"

"Just since last week," she replies.

Geri and Raphael exchange gleeful small talk about people I don't know and places I've never been while I smile like an idiot. This happens all the time when I'm with Raphael.

Finally, Geri takes our drink order. I'm having a margarita, but Raphael wants something called a Golden Cadillac. Geri winks at him and tells him that technically he's not supposed to get anything but a margarita two-for-one, but she'll make an exception for him.

As Geri sashays away, I ask, "Raphael, do you know everybody in Manhattan?" I reach for a chip before remembering. The date. The dress. The gut.

I pull my hand back and sit on it.

"Not *everybody,* Tracey," he says, dead serious. He sneezes, then adds, "He used to date my friend Jacob."

"God bless you. He? Who?"

"Thank you. Jacob. You know. From the *Sondheim Review.*" He blows his nose loudly.

Actually, I don't know Jacob from the *Sondheim Review.* Nor do I have a clue what he's talking about.

Mustering my patience, I try again. "Who used to date your friend Jacob from the *Sondheim Review?*"

"The waiter."

Waiter?

I glance over at the bar, where Geri—rather, I suppose, Jerry—is waiting for our drinks. His cleavage is spectacular. So is the bulge beneath the fly of his black toreador pants.

I sigh. You'd think by now I'd be used to Raphael, human magnet for all manner of bizarre life forms.

"Tracey, I can't wait to meet Jack," Raphael announces, munching a chip, then promptly double-dipping in the salsa.

Ew. So much for temptation. I wouldn't touch the stuff now. Raphael has a horrible head cold. He kept me up most of the night with his sniffles and coughs.

When I suggested that he cancel his date with the construction worker, he looked at me like I'd advised him to join the Franciscan friars.

"Ooh, Tracey, you have to taste this!" he exclaims, crunching. "It's fresh. Mmmm. It's so cilantro-y."

"You're not going to meet Jack, Raphael," I say, retrieving my hand and shoving the bowl of fresh and germ-ridden cilantro-y salsa toward the opposite side of the table.

"I'm not going to meet Jack?" He looks crushed. "Why not?"

I look at Raphael, taking in the leopard-spotted hair scrunchy he's wearing on his wrist as a bracelet, the denim culottes, the red-patent-leather pointy-toed boots.

"Not to be mean or anything, Raphael, but you might scare him."

"Oh, never mind, Tracey. By the time he gets here, I'll be long gone. Carl should be here any second now."

"Carl's coming *here*?"

"Didn't I tell you?"

"No. I thought you were meeting him at Oh, Boy."

"Change of plans. He's coming here." He blows his red nose and moves the scrunchy aside to shove the used tissue up his sleeve. "Oh, look, there he is now. Carl!"

I turn to see a strapping boots-and-flannel-clad giant stepping in off the street, a legend come to life.

I blink.

Holy Paul Bunyan, Batman.

"Isn't he masculine, Tracey?" Raphael gushes, pretty much swooning into the guacamole.

"All that's missing is Babe the Big Blue Ox," I mutter, as Jerry the gender bender sets my drink in front of me.

Carl joins us.

I take a big, hearty sip of my slushy lime drink. Instant head freeze.

I know I should go easy, considering my empty stomach.

Yeah, right.

The next thing you know, I'm sipping the last of my first margarita while my freebie one stands by. Raphael and his strapping gentleman friend are already on their second freebie Golden Cadillacs. Meaning, their fourth drinks in the hour or so we've been sitting here.

Actually, Carl isn't so bad after a stiff drink. The three of us swap New York apartment horror stories, always a scintillating topic.

"So when's the merchant marine getting here?" Carl wants to know.

Uh-oh.

"Who's the merchant marine?" I ask Raphael, picturing some bizarre nautical drag queen pulling up a chair.

He blows his stuffy nose into a cocktail napkin and shoves that up his sleeve, too. "I guess he means Jack."

"My Jack?" I echo incredulously. "He's not a merchant marine."

"He's not?" Carl looks confused.

"No. Who said he was a merchant marine?"

"You did," Carl slurs.

"I did not! I said he was a media planner."

"No, you didn't. You said he was a merchant marine," Carl accuses in his booming baritone lisp.

I look at Raphael. He nods. His nostrils are as raw and red as the salsa. "I think you did, Tracey."

"You had four Golden Cadillacs and God knows how many Tavist-D, Raphael. You have no idea what I said."

He giggles. "You're right. I don't."

"Well, I do," Carl says, "and you said this guy Jack is a merchant marine."

Right. Merchant marine, media planner. I get the two mixed up all the time.

Carl informs us, "I've never met a merchant marine."

"That makes two of us," I retort.

"When's he coming?"

I shoot a pointed look at Raphael, then hold up my watch and tap it.

He just giggles again and polishes off his foamy white cocktail of yesteryear, foolish drunkard that he is.

"Shouldn't you be leaving now, guys?" I suggest.

"Not till we meet the merchant marine," Raphael bellows.

"Yeah, the merchant marine," resounds his brutish buffoon of a date, plunking his empty glass down on the table so hard I'm surprised it doesn't shatter in his paw.

"Where is he?" Carl asks, pressing his face against the window. "When's he coming? Does he wear his uniform?"

I glare at Raphael.

He grins happily at me.

I step outside to smoke a cigarette, freezing my ass off on the sidewalk.

A few times, I think I spot Will. Once, crossing the street with beautiful blond Esme on his arm, and once, in a passing cab.

Both times, it isn't him. It isn't Esme, either.

I try to put Will out of my mind and concentrate on looking up and down the street, wondering where the hell Jack is. He's late.

Then I see Carl's face still plastered against the window and I'm thanking my lucky stars Jack is late.

I stub out my cigarette and go back inside to get rid of him.

"Raphael," I begin, just as he sneezes so loudly he can't possibly hear me.

Outside, a woman walks by with a poodle. She's wearing a fur coat and one of those tall, furry Russian-looking hats.

"Hey, great hat!" Carl calls, tapping on the glass. "I want that hat! I'd look good in that hat."

"You would look good in that hat," Raphael agrees, sounding hoarse, and coughs. "Does anyone have a Halls?"

"No, he wouldn't look good in that hat," I say, too exasperated to dig a cough drop from the bottom of my purse. "He'd look like the Empire State Building with a hairy ape draped over its spire."

"Hey! Are you making fun of me?" Carl shouts.

"Me? No." I shoot Raphael a pleading look. He's too busy rummaging in his purselike shoulder bag to notice.

The bartender comes over. "You need to keep it down over here, okay?"

Carl doesn't want to keep it down. Carl wants to speak.

Loudly. About merchant marines, and tall furry hats, and some other stuff.

Carl also wants another foamy white cocktail of yester-year.

The bartender doesn't want Carl to have another anything with liquor in it.

Carl protests.

The bartender asks Carl to leave.

Carl doesn't want to leave.

I look at my watch, and then at Raphael, who's in the midst of another coughing fit.

"This isn't happening," I tell him. "Jack's going to show up any second and find me getting kicked out of the bar."

"He's not kicking *you* out, Tracey, just Carl," Raphael protests as his date loudly accuses the bartender of being homophobic and threatens a lawsuit.

"Raphael, take him and go, will you?" I plead.

"But, Tracey, he *really* wants to stay."

Yeah. And I *really* want to wring his big old lumberjack neck.

"Do this for me, Raphael."

"How am I going to get him out of here?"

"I don't know…a hand truck? Bribery? I don't care, just do it."

"Oh, all right. Carl, hon…" Raphael stands on his tiptoes and whispers something in Carl's ear.

"When?" Carl asks, tilting his head thoughtfully.

"Now," Raphael promises with a wink.

He throws a couple of twenties on the table and the two of them stroll off into the evening arm in arm, headed for…

I don't even want to know.

I suck down half of my second drink before I remember that I'm suppose to be nursing it, and I suck down the other half when I realize that Jack's forty-five minutes late.

Is he standing me up?

I've never been stood up. Not even by Will.

"You want another margarita?" Jerry asks. "It's still happy hour."

Not for me, it isn't.

But I order another drink because what else can I do? Leave?

Okay, I guess I can leave, but what if I do and Jack shows up a minute later?

I can't leave.

Fifteen minutes and a third of the way through the new drink later, he blows in the door, wearing jeans and black boots and a black cable-knit turtleneck sweater under a navy pea coat. His cheeks are red from the cold, and his wavy brown hair is wind-tousled.

"Tracey, I'm so glad you're still here. I'm so sorry. You'll never believe what happened." He collapses into the chair recently abandoned by Carl the merchant-marine-obsessed gay construction worker.

I'm not good at being pissed off, so I smile and say, "Try me."

He's so freaking cute, I think as he runs a hand through his hair. I find myself wishing he didn't live with Mike, because despite my vow not to sleep around, I want to sleep with him. Just once. Tonight.

There's always my place….

But if he stays at my place, Mike will know I slept with someone on the first date. I won't get promoted.

Will I?

Can you not promote somebody because of sex?

*Who knows?*

Gazing at cute Jack, I find myself thinking, *And who cares?* Being a secretary isn't *that* bad.

"So I decided to run home to Brooklyn to take a shower before coming down here," Jack is saying.

Naturally, I immediately picture him naked in the shower. Steam, lather, rippling muscles—and me there with him.

Oblivious to the late-night Cinemax movie screening in my head, Jack goes on. "I was on my way to the subway when this little old lady stopped me and asked me if I knew where Grand Central was. So I told her that was where I was going, and I offered I'd take her there."

"That was nice of you."

He flashes those famous (well, to me, anyway) dimples. "I'm a nice guy. And I was going anyway."

Jerry pops up at his elbow. "You showed up! She was getting worried."

"You were?" Jack looks at me. "Did you think I'd stand you up?"

"Not really. I mean…I hoped you wouldn't."

Jack touches my hand. "I wouldn't."

We smile at each other. It's a touching moment until Jerry butts in.

"It's actually a good thing you were late, because her friends—"

"Hey, wasn't I supposed to get another freebie margarita, Jerry?" I interrupt, before colorful tales of Carl the unruly urban lumberjack spill from Jerry's pink lipsticked mouth, which, I now notice, is topped by a barely visible fringe of five o'clock shadow.

I don't need or want another drink, but Jerry brings it and I sip it as Jack drinks his Dos Equis and finishes telling me why he was late.

"So, anyway, there I am, escorting this little old lady—who tells me her name is Henrietta but I should call her Henny—to Grand Central, and it's rush hour and the sidewalks are jammed, and she's walking, like, two inches an hour."

He stand up and demonstrates and I crack up.

"I'm totally serious. And *then,*" he says, sitting across from me again, "these three *other* little old ladies stop her and ask her if she knows where Grand Central is. She says, 'That's where we're going, come with us! I'm Henrietta but you can call me Henny, and this is Jack.'"

His voice is little-old-lady high-pitched and crackly, and he pulls his lips back over his teeth to look little-old-lady gummy. I'm laughing hysterically.

"So now I've got four little old ladies all shuffling along with me like I'm the Pied Piper, and people are trying to mow us down...." He shakes his head and bites a chip.

"I forgive you for being late," I say, wiping tears from my eyes. "Good citizenship is an acceptable excuse."

"Wait, I'm not finished. When we finally get to Grand Central, the old ladies are even more confused, so I offer to help them get on the right subway. So the five of us are on our way down the stairs when I hear somebody calling, 'Help! Help!' from up at the top."

I'm hanging on every word, still half laughing, but half not sure if he's bullshitting me. I mean, this is so far-fetched—and then again, it's New York, where nothing is far-fetched.

"So I look up, and there's a guy in a wheelchair with no arms or legs. I have to go back up and get him and carry him down the stairs, then go back for the wheelchair and carry that down the stairs...and by the time I got Henrietta—"

"You mean Henny—"

"I mean Henny," he agrees, "on her train and the other three on their train, I realized I was going to be late but I really needed a shower because the guy stunk, and thanks to him so did I."

"Are you serious?" I say, laughing.

"Dead serious. He had terrible BO."

"Not about the stink. About...the old ladies. And the wheelchair. I mean...that's some story."

"All true." He grins. "Hey, Tracey, could I possibly make up something like that?"

I consider it. If he could, I'd probably be even more attracted to him. I like a guy with a creative imagination.

Suddenly I have to pee.

"I'll be right back," I tell Jack as I grab my purse from the back of the chair.

He nods, lifting his beer to me in a silent toast.

The second I stand up, I realize that all that tequila on an empty stomach was a huge mistake.

I'm not drunk—not really. I'm just...

*Sick.*

I barely make it to the bathroom before the margaritas are backing up my throat and regurgitating right out of me. Oh, ick.

I flush, rinse my mouth with cold water, and stand in front

of the mirror. My face is pale and I puked off my lipstick, but other than that, I look pretty good.

And the date was going so well.

Then again…was it? Between Carl being thrown out and Jack being late and now this…

Maybe I should take it as an omen. Maybe I should tell Jack I'm sick and just go home.

Nothing can come of this anyway. It's not like we have a future. Everybody knows you don't fall in love with the first person you date after a breakup.

I might think I'm totally attracted to him—okay, I know I'm definitely totally attracted to him—but this is sheer rebound stuff. It's an illusion. I'd be attracted to anyone right now. The fact that he seems like the perfect guy for me means nothing.

After all, Buckley also seems like the perfect guy for me. But I had Will when we met, and then, when I didn't have Will, Buckley had Sonja.

*What if Buckley and Sonja break up?* a familiar little voice pipes up. *What if you and Buckley fall in love then?*

I see that I'm smiling at myself in the mirror, this sappy thinking-of-Buckley smile.

*Stop it, Tracey. Why do you have to think of every cute guy as a potential boyfriend?*

Because after three years of being part of a couple, being alone doesn't feel right. It feels…

Lonely.

But I can't jump into another relationship just because I'm lonely. That would be as big a mistake as holding on to Will for three years turned out to be. I clung to him because I was afraid to let go.

Now here I am looking around for somebody else to grab on to.

Kate was right.

I'm still healing. I'm not ready for a relationship yet.

First I need to figure out who Tracey is on her own.

I pull my lipstick from my bag and put it on, blotting my lips on a paper towel. Then I find the Halls cough drops in the bottom of my purse and pop one into my mouth, hoping mentholatum kills vomit fumes. For good measure, I find a fragrance sample tube in the change purse of my wallet and dab a little Ralph Lauren perfume behind each ear.

There. At least I'll look and smell divine when I tell Jack that I'm sick and have to leave right away.

As I leave the ladies' room, I tell myself that it's the right thing to do.

After all, he was an hour late—why should I feel bad about leaving early?

Maybe he'll be relieved. Maybe he wasn't into going out with me anyway, and just asked me because of Mike. Maybe Mike and Dianne told him about the depressing state of my love life and they all felt sorry for me.

Maybe…

I arrive at the table.

"Hey, there you are. I missed you," Jack says with a heart-melting, dimple-punctuated grin.

Maybe…

Maybe I should leave, before…

Before I stay.

7

$F$or the first time in weeks, I'm not freezing to death when I wake up.

That's because I'm snuggled against the human furnace that is Jack.

Oh, and his last name is Candell.

I'm telling you that—smugly—because I don't want you to think I slept with somebody whose last name is a mystery.

I even know how you pronounce it—with the emphasis on the second syllable. Not like Candle. It's Cand*ell*.

See?

I know other things about him, too. Things like:

When he was seven, his family moved out of the Bronx to the suburbs, and he lay awake for hours every night because it was so quiet he couldn't sleep.

When he was ten, his parents sent him to sleep-away

camp in Massachusetts against his will, and he was home-sick, and it took him all summer to learn how to swim.

When he was twelve, his dog ran away and got hit by an ice-cream truck.

No, I don't know the dog's name.

Should I have found out the dog's name before I spent the night with Jack?

Probably. I probably should have found out a lot more, too. I probably should have waited. In fact, I probably should have kept my promise to myself—and to Kate—and not have slept with him at all.

But right now, with the gray Saturday-morning light filtering in through the cracks in the blinds and Jack's arms around me and my head on his chest and his even breathing warm against my cheek, I could care less about *shoulds*.

You're probably wondering how we ended up here after I swore this wouldn't happen.

Let's just say it was a natural progression.

You know how it goes: first drinks, then vomit, then dinner, then coffee and pastry at a great little place on the corner of Mulberry and Broome in Little Italy…then mind-blowing sex.

Okay, maybe you don't know how it goes. But trust me, that's how it goes. At least, that's how it went with us, and it felt right at the time. It still does.

Even this—waking up in Jack's arms the morning after—feels right.

There's no awkwardness, no panic attack, no sudden urge to flee—which is a good thing, since I'm home.

Going to his apartment was out of the question. He suggested it, but I pointed out that my place is closer to the corner of Mulberry and Broome, so we'd be here quicker. At the time, since we couldn't seem to keep our hands off of each other, that was important.

I also pointed out that as far as I knew, *his* boss wasn't sleeping on the other side of my bedroom wall.

So here we are, me and Jack, all snug and snoozey in the big, oak sleigh bed I bought a few months ago. It's my first real piece of furniture, and Jack is my first real overnight guest since I got it.

I can't count Raphael, because I made him sleep on the floor Thursday night, which pissed him off, even when I explained that I didn't want to catch that juicy cold he's got.

But Jack—well, no way was I going to make him sleep on the floor. So he and I christened my new bed—a few times, in fact—and I really wanted to tell him that he'd always be special for being the first person to share it with me. But I didn't.

I didn't tell him a lot of things I was tempted to blurt out in the dark, as we were cuddling and drifting off to sleep.

I figured some things are better left unsaid.

Things like *I was dumped by the love of my life a few months ago and you're my Transition Boy and I wasn't supposed to have sex with you.*

Jack wakes up, gently traces my cheek with his finger, says, "Hey, good morning. You look so serious. What are you thinking?"

"That Kate is going to kill me."

"Who's Kate?"

"My friend."

"The one who's having an obsessive love affair with her camera?"

"No, that's Latisha, and actually, that was my camera she had the other night. Kate doesn't work at Blaire Barnett."

"Where does she work?"

"Well, she *thinks* she's a Relationship Guru, but technically, she's unemployed."

"And she's going to kill you because…?"

"Because I did something she warned me not to do."

"Does it have something to do with me?"

"What are you, psychic?"

He shrugs. "What else can it be?"

"Well, it can be lots of other things," I say. Kate is always giving me advice and warnings, solicited or not. "But actually, you hit it on the head."

"Your friend told you not to go out with me?"

"No, she told me to go out with you, but not to sleep with you." Oops, that sounds bad. "I mean, it's not like I do stuff like this all the time. I never do, really. It's just…I just went through a breakup. And she's worried that I'm going to, uh, get…"

Get what?

Hurt?

Dumped?

Impregnated by my boss's roommate?

All of the above?

"Oh." Jack's nodding. "I get it."

"And the thing is—I mean, I've never done this before. Especially not on the first date."

I shove away a disturbing vision of my one-night tumble in the *Star Wars* sheets. That wasn't a date, so it's not a lie. That was a bar pickup. There's a difference, right?

I wait for Jack to tell me he doesn't usually do this on the first date, either. But he doesn't. He just yawns and rolls onto his back, stretching lazily.

Obviously, he's not in any hurry to get dressed and leave.

I plot of ways to keep him here for a while. Or maybe, for the rest of the day. Or even forever.

I know, I know…he isn't my Forever Man.

But a girl can fantasize. A girl can look at Transition Boy and envision Forever Man.

She can look into his eyes and catch a fleeting glimpse of in-laws and Lamaze classes and house-hunting in the suburbs and SUVs and first communions and curfew arguments and college loans and mother-of-the-bride dresses and silver anniversaries and golden anniversaries and shared headstones.

A girl can want all of those things so badly that she can practically taste the wedding cake and champagne.

Jack turns his head toward me. "What are you thinking?"

Do you think he'll run screaming into the street if I tell him I'm thinking about wedding cake and champagne?

Yeah, I think so, too.

So I shrug and lie. "I was just thinking about all the Christmas shopping I've got to do this weekend for my, uh, Secret Snowflake."

"Secret Snowflake?"

"You know—it's like the Secret Santa thing. Aren't you in it?"

"Nope."

"Merry said it was mandatory."

He shrugs. "She says that every year. Nobody in our department ever does it."

"You're kidding."

"Nope. She just says it's mandatory because otherwise nobody would sign up."

"So she tricked me?" I groan. "And now I have to buy five gifts for Myron for no good reason?"

"Mail-room Myron? He's a good guy."

"I know he is, but he's not usually at the top of my Christmas gift list," I tell Jack. "And what am I supposed to get him on a fifteen-dollar limit for the whole week?"

"There's a lot you can get him for that."

"Like what?"

"Off the top of my head? Lottery tickets, candy, a tree ornament, a book—"

"Hey, I've got an idea. How about if you pinch-hit my Snowflake shopping?"

"Or maybe I can just come with you. Are you going today?"

"I *can*," I say casually, as though my life doesn't depend on it.

"Great. I've got shopping to do for my sisters, too."

"Sisters? How many do you have?"

"Four. Three older, one younger."

"Let me guess. Your dad always wanted a son…and the baby of the family's nickname is Oops."

He laughs. "That's pretty much it. But she's my parents' favorite, so I guess they have no regrets about having five kids."

"My parents had five kids, too," I tell him, reminding myself that one coincidence does not happily-ever-after make. "I'm the youngest, but I'm not the favorite."

"Who is?"

"Everyone but me. My sister and my brothers all stayed in Brookside, like they were supposed to."

He laughs.

Too bad I'm dead serious.

"So Brookside—that's your hometown?"

I nod. "It's upstate. Like, as far upstate as you can go and not be in Lake Erie."

"And your whole family lives there?"

"Yup. My sister, Mary Beth—she just reconciled with her idiot husband. They have two little boys. My brother Danny and his wife, Michaela, have one little boy. Then there's my brother Joey and his wife Sara. And my brother Frankie. He's engaged and his fianceé is from Brookside. I'm the only one who ever left."

And the only one who's unattached. At twenty-three, if you're still single in Brookside and you haven't had a spiritual calling, lesbian rumors abound.

Jack asks, "Why'd you leave?"

If ever there was a question with a one-word answer, that's it.

*Will.*

Will is why I left. He was like my own personal spiritual calling. I met him in college, and I would have followed him anywhere. Luckily for me, he was only going as far as New York City.

But I don't want to talk about Will with Jack, so I say, "I wanted to be a copywriter. And writing classifieds for the *Brookside Observer* didn't sound very exciting, so…here I am. Still not a copywriter, but…"

"Mike says you're going to interview for a position in Creative when one opens up."

"He did?"

This makes me happy. Not just because it proves Mike

hasn't forgotten about our deal, but because it proves Jack was asking him about me. Unless Mike just volunteered that...and other, potentially embarrassing, information.

"What else did Mike say about me?" I ask, suddenly filled with trepidation.

"Not much. Dianne was there."

"Oh, Dianne. She's so sweet."

He snorts. "Yeah, sweet like a lime."

"You don't like Dianne?"

"She's a bitch."

Guess that means he doesn't like her.

"I'm so surprised. I mean, she's really nice to me on the phone."

"That's fake. She's evil."

Suddenly, I remember something.

*Mike has a roommate, but he's a real asshole.*

How could I have forgotten all about that? Dianne said it that day on the phone when we were talking about my breakup with Will and how she wished she knew somebody she could fix me up with.

Jack doesn't seem like a real asshole. But then, I haven't exactly been the best judge of assholeness in the past.

What if Dianne's right and he really is an asshole?

What if Jack's right and she really is evil?

Hard to tell, at this point, whom to believe.

"Why is Mike with Dianne?" I ask. "Because she's pretty?"

"Pretty? Dianne?" He shudders.

"I think she is. I've seen her pictures." Framed, on every surface in Mike's office. She's perky-looking, with a dark pageboy and elfin features.

"Forget it. Let's not talk about Dianne. It puts me in a bad mood."

"Sorry."

He pulls me toward him. "Want to know what puts me in a good mood? One guess."

"Um, Christmas shopping?" I laugh. A girly giggle-laugh, the kind that tends to spurt out of me without warning when I'm flirting.

Jack kisses me. "Wrong. Not Christmas shopping."

"Can you give me a hint?"

He nuzzles my neck.

I guess again.

And this time, I'm right.

Along about noon, we wake up again.

"So you really want to go Christmas shopping, Tracey?"

"Definitely!" *Down, girl.* "I mean, if you do."

"Sure. Can I take a shower?" Jack asks, sitting up and stretching as I ogle his naked back from my pillow.

"Go ahead. The bathroom's that way." I point, like he could possibly get lost in an apartment the size of a ring box.

An engagement ring box that contains a pear-shaped diamond on a platinum band…

*Mental Note: You are not, nor will you ever be, engaged to Jack. One does not go directly from Christmas Party Don't to I Do. Period.*

Fantasy curtailed.

As much as I'd love to check out Jack's bare butt as he walks naked toward the bathroom, I'm just not that brazen in the broad light of day. I roll over and stare at the wall, content to relive every moment of this morning's encounter.

Jack goes into the bathroom and comes right out again.

"Tracey? Do you want to, uh, take your stuff out of the tub?"

"What stuff?"

"Your panties?"

My *panties*?

My panties aren't in the tub; they're somewhere in the heap of hastily discarded clothes by the bed.

But he's waiting, so I wrap myself in my quilt and hoof it barefoot from the drafty parquet floor to the ice-rink-like ceramic tile.

There, I gaze in absolute horror at the zebra-print thong draped over the faucet in the tub.

It's panties, all right. But it's sure as hell not *my* panties.

"Those belong to a friend," I say.

Jack just looks at me like he's a cop and I'm a shirtless stoner trying to explain away the baggie of pot in my pocket.

"Really," I say.

Yeah. Uh-huh.

I take a deep breath. "My friend Raphael spent the night here last night because his apartment was being fumigated, and he must have forgotten them." Then, lest Jack get the wrong idea, I hastily add, "Raphael's gay."

As if that were necessary.

As if any remotely heterosexual man would be caught dead in a zebra-striped thong.

"You don't say," Jack replied dryly.

"So you can just move his, uh, panties and—"

"That's okay. You can move them."

"I can?"

He grins and steps aside with a sweeping gesture at the tub. "Be my guest."

I stare at the panties.

Cue *Jaws* music.

"I'll be right back," I tell Jack.

In the three-linoleum-tiles-long patch of floor that is my kitchenette, I grab a long-handled, two-pronged barbecue fork left behind by a previous tenant. I've been meaning to get rid of it since I moved in, since God only knows why anyone would need a barbecue fork in a Manhattan studio.

Returning to the bathroom, I find Jack still eyeing Raphael's panties with repugnance. He doesn't look the least bit surprised to see me armed with a fork. Nor does he offer to take the fork and be my hero.

Terrific.

I gingerly approach the tub, spear the panties with a deft stab of the fork and shudder.

"Now what?" Jack asks, amused.

I carry the panties to the kitchen garbage can, step on the pedal that raises the lid and deposit them into the trash.

"That's what," I say, removing my foot from the pedal and closing the lid with a clank.

"What if your friend comes looking for his, uh, panties?" Jack asks from the bathroom doorway, amused.

"Sadly, he probably won't even miss them. I'm beginning to suspect he's the kind of guy who leaves his panties all over town."

Jack just laughs and heads for the shower as I return to the warm, rumpled bed and my naked Jack—but not fiancé Jack—fantasies.

★ ★ ★

You would think Christmas shopping with someone you barely know on the day after you slept with him would be extremely awkward.

You would think there would be nothing to talk about, and the crowds would get on your nerves and you'd both make excuses to cut the day short.

You would be so wrong.

Shopping with Jack is the most fun I've had since...

Well, *ever*.

I really wish I were exaggerating, but I'm not.

Shopping with Jack isn't as intense as shopping with Raphael, and it isn't as exhausting as shopping with Kate.

Shopping with Jack ranks right up there with shopping with Buckley; Jack makes me laugh just as hard as Buckley does. The reason this is better is because Jack and I hold hands, and we keep stopping to kiss.

We spend the whole afternoon browsing around the Village, buying stuff. At one point, when the rain briefly turns to flurries of snow, Jack sings "Winter Wonderland."

He sings it horribly off-key but he doesn't care, and neither do I.

I can't help comparing Jack to Will, who, when he sang in public, always seemed to expect people to stop and listen and applaud.

Not Jack. He just sings because he wants to, and he doesn't give a damn who hears or what they think. I even join in. When I was with Will, I never dared sing out loud, for fear he would criticize my vocal talent—or lack thereof.

But with Jack, I sing my heart out, and it feels great.

I only think of Will two other times all day: once when

Jack and I pass the cabaret place where Will and I went on our first date after I moved to New York, and once when, out of the corner of my eye, I think I see him walk by. I do a double take. It isn't him. In fact, it's a black man walking a dog.

Will isn't black and he's allergic to dogs.

I get five small gifts for Myron, and Jack gets beautiful handmade sweaters for all of his sisters.

In the late afternoon, it starts pouring suddenly, so we duck into a little diner off Washington Square. We have coffee and onion rings dipped in mustard, and somehow they go together perfectly.

We sit there talking about deep-fried foods and Billy Joel songs and state capitals, and I'm shocked when I glance at the rain-spattered window to see that it's dark in the street.

"How long have we been sitting here?" I ask Jack.

"Too long," he says, glancing at his watch. "Unfortunately, I've got to get going."

"Oh...I should get going, too," I say, as though I've got someplace to be.

I don't, but something tells me he does.

He insists on paying the check—Will and I always split it—and we carry our packages out the door. We stand under the overhang and zip our coats, and I try not to be obsessed about his plans for tonight.

Does he have a date?

After all, it's a Saturday night.

I don't want him to have a date. I want him to come home with me. But I don't dare ask him to.

"I've got to go west to get the F train. But let me get you a cab home first," he says, glancing around.

There are dozens of cabs, all of them occupied.

"No, that's okay, Jack. I'll take the subway. It's only one stop."

"Are you sure?"

"Positive." Too bad I have to walk east to get my train. Otherwise, I could walk with him and try to get more information out of him.

But east is east and west is west, and I guess this is where we part ways.

It was good while it lasted.

"I'll call you," Jack says, giving me one last kiss.

"Okay."

We splash off in opposite directions, Transition Boy and me, and I wonder if he really will call.

I don't know what I'll do if he doesn't.

Then again, I don't know what I'll do if he does.

8

On Sunday morning, I wake up to a ringing alarm, thinking it's Monday. Until I remember why I set it.

Oh. Church.

It's so tempting to roll over and go back to sleep. But I drag myself through a cold downpour to mass at St. Fabian's near Washington Square, just as I promised I would. My inner Catholic schoolgirl can be a real pain in the ass.

But when I get to church, I'm glad to be there.

The altar is decorated with poinsettias and greens and twinkly white lights, and the priest gives an uplifting homily about loving our fellow man.

I have to remind myself that he doesn't mean it literally—at least, not in the biblical sense. That, in fact, the whole reason I'm here in the first place is because I'm guilty of loving my fellow man—er, men.

I take communion out of habit, wondering only after I've

swallowed the host whether I should have gone to confession first.

Is sex before marriage—okay, sex with zero prospect of marriage—technically a sin?

Hard to tell, given the archaic language Moses used in the Ten Commandments. I mean, Jack isn't my neighbor's wife. And we didn't have sex on the Sabbath Day or anything....

Still, when in doubt, cleanse the soul—that's what I always say.

Well, not *always.*

In fact, I've never said it until now, but then, my soul—if that's what you want to call it—has never been this, um, for lack of a better word, *dirty.*

So on the way out, I dutifully pick up a bulletin and check to see when the priest hears confessions. I make a note to make a note in my day planner to go on Tuesday night.

There.

I'm almost feeling like my old chaste self again.

Sunday afternoon, Buckley and I go to see the new Julianne Moore movie. It's still pouring out, and the trains are messed up and I can't get a cab, so I'm late meeting him at Loews.

I spend the whole movie thinking about Jack. Buckley and I don't have a chance to talk until we're on our way across the street for a beer.

Naturally, I light up the minute we leave the theater.

"Do you have to smoke?" Buckley asks, holding an umbrella over me and my cancer stick, and wrinkling his nose.

"Yup. I'm way below my daily quota," I say, trying not to exhale in his direction. But there's a raw wind, and the smoke blows right back at us, swirling around his head. He makes a face.

"Why don't you just quit, Tracey? I mean, the only places in the whole city you can smoke are the sidewalk and your apartment. Give it up already."

I glance at Buckley. Cranky nagging isn't like him.

"What's wrong, Buckley?"

"Nothing. I just don't like to breathe in secondhand smoke."

"Yeah, but that's not it. Something's wrong."

"Sonja and I broke up."

"Oh, no."

"Oh, yes."

I am legitimately sorry, even though there's a part of me slapping high fives and shouting, *Yessss!* After all, this is what I've been hoping for ever since Will dumped me. It's hard to be attracted to one of your best friends when he has a girlfriend and you know you have no chance.

It's also hard to see your best friend so down.

"Yeah, I figure it's better this way," he says, holding open the door of the pub with his foot as he lowers the sopping umbrella.

I reluctantly drop my half-smoked cigarette into a puddle and step inside. The place is empty, aside from the bartender, who's watching the Giants game on the big-screen television.

We sit at the bar and order two Buds.

"So what happened?" I ask Buckley.

"It was mutual. We talked last night, and she tried to give me an ultimatum. I told her I don't want to move in with her. So she left."

"Are you okay?" I ask as the bartender plunks two brown bottles in front of us and goes right back to his football game.

"I *will* be okay," Buckley says resolutely. "It just sucks right now."

"I know the feeling."

He looks at me. "Yeah, I guess you do."

"You'll survive."

"I know I will. I've done this before, remember?"

Buckley had a girlfriend before Sonja. They broke up right before I met him. Like I said, I had Will at the time. And then I didn't have Will. But Buckley had Sonja.

Now I don't have Will, and Buckley doesn't have Sonja.

We're both free.

Except…

Jack.

Hearing about Buckley's breakup made me forget all about him. But now that I remember, I am oddly compelled to blurt, "Hey, I met someone."

Buckley blinks a *why-are-you-telling-me-this?* blink.

I have no idea why I'm telling him this, but it seems important that I do it right away.

"He works at Blaire Barnett, in media. I met him at the company Christmas party last week. And we went out on a date Friday night."

"That's great." Buckley's voice is hollow. He doesn't look at me. He's busy tearing the wet edge of the red label off the beer bottle.

"Yeah. His name's Jack. He's nice, and really funny, and smart…he knows all the state capitals…."

*Shut the hell up, Tracey. Can't you see Buckley's in pain?*

I can see it, but for some reason, I feel like I can't respond to it.

"He knows all the state capitals?" Buckley asks, looking up at me.

"Yep," I say brightly, as though I've just announced that Jack waved his hand and resurrected the Twin Towers.

"Gee, I didn't know that meant so much to you, Trace."

Frankly, I didn't either.

Will didn't know any state capitals. Why would he? After all, American geography has very little to do with him, personally. And as I've come to realize, if it isn't about Will, Will doesn't want to know about it.

I try to explain to Buckley how refreshing it is for me to have met a guy who cares about—well, all sorts of things. Including, apparently, *me*.

But Buckley doesn't seem to be listening. He's too busy shredding his beer bottle label and spinning the bottle around and around on top of the bar, leaving a series of interlocking wet rings on the sticky wood.

Finally, I drop the topic of Jack and bring up Sonja again.

"Do you think she'll change her mind, Buckley?"

Buckley snaps to attention. "Why? Do you?"

"I don't know…. I mean, if she's serious about wanting to live with you, then…" I shrug. "How about you? Will you consider changing your mind about moving in together?"

He doesn't even hesitate. "Nope."

Typical guy response, I think, fighting the urge to roll my eyes. I love Buckley, but sometimes he sounds like one of my brothers. With them, everything is black-and-white.

Were the Buffalo Bills robbed in their first Super Bowl? Yep.

Should my Aunt Carm put raisins in her meatballs? Nope. It's that simple. Most things are.

At least, for them.

"Care to elaborate, Buckley?" I ask.

"I just don't think moving in together's a good idea," Buckley says with a shrug.

"Why not?"

"We've only known each other for a few months."

A lightbulb goes off.

"Buckley, Sonja's your Transition Girl!"

"My what?"

"She's the person you're meant to be with between your old girlfriend and the woman you're going to marry. Everyone has a Transition Girl—" *or Transition Boy* "—after a breakup."

"Where'd you hear that? *Oprah?*"

No, Kate. Same difference.

But I don't tell him that.

I just say, "The thing about a transition relationship is that it can't last. It isn't meant to. You're still healing. You're not ready for anything permanent. You're still trying to figure out who you are on your own."

Buckley surprises me by saying, "That makes sense."

"It does, doesn't it? You can't jump from the wreckage of one relationship into something long-term. You have to realize that when you're on the rebound, your instinct is to become part of a couple again. You have to fight that instinct. It's too soon for you to fall in love again."

"Okay…. So how long does it take till you're supposed to be ready to fall in love again?"

"I don't know…." I wing it. "A year?"

That sounds about right.

But in my case, do I count the year from when Will left for summer stock in June, or when he stopped calling in July or when he officially dumped me in September?

"So now I have to wait another year before I start a new relationship?" Buckley is asking.

"No! You don't have to wait a year after Sonja, because she was your transition person. She doesn't count. You just have to wait a year since you broke up with your original girlfriend. The one before Sonja."

"This sounds way too complicated, Tracey."

It does.

Depressing, too.

Because all night, I dreamed about Jack, and all day, until Buckley's news, I thought about him. Even in church.

I managed to completely overlook the fact that in my subconscious mind, Jack is just a replacement for Will, whom I'm still mourning.

Even if I count back to June, when Will left, that still gives me at least six months to wait before I'll be ready for a new relationship.

"You know, maybe a year is too long," I tell Buckley. "Maybe you need to only wait six months after a breakup."

"I did break up with my girlfriend six months before I met Sonja…."

"Oh."

"In which case, Sonja isn't my Transition Girl."

"Right."

But I want her to be his Transition Girl. I don't want her to be his Ms. Right.

Because I might want Buckley for myself. When I'm ready.

But, wait. Don't I also want Jack for myself?

Yup. I want both of them.

And according to Kate, I can't have either one of them. *Yet.*

"I don't know what I want," Buckley says with a heavy sigh. "I just know what I *don't* want."

"A live-in girlfriend."

"Right."

"Or a June wedding."

"Sure as hell not *next* June." He plunks his bottle down. "Want another beer?"

I do, but I can tell that he doesn't.

So we leave.

Buckley takes the subway back uptown, and I walk home through the rain. I need the exercise. Now that the weather's so crummy, I haven't been walking back and forth to work anymore.

I don't think I'll ever get past the deep-seated dread of regaining all that weight.

Look, I'm not as self-involved as Will is. I *know* that there are worse things that can happen in the grand scheme of things. *Far* worse things. War, plagues, terrorism.

I have more than my share of anxiety when it comes to potential global disaster, even *with* my happy pills.

But on a personal level, aside from getting lung cancer or being shoved in front of a number seven train by a street psycho, one of my greatest fears is being fat again. Because when you come right down to it, being overweight is pretty damned horrible.

If I were still overweight, a guy like Jack never would have asked me out.

Will pops into my head. Will, who was my boyfriend when I was fat.

That I even *had* a boyfriend when I was fat is sometimes hard to fathom. But, of course, Will never really cared about me. For him, the big—the *only*—attraction was that I was as obsessed with him as he was.

And anyway, I didn't really *have* him when I had him. He cheated on me the whole time we were together, with skinny girls. He left me for a skinny girl.

And even though I know I'm better off without him, there's a hurt, wistful part of me that can't help but wonder how Will would feel about me if he could see me now, as a skinny girl.

We've talked, but only on the phone. The last time I saw him—and he saw me—was the night he broke up with me. In the three months since, I've lost almost twenty more pounds.

Standing on the corner of Broadway, waiting to cross, I catch sight of myself in the window of Tower Records. I look like a drowned rat. But a svelte drowned rat.

Am I skinny enough, now, for Will?

*It doesn't matter,* I remind myself sternly. *Will is a narcissistic jerk, and even if he wanted you back, you wouldn't want him.*

After all, I didn't just change on the outside; I changed on the inside, too. I'm different now than I was when I was with Will. Stronger. Happier. More self-confident.

*Yeah, right. If you're so self-confident, why are you checking to see if your reflection is as slender as Esme Spencer's?*

The light changes.

I splash into the street.

Why does the old, insecure, not-good-enough Tracey keep rearing her sorry head, questioning everything?

Everything from whether I'll really get a shot at being a copywriter to whether I'll ever be a bride to whether, if I splurge on a knish, I'll gain back fifty pounds, and then some.

By the time I reach my apartment, I'm cold and wet and sick of myself. All I want is a hot shower and flannel pajamas and a cup of tea and the new Jane Smiley novel I bought last week and haven't had a chance to start.

I'm so focused on those things that I never even think to check the answering machine.

It isn't until I'm shuffling past it in my slippers, carrying my tea and the *TV Guide*, that I see the red light blinking.

Hmm. A message. Even then, it doesn't occur to me that it might be Jack.

I press the button and flip the *TV Guide* open to Sunday, sipping my tea as the tape rewinds.

"Hi, Tracey, it's me, Jack."

Startled, I swallow a gulp of scalding tea, scorching my esophagus.

"I just wanted to say hi and tell you that I had a great time yesterday. We should go out again. Give me a call if you want—the number's 718-555-7455—or I'll try to stop by your desk tomorrow at work. Bye."

I stand there, throat burning, staring at the answering machine.

He said he'd call.

He called.

And I'm tasting wedding cake and champagne again, dammit.

# 9

Monday morning, I get to work early enough to leave my first Secret Snowflake in Myron's cubby in the mail room. Jack told me Myron's a huge Jets fan, so I got him a gummy sucker shaped like a football player wearing a Jets uniform. Very cute; very affordable: It was only a buck fifty.

It's so early that I have to turn on all the lights and make the coffee in the kitchenette on my floor. I stand there while it's brewing, trying to warm my icy hands in the pockets of my brown blazer, and thinking about Jack.

I decided not to call him back last night.

For one thing, it can't hurt to play hard to get.

After all, I did the opposite with Will, and look what happened.

For another thing, I was afraid that Mike would answer the phone if I called. I know it's stupid, but I just can't seem to get over the weirdness of Jack being Mike's roommate.

For yet *another* thing, I was supposed to have one date with Jack and move on. I wasn't supposed to sleep with him, and I sure as hell wasn't supposed to start fantasizing about a relationship with him.

The final reason I didn't call Jack back is that Buckley called me. He kept me on the phone for over an hour, dissecting his relationship with Sonja. I could hardly make an excuse and hang up. Not after I had done exactly the same thing to him—repeatedly—when Will and I broke up.

The more I talked to Buckley, the more I wondered if fate wants us to be together. Me and Buckley, that is.

I mean, I've been attracted to him from the moment I met him. And he was attracted to me, too.

Now that we're both unattached, are we meant to fall madly in love?

I try to picture myself walking down the aisle toward Buckley. To be honest, it isn't hard to do.

I try to picture myself walking down the aisle toward Jack. That isn't hard, either.

But then, at this time last year, I had every detail of my wedding to Will planned, unwilling to believe that the closest he intended to get to a wedding cake was serving it as a waiter for Eat Drink Or Be Married.

How could I have fooled myself for so long?

You know, my Monday-morning brain hurts from all this complicated thinking. Too bad my next shrink appointment is still two days away.

I pour myself a cup of coffee and head to my cubicle. Maybe I'll have an e-mail from Jack. It'll be easier to respond in writing than in a telephone conversation, because I can edit myself. When I'm nervous about something, I tend to blurt embarrassing things.

When I get to my desk, I see a package sitting on top of my keyboard. It's a gold foil-wrapped box with a red velvet bow, and I instantly recognize the distinctive shape.

Godiva.

A one-pound box, at that.

Yowza.

Who do you think it's from?

I lift the box and turn it over, looking for a note. There isn't one.

"Whatcha got there, Chief?"

I look up to see Mike poking his head into my cubicle.

"Chocolates."

"Wow. Nice."

"Yeah."

Is it my imagination, or are his eyes ultra-twinkly?

Jack. The chocolates are from Jack. Yup, they're from Jack, and Mike knows about them. That's why he's all ultra-twinkly.

"Guess your Secret Snowflake really likes you, huh?" Mike says.

Ah, I see. A ruse. He wants me to think they're from my Secret Snowflake to throw me off Jack's trail. How cunning.

"They can't be from my Snowflake," I point out. "This candy costs more than twice as much as we're supposed to spend on our Snowflake for the whole week."

He dismisses that with a wave of his hand. "Maybe your Snowflake got them on sale."

Now I'm convinced he's covering for Jack.

Although, come to think of it…why wouldn't Jack want to take credit for a pound of Godivas? I look again for a note, wondering if I somehow missed it.

"Ooh, chocolate for breakfast!" Brenda squeals from over Mike's left shoulder. "What's the occasion? Are you sharing, Trace?"

"Of course I'm sharing." In fact, I'm not touching these things. After the onion rings on Saturday and the movie popcorn yesterday, I might as well apply premium Belgian truffles right to my hips.

I carefully remove the bow, which is tied with a Christmasy doodad. Then I open the box and set it on top of a file cabinet.

"Help yourselves," I tell Mike and Brenda.

They do.

Then they leave me alone with the chocolates, the ribbon-entwined doodad and an inquiring mind.

Later that morning, I'm still wondering whether they're from Jack when the man in question shows up by my desk.

"Hi," he says cheerfully. He's wearing dark suit pants, a pressed white dress shirt, and a strangely familiar black-and-white patterned tie.

"Hi, Jack!" I respond, just as cheerfully.

"Chocolate," he says, looking at the still-open box of Godivas, which is half gone. Thanks to willpower of steel, I've only eaten one.

"Yeah, chocolate." I try to read his expression. "You want some?"

"No, thanks. I don't like chocolate."

"You don't *like* chocolate?"

Not only have I never met a human being who doesn't like chocolate, but...

Why would you send somebody something you don't like?

So maybe I was wrong. Maybe he didn't send them.

But if he didn't, who did?

"Nope. I don't like chocolate," he repeats. "Not candy, anyway. It gives me a headache."

"All chocolate?"

"Not chocolate cake. I do like chocolate cake. I don't suppose you'll be serving any of that later?"

I laugh.

So does he.

We fall silent.

You'd expect silence to be awkward, but it isn't.

Still, I'm compelled to fill it, because...well, because I trained myself to do that with Will.

"Nice tie," I comment. "It's Mike's, huh?"

"Nah, it's mine. But Mike borrows it sometimes."

"He does?" It's funny to picture him and Mike raiding each other's closets. I thought only women did that.

"Yeah, Dianne hates it when he wears my ties. She usually picks out all his clothes. She has expensive taste. Really expensive, and really boring. Which isn't surprising, considering that *she's* really boring."

"Is there anything you *like* about Dianne?" I ask, lowering my voice. Mike's supposedly out at a client meeting, but you never know.

"Absolutely nothing," he says. "She's a one-woman axis of evil."

"Then why is Mike with her?"

"Because he has no spine. And because he's infatuated

with her, and God only knows why. I don't like her. None of his friends like her. But he won't listen to us. He has blinders on when it comes to Dianne."

It sounds uncomfortably close to a Tracey-Will relationship. So close that I must change the subject immediately.

"How was your weekend?" I ask. "The rest of it, I mean."

He shrugs. "I had to go to my cousin's birthday dinner Saturday night up in Scarsdale."

Elated, I ask, "How was that?"

"The caterer was great. My cousins are stuffy. What'd you do?"

*Sat around and worried, needlessly, that you were out with another woman.*

"Not much. Your family lives in Scarsdale?"

"Just that branch—my father's brother, his wife and their kids. My parents are up in Bedford."

I may not know much about the northern suburbs, but I know that Scarsdale and Bedford are where all the rich people live. Okay, maybe not all of them. Most of them.

Jack doesn't *seem* rich.

Then again, if he's sending Godiva chocolates on a media planner's salary, he might just have a trust fund or something.

Feeling like a brazen contestant on *Joe Millionaire,* I size up his suit and take a peek at his shoes. Not that I know anything about men's shoes. His are polished and black.

He looks down. "Did you drop something?"

"No! I, uh, I thought I just saw something scurry across the floor. Like maybe a mouse, or, uh, a cockroach."

Good going, Tracey. How romantic.

*Reminder to self: In future, avoid mention of rodents and/or roaches during flirtation.*

Jack has jumped back a few feet, gaping at the floor and then at me.

I can't help laughing at his squeamish expression.

He laughs, too. "Sorry," he says. "When it comes to roaches…"

"I know." I shudder. Then, in case he's thinking of fleeing my vermin-infested office, I conclude brightly, "Maybe it was just an ant."

An ant. Uh-huh. An oversized ant, in a Manhattan office building, in the dead of December.

"You might want to cover your chocolate, just in case," Jack suggests, glancing at the box.

Then he asks, casually—*too* casually, I think—"Who's it from?"

"I'm not sure. I found it on my desk this morning. There wasn't a card."

"Must be your Secret Snowflake."

"It can't be. There's a fifteen-dollar limit for the week."

"This is over the limit?" he asks, the picture of innocence, as he puts the gold foil cover on the Godivas.

"Um, ye-ah," I say in my best teen girl *duh* tone.

"Oh. Well then, maybe you have a secret admirer."

"Maybe," I say coyly, leaning forward on my desk and resting my chin in my hand, inviting him to fess up.

"Well, I've got to get this up to Creative." He holds up the manila folder in his hand.

"Okay." I deduce he's not going to fess up now.

Or that maybe he didn't give me the chocolates.

But then, who did? Santa Claus?

"Want to go out again?" he asks, lingering in the doorway of my cube.

I pounce on that like Raphael on a new issue of *International Male*. "Sure! When?"

Do you think I sound too eager? I can't help it. I can't wait to be alone with him again. I don't know how I'll get through until—

"Tomorrow night?"

"Tomorrow night?" It's all I can do not to jump on him and wrap my arms around his neck and my legs around his waist.

*Please remain calm* blares the public address system in my brain.

"I think I'm free," I say sedately. "Let me check."

I snatch the big black bag from under my desk, grab my day planner and wildly flip through the pages.

Under Tuesday, it says only *CONFESSION* in huge black letters, underlined.

"Um, yeah, I'm free tomorrow night," I tell Jack, holding the day planner so that he can't see *CONFESSION*. Like I want to explain *that*.

I look at him.

His dimples deepen.

*I'm melt-innnngggg...*

"Tuesday sounds great," I say.

The minute he leaves, I cross out *CONFESSION* and beneath it write *JACK*. I underline it twice.

I mean, why confess my sins if I'm just going to run right back out and sin again?

So much for chastity and soul cleansing. I might as well wait until after the date and kill two birds with one stone. The two birds being sleeping with Jack twice.

On the other hand...

Okay, here's a novel idea: I could *not* sleep with him.

Or I could just not go out with him at all.

What kind of idiot idea is that?

Nobody said you can only go out once with a Transition Boy. I mean, what kind of transition is that?

I need to get used to dating again.

And I have a foolproof way to make sure I won't sleep with him this time.


"You want me to sleep over tomorrow night, Tracey?" Raphael narrows his permed eyelashes at me across the pile of dirty clothes I'm sorting.

Since we both live in buildings without laundry facilities, our tradition is to meet at a Laundromat once a week for suds and suds—we always bring a six-pack with us.

Tonight, however, the six-pack is for me.

Raphael brought a thermos full of something with brandy, rum and curaçao in it. It's called a Between the Sheets. Naturally, Raphael thought it was apropos for our laundry date. I don't feel like getting plastered on a week-night, so I'm sticking with Rolling Rock.

"Yup, I want you to sleep over tomorrow night, Raphael," I confirm. "Will you?"

"But why?"

"Please, Raphael, just do it."

"Tracey! I can't just agree to something like that without knowing why."

"What difference does it make?"

"I need to know."

"Raphael, you sleep all over Manhattan with God knows who. Why can't you spend one night at my place?"

"I already spent one night at your place this week."

"So spend another night."

"On the floor? No, thank you."

"You can have the bed this time," I promise, tossing a pair of jeans onto the darks pile with my left hand and raising my bottle of Rolling Rock to my mouth with the right. I take a swig, then ask, "You're over your cold, right?"

"Almost. Aside from the phlegm."

He makes a spasm gesture and coughs, like he's trying to raise a fur ball.

I wince.

"Come on, Raphael, I need you."

"This is the second favor you've asked for in five minutes, Tracey."

Yeah, like he really minds helping me find a male stripper for Yvonne's bachelorette party next week.

"I know, Raphael, but you're the only one who can help me. I need you to sleep over."

"Why?"

"I'm, uh, scared to be alone," I lie. "I heard there's a prowler in my building."

A prowler in the building? Who am I, Lucy Ricardo? There are no prowlers in New York these days. Rapists, yes. Packs of wilding kids, yes. Serial killers, yes.

As far as Manhattan goes, prowlers seem as quaintly old-fashioned—not to mention obsolete—as the Automat, the Brooklyn Dodgers and subway tokens.

Raphael asks, "Can I bring Carl?"

"No!" I just spent fifteen minutes listening to Raphael's uncensored account of Friday night after they left Tequila

Murray's. Believe me, it was *T.M.I.* In fact, any *I.* when it comes to Raphael and Carl is T.M.

"But if there's a prowler, Tracey, we might need Carl to protect us."

"That's supposed to be *your* job."

He casts a dubious downward glance. In his tummy-baring sweater halter, wide patent-leather belt and purple crushed-velvet bell-bottoms, he looks, below the neck, like somebody's kid sister.

"Okay, Raphael, I don't need you for that kind of protection," I admit, throwing my last towel into the heap of whites. "I need you to sleep at my place for—well, it's like insurance. I'm going out with Jack again…."

"The merchant marine?"

"Oh, Lord. Don't even start with that, Raphael."

"Just kidding, Tracey," he says, all innocence.

"Anyway, I want to make sure I'm not tempted to bring him home with me. If you're there, I can't."

"Is he cute?"

"Very."

"Then bring him home with you anyway. I'll be waiting. In bed." He flashes a lascivious grin before swigging from his drink. It's in a real martini glass, of course, with a cherry garnish. And a paper umbrella.

"Sorry, Raphael," I tell him, "I don't think Jack would be into that."

"Don't be so sure, Tracey."

I roll my eyes. Like I said, Raphael thinks every man is secretly gay.

"Oh, Tracey, look who's here!" he hisses. "It's One-Sock Sally."

I narrow my eyes at the woman who comes in the door.

I have no idea what her real name is, but One-Sock Sally, as Raphael and I refer to her, is our archenemy. There are way more working washers than dryers in this place, so a lot of times, you have to wait with a cartload of wet clothes until one opens up.

One-Sock Sally always cleverly beats the system by putting one sock into a dryer and turning it on the second she gets in the door. Sometimes, she even lays claim to two or three, if they're available. That way, when her clothes are done washing, she just adds them to the sock and never has to wait like the rest of us.

Raphael and I, who every week have to scrimp together enough change to do our laundry in the first place and can't afford to waste it on an empty dryer, like to pass the time by plotting elaborate revenge schemes on old One Sock.

We glare at her as she marches over to the lone available dryer, puts her sock in and feeds quarters into the slot.

She ignores us. She always does.

"So will you sleep over?" I ask Raphael, as One-Sock Sally begins sorting her laundry on the opposite side of the room.

"If you promise I can definitely have the bed. Your floor was freezing Thursday night, and I need a good night's sleep. I'm exhausted. Carl and I went out again last night, and—"

"Stop right there." I hold out my hand like a traffic cop to stave off more tales of unbridled lumberjack passion. "And do me a favor, Raphael. Don't mention this to Kate."

"What? Carl? Tracey, I already told her—"

"Not Carl. Jack and me. Don't tell her I'm going out with him again, okay?"

"Why not?"

"Because she doesn't think I'm ready for another relationship. She thinks I'm on the rebound."

"You *are* on the rebound, Tracey."

"I know I am. But that doesn't mean I can't go out with this very nice guy again."

"Or sleep with him again."

"Who said I slept with him?"

"Tracey! You can't fool me. You slept with him Friday night, didn't you?"

"No!" I avoid eye contact, wheeling my wire cart full of whites toward a vacant machine.

Raphael follows me, carrying his martini glass. "Yes, you did, Tracey! Otherwise, you wouldn't be worried about bringing him home with you tomorrow. You wouldn't need me in your bed as insurance."

"Raphael…" I swear he has some sick kind of sixth sense when it comes to sex.

I sigh. "Okay. I slept with him. But I'm not going to sleep with him again. And I know Kate won't believe me."

"I don't believe you, either. Tracey, you need to be careful. You're on the rebound."

"I am being careful." I fish six quarters out of my pocket and feed them into the machine. "That's why I need you, Raphael."

"I'll sleep over this once, but I can't always be there in your bed, Tracey. I have my own bed to sleep in, you know."

"I know, Raphael, and I really appreciate it."

"Anytime, Tracey. I'm always here for you. Really."

"Thanks. You're a good friend, Raphael."

We share a sappy smile.

It's a beautiful moment.

Until Raphael hacks up a major phlegm ball and spits it into a dirty T-shirt.

When I get home, I deposit the sack of clean laundry just inside the door and go straight to the cupboard to see what there is to eat. The beers have lowered my willpower, and I've got a fierce carb craving.

I'm out of pasta and rice, and the seven-grain bread is covered in a lovely green fuzz, but there are a few new red potatoes left in the bag I bought a few weeks ago. Three of them have disgusting spongey spots and smell like vodka, but the last one is fine as soon as I pull off a few sprouty growths and scrub it under the tap.

I wrap the tiny potato in foil, pop it into the oven to bake and change into workout clothes. I'm bone tired and I'd love to just curl up with my Jane Smiley book, but if I'm going to eat carbs this late in the evening, I'm sure as hell going to work out first.

I'm halfway through the Tae-Bo video when the phone rings. Normally, I'd let the machine get it, but it occurs to me that it might be Jack, calling to own up to the chocolates.

I snatch up the phone with a breathless "Hello?"

"It's me."

"Kate!" Dammit. Not just because it isn't Jack, but because there's only ten minutes until *CSI* starts, but Kate likes to talk. And talk. And talk.

"What's new?" she asks.

"Not much. How about you?"

"Billy's watching *Monday Night Football* and I'm bored to tears."

"I thought you like watching football with him."

She lowers her voice. "That's just what I say. Guys like girls who like sports."

Right. Sometimes I forget Kate is a graduate of the Southern Belle Academy of Feminine Wiles. You know, the one whose curriculum includes Intro to Drinking Bourbon Like a Lady and How to Avoid Letting Him See You Without Makeup Before You've Got a Ring on Your Finger 101.

"You never answered my e-mail," Kate says.

"I haven't checked it all weekend. I've been busy."

"I just wanted to know how your date on Friday night went."

"Fun. Really fun."

"You slept with him."

"Kate! You made me swear I wouldn't, remember?"

"You slept with him."

"You were right about him being just a Transition Boy," I go on, as if she hasn't spoken. "I mean, I can't get into a relationship right now."

"Answer the question, Trace. You slept with him."

"That's not a question, Kate."

"You're right, it isn't. Because I know you did."

Apparently, Kate also went to the Voodoo School of In-Your-Face Sex Clairvoyance with Raphael.

"Okay, Kate, I did sleep with him. And I don't regret it."

For a moment, all I hear on her end is football-game noise

in the background—cheering fans, a fast-talking commentator and Billy shouting something.

Then Kate says heavily, "You're fragile right now, Tracey. It's too soon to fall for somebody."

"I didn't say I fell for him. I said I slept with him."

"On the first date? That's—"

"You slept with Billy on the first date."

"I wasn't on the rebound."

"Maybe I'm not either."

Okay, who am I kidding? I'm so on the rebound I've got backboard burns on my ass.

I clear my throat. "Kate, I know you're just trying to be a good friend, but really, I can take care of myself. I'm just dating this guy. And I won't sleep with him again. I can't."

"Why can't you?"

I fill her in about Raphael the human chastity belt.

"Well, that works for now," Kate says, "but what about next time?"

"Who says there's going to be a next time?"

"He might keep calling you, Tracey."

A thrill shoots through me at the thought of it, but I do my best to sound blasé about it. "I doubt that. He's not really my type."

"Then why even bother going out with him again?"

"Because…he's nice. And funny. And smart. He knows all the state capitals."

"What?"

Forget it. She can't possibly understand.

"Never mind. I have to go eat my baked potato and watch *CSI.*"

"Lucky you, to have the TV remote all to yourself."

Yeah, sure. Lucky me.

All alone in the world's smallest apartment with the world's smallest baked potato.

Woo-hoo.

# 10

Tuesday morning, I get to work early and sneak a hot-chocolate packet and drugstore Christmas mug into Myron's cubby.

When I get to my desk, there's a gorgeous, gigantic pink-and-white poinsettia waiting for me. It's wrapped in cellophane. No card.

I suspect it's from Jack, but I can't figure out how to mention it when he calls me to confirm our date.

"Maybe it's from your Secret Snowflake," Brenda suggests as we fill our plastic salad containers in the deli at lunchtime. "Maybe the chocolates were, too."

"They can't be. There's a fifteen-dollar limit for the week." I swear, I'm getting so tired of saying that.

"Well, maybe your Snowflake wants to spoil you. And, anyway, you didn't get any other anonymous gifts yesterday or today. So if the chocolates and the plant weren't from your Snowflake, your Snowflake forgot all about you."

True.

But that makes more sense than a Snowflake who's already spent at least fifty bucks on me.

I prefer to think that my Snowflake's got Alzheimer's and that a smitten Jack is showering me with flowers and candy.

Tuesday night after work, Jack takes me to dinner at the Sea Grill restaurant under Rockefeller Center.

We sip wine and eat scallops and watch the skaters through the plate-glass windows. Afterward, we stroll across the plaza to see the tree.

"When I was a kid, I always wanted to come to New York at Christmastime and see the tree in person," I tell him, shivering in the cold, still evening air as we come to a stop by the metal railing at the base of the tree.

"It's gorgeous, isn't it?"

I nod, my breath puffing white as I say, "Sometimes I can't believe I really live here."

He puts his arms around me from behind and pulls me close, my back against his chest as we look up at the brilliant-colored lights stretching into the night sky.

We stand there for a long time.

People rush past us: tired office workers carrying briefcases, suburban women loaded down with shopping bags, harried families holding programs from Radio City Music Hall's Christmas Spectacular around the corner. Taxis honk and sirens wail and a jackhammer rattles at an all-night construction site.

I try to memorize every detail, knowing I'll want to relive it all later, when I'm alone.

Jack's body heat radiates against my back, and he smells

like wine and herbal soap. I can feel his warm breath stirring the hair behind my ear, and his hands are tucked into my coat pockets with mine.

"It's snowing!" I realize, catching sight of white flakes swirling down in a floodlight's glow. "Oh, my God! Jack! It's snowing! It's perfect!"

He kisses me, and it's even more perfect.

We stand there, shivering and kissing and snuggling against each other for warmth.

He sings "Winter Wonderland" in my ear, and then he sings "Let It Snow." He definitely can't carry a tune, but it's wonderfully romantic anyway.

Minutes pass—long, cozy, teeth-chattering minutes.

It's snowing harder. Real snow.

*It's A Wonderful Life* snow.

Heated kisses.

Frozen toes.

"Let's go," Jack murmurs in my ear.

Already? I don't want to go. I want to stay here, with him, kissing by the Rockefeller Center Christmas tree.

"Come on," he says, tugging my hand. "We'll get a cab downtown."

"Oh…" I smile. I get it. He's coming home with me.

He's coming home with me?

"Oh!"

"Tracey? What's wrong?"

"Um, we can't go to my apartment."

"We can't? Why not?"

"My friend's sleeping over tonight."

"The one with the leopard-print thong?"

"It was zebra print, and yes, that's the one."

"His apartment is *still* being fumigated?"

"Yes. It was really infested."

Jack winces.

*Mental Note: Any mention of "infestation" kills romance.*

We stand for a bit, staring up at the tree through the falling snow.

Then we start kissing again.

When we take a breather, Jack suggests, "We could go to my apartment."

"Is Mike there?"

"Probably."

"Doesn't he ever sleep at Dianne's?"

"I wish. She lives with her mother."

"That sucks."

He laughs. "Tell me about it. She's always at our place. But I don't want to talk about her."

In fact, he doesn't want to talk at all. I close my eyes in complete and utter rapture while Jack nuzzles my neck.

It's snowing harder.

I can feel the flakes catching in my eyelashes, feel wet trickles down my cheeks. They're probably tinted black with mascara. Lovely.

Okay, we can't stand here all night. A decision must be made.

"Let's go to my apartment," Jack whispers.

"I can't," I whisper back, wiping at and undoubtedly smearing the wet eye makeup.

"Why not?"

"A lot of reasons. Mainly, Mike."

"He doesn't have to know you're there. We'll sneak in."

"He might hear us and think we're prowlers."

"Prowlers?" He laughs. "I doubt it. But just in case, we could get you a disguise. I bet you'd look great as a blonde."

Feeling vaguely insulted, I shake my head. "I can't. I'd be too freaked out if Mike found out. I should just go home."

He looks so disappointed, I'm no longer insulted. Clearly, he's into me, brunette, snow-soaked hair, smudged black eyes and all.

He squeezes my hand. "Are you sure, Tracey?"

"I'm positive. I'm sorry."

We kiss again.

"Maybe you could kick your friend out of your place?" Jack murmurs.

Yeah, right. After I begged him to stay? Fag-hag divorce grounds, for sure.

"I can't," I say, cursing phlegmy Raphael in my bed. "He has nowhere else to go."

Aside from his newly fumigated and perfectly inhabitable apartment, of course.

I'm such an idiot.

Jack kisses me.

Dammit. I want to be alone with him. But where?

Too bad I don't still have Raphael's keys. He had to change all the locks after the nasty breakup with Wade, and he hasn't gotten around to giving me a new set.

I look longingly at Jack.

The wind blows granular snow into my upturned face.

Jack brushes it off, gently, with the edge of his soft black scarf.

I compare him to Will, who I'm positive would let me be buried up to my eyebrows in a snowdrift before he'd clean me off with *his* cashmere scarf.

Jack kisses me again.

"Are you sure you can't come home with me, Tracey?" he asks.

"I'm sure," I say.

He kisses me again.

And again.

And again.

And five minutes later, of course, we're on a subway to Brooklyn.

"Tracey?"

"Hmm?" I burrow beneath the warm quilt.

"The bathroom's free."

"Mmm-hmm."

"Tracey…"

Bedsprings creak.

Jack kisses my cheek. He smells soapy and minty, like he just showered and brushed his teeth.

Conscious that I haven't yet showered or brushed my teeth, I tilt my head and talk into the pillow. "Five more minutes?"

"Not if you want to take a shower and get out of here before Mike wakes up. That's what you swore you wanted to do last night. His alarm doesn't go off for another twenty minutes, so—"

That's all I need to hear.

I catapult out of bed, wrapped in a blanket, still not comfortable enough with my newly slimmed-down body to walk around naked in front of anybody, and certainly not Jack.

"There's a new toothbrush in the medicine cabinet," he

calls after me as I bolt for the hallway and the bathroom I vaguely remember sneaking into last night.

I'm careful not to make a sound as I hurry past the closed door, knowing Mike is asleep behind it. How bizarre is that? Me, creeping naked past my boss's bedroom door.

Well, not naked, but close enough. The blanket I grabbed is little more than a throw.

It doesn't occur to me until I'm in the shower-steamy bathroom with the door closed behind me that I've brought nothing to wear on my return trip to the bedroom.

*Rut-roh.*

I'd better hurry. I can't think of anything worse than running into Mike in the hallway when I'm half-naked.

After checking the door repeatedly to make sure I'm locked in, I drop the blanket, find the new toothbrush in the medicine cabinet and unwrap it. The crinkling cellophane is deafening. So is the tap when I turn it on.

The bathroom is old, with pink-and-black tile and stains in the grout. It's not that clean, either. When I pick up the soap and see a coarse, curly black hair embedded in it, I'm so horrified that I drop the whole bar into the tub.

I don't even want to speculate about whose crotch it fell out of.

I wash without soap, and as I do, I think about Jack and last night.

And Jack's apartment.

It's a third-floor walk-up in one of those boxy brick apartment buildings that line the streets of the outer boroughs. We pretty much went straight to the bedroom when we got here, but I glimpsed enough of the tiny place to know that it's your run-of-the-mill bachelor pad. Mismatched hand–me–down furniture, no rugs, no pictures on the walls, and it smells faintly of old beer and steam heat and Comet.

Jack's room consists of a full–sized mattress and box spring sitting right on the floor, a tall dark dresser that looks like it came out of his childhood bedroom and some stacked plastic milk crates filled with books and CDs and papers.

So much for my trust–fund theory. Jack is clearly living on his media planner's salary. Which makes a forty-dollar box of imported chocolate and a shrub-sized poinsettia plant all the more impressive. *If* they really are from him.

Dammit, the tub isn't draining right, which leaves me standing in a shin-deep pool of soap scum and floating hairs. Oh, ick.

Plus, several of the holes at the top of the vinyl shower curtain are torn right through. So it droops on one end and I don't realize the floor is getting soaked until I'm done with the shower.

"Shit!" I whisper-scream when I see the flood.

I climb out of the tub and try to sop up the mess without using all three towels that are in the barren linen cabinet, reasoning that I need one and Mike will need one. But it takes two towels to even semi-dry the puddles. I'm left still dripping wet and naked myself, and wondering if I dare use the last dry towel.

What are the chances that there's a clean, newly laundered, just-folded load sitting just outside the door in a laundry basket?

I know, I didn't think so, either.

I have no choice but to grab the last dry towel from the

shelf, do my best to blot my hair and the rest of me. My feet are slippery up to my ankles from standing in the soap slick in the tub. They'll probably be all itchy later. Lovely.

I wrap the towel around myself, and drape the blanket over my shoulders for good measure.

Then I open the door, peer cautiously into the hall and step out of the bathroom.

All is dark and quiet.

Safe.

I take two steps…and skid in my still-damp, slippery feet on the hardwood floor.

I go down with a crash and a screech.

"What the—"

"Tracey?"

Two doors open simultaneously.

Two men rush out of their rooms.

One is Jack.

The other is Mike Middleford, boss of Tracey.

Did I say that I couldn't think of anything worse than running into Mike in the hallway when I'm half-naked?

I did?

Well, guess what? I just thought of something far freaking worse.

I scramble to rewrap the towel and blanket around myself as Mike gapes, standing there in—you guessed it—his underwear.

They're not boxers, like Jack has on.

Nor are they a zebra-print thong, à la Raphael.

But, God help me, they're something in between. I believe the proper term is tighty whities.

*Oh, the horror,* cries a news commentator in my head, who

apparently hasn't seen anything this bad since the Hindenburg crashed and burned.

Tracey: sprawled, nearly naked.

Mike: tighty whities.

*Oh, the horror. Oh, the humanity.*

Face flaming, I get to my feet and speed-skate toward Jack, who hustles me into his room and closes the door behind me.

"Are you okay?" he asks.

"That was…that was…" I can't even find the words to describe it. I bury my face in his bare shoulder, trembling.

"Did you hurt your leg?" he asks, holding me at arm's length and looking down.

"No."

"You're bleeding."

Dammit, I am bleeding. Ouch. My knee has one of those brush-burns you get when you're seven and fall off your two-wheeler onto the asphalt.

Oh, to be seven again.

Oh, to be fully clothed and falling off a two-wheeler.

Jack takes a corner of the towel that's slipping off me and kneels at my feet, gently dabbing my knee.

I wince.

"Does it hurt?"

It stings like crazy, but that's nothing compared to the utter, soul-searing humiliation I feel.

"It's not so bad," I tell him, meaning the knee.

He dabs at it again.

"Do you think Mike saw anything?" I ask.

Which is like Michael Jackson asking if anybody's noticed he got his nose done.

"Nah," Jack says, unconvincingly. "Come on, let's go clean up your knee. I'll get you a Band-Aid."

The Band-Aids, as I recall, were next to the toothbrush in the bathroom cabinet.

"I can't." I plop down on the edge of his rumpled bed, wishing I could smoke. But my Salems are in my bag, which is hanging on a hook somewhere beyond Jack's bedroom, so it's out of the question, since I can't leave this room. Ever.

I say exactly that to Jack.

Jack grins. "Really? I kind of like the idea of you in my bedroom 24/7."

"Jack, I'm not kidding. How can I ever face Mike again after that? I work for him!"

"It's not that big a deal, Tracey."

Easy for him to say. *He* wasn't sprawled naked at his tighty-whitie-clad boss's feet. In fact, I think it's safe to assume that in the whole history of the world, no other human has ever been sprawled naked at their tighty-whitie-clad boss's feet.

Jack sits beside me on the bed.

"Do you want me to go talk to Mike?"

"No!" I narrow my eyes at him. "What could you possibly say? Pretend you didn't see that? I don't think it's an image he's going to forget any time soon."

I know I won't.

Every time I look at Mike, I'm going to see his toothpick legs and his scrawny but hairy chest and the disconcerting bulge in his—

"I can't stand it," I wail, closing my eyes to block out the image.

Jack gives my shoulder a *there, there* pat. It doesn't help.

I can't think of anything that might help, aside from maybe a cigarette. Or being shot with a tranquilizer gun.

We hear footsteps in the hall. A door closes, and a few seconds later, the tap is turned on.

"He's in the shower!" I tell Jack, springing into action. "I have to get out of here before he comes out."

Jack looks down at his boxers. "But—"

"Now!" I bark in a guttural voice.

He looks taken aback, so I sweetly smile and say, "Sorry."

"It's okay," he says, but I can tell he's wondering if there's a scary hidden ax-murderess side of me.

Ten minutes later, we're both dressed for work and walking through the brisk gray morning to the subway. My hair is still wet and I'm wearing the same thing I had on yesterday, of course. I have to stop home and change before I go to the office.

I tell Jack to continue on uptown when we reach my stop.

In my apartment, I find Raphael snoring in my bed and the television on. It's tuned to a porn station; a closeup action scene of a big wet tongue on the most enormous nipple I've ever seen in my life.

Oh, for God's sake.

I turn it off, take another shower—this time with soap above the ankle and proper rinsing below—dry my hair, and get dressed. Raphael sleeps through it all.

I can think of a billion places I'd rather spend today than the office. Like, say, in the confessional at St. Fabian's. Or Baghdad.

But I can't call in sick. I'd have to call Mike, who knows I'm not sick. Who now knows everything about me, come to think of it.

I slink into the office fifteen minutes late. When I see Myron wheeling his mail cart by the reception area, I realize I forgot to bring the paperback sports biography I bought him as today's Secret Snowflake gift.

*Mental Note: Run down to Korean market and find something—nice shiny apple?—to leave for Myron at lunch hour.*

Mike's in his office with a couple of production guys. Thank God he's busy for now. That gives me time to brace myself before I see him again.

"Morning, Tracey!" Merry chirps, passing me in the corridor as I hang up my coat.

"Merry! Wait, I need to ask you something."

"Hmm?" She turns around. She's wearing one of those acrylic Christmas sweaters with a sequined candy cane on the front, and a plastic pin shaped like Rudolph's head. The nose is a miniature lightbulb that's glowing red.

"About the Secret Snowflake…how much are we supposed to spend on gifts for our person?"

"Fifteen dollars for the week. Is that a problem?"

"No! I just, um, wanted to make sure."

She says dramatically, "Isn't your Snowflake leaving you little gifts, Tracey? Because if there's a situation…"

A situation.

Judging by her expression, there's nothing more ominous—at least, not to Mary the One-Woman Goodwill Gestapo—than a Secret Snowflake *situation*.

"No, there's no situation," I assure her, unwilling to admit that my Snowflake is either neglecting me or overspending. For all I know, that's grounds for a Secret Snowflake tribunal, and who has time for that?

Merry goes on her merry way, *Tra La,* and I head to my

cubicle, praying Mike will spend the rest of the morning—or, with any luck, the rest of both our careers—in meetings.

I stop short in the doorway to my cube.

A white envelope is propped on my keyboard. My name is scrawled on it in black Sharpie.

Thank God my stomach is empty, because I'd probably throw up if it weren't.

For a split second, I'm convinced that it's from Mike. That he's firing me.

*Okay, get a grip, Tracey. He can't fire you for being naked in his apartment.*

But can he fire me for letting him unwittingly take a shower with nary a dry towel in the bathroom?

My hands are shaking as I tear the envelope open.

Inside, there's a little cardboard folder that contains a twenty-five-dollar gift certificate to Sephora.

Okay, I'm not fired.

That's a good thing.

Somebody is treating me to upscale beauty products.

Also a good thing...

Unless it's a major hint.

As in, "You need a makeover, Tracey Spadolini, and if you're not going to spring for it, I will."

Whoever *I* is.

Nah. Twenty-five bucks at Sephora wouldn't transform me into a new woman. I'm not even sure it would buy me blusher and a lipstick.

I have no idea who left this envelope, but after further investigation, I have to conclude that it probably isn't from Jack. The gift certificate is timed and dated, and I was with him last night when it was purchased.

Which means the chocolates and poinsettia weren't from Jack, either.

Not a good thing.

Can my Secret Snowflake really be behind this?

Frankly, I'd rather be ignored and forgotten, like I forgot poor Myron today.

I mean...I'm going to run out and get him a nice shiny apple? Who am I, the old hag from *Snow White?*

Meanwhile, my Snowflake is giving me better presents than I'd buy my own mother.

That's just *wrong*.

And creepy as hell.

"How's it going, Chief?"

I look up to see Mike standing over me with a stack of papers in his hand.

"Hi, Mike." Instant flaming face.

"Nice flowers." He's fully clothed...in person. But not in my mind's eye.

Oh, Lord.

"Thanks," I say, sounding hoarse.

"Secret Snowflake again?" he asks.

"I, uh, guess so." I try not to stare at anything but his face and hope to God he's not having the same struggle.

"Listen," he says, holding out the papers. "I need four copies of this presentation by the end of—"

"No problem." I snatch the stack out of his hand and take off for the copier.

Good thing I have an appointment with my shrink after work tonight.

Maybe she can make some sense of my life, because I sure as hell can't.

★ ★ ★

"Do you think a person can fall in love with someone new within months of breaking up with somebody they were with for three years?"

Dr. Schwartzenbaum—whose real name is Beatrix but goes by Trixie and has repeatedly invited me to call her that—studies me over the top of her half glasses. "You've met somebody new, Tracey?"

"Sort of. I mean, I definitely did meet him. But he's my boss's roommate."

She nods. Waits.

Twenty-three stories below, sirens wail along Twenty-ninth Street.

I shift my weight on the leather couch. It makes a deafening sound that sounds exactly like a blast of intestinal gas. Nice. I shift my weight again, hoping it will make the same sound so she'll know it wasn't a fart, but the couch won't cooperate.

I look up.

She's just watching me. It's hard to tell from her expression whether she's wondering whether flatulence fumes are about to hit her in the nostrils or if she's merely still waiting for me to expand on what I was saying.

That's the one thing I hate about Dr. Schwartzenbaum. She spends a lot of time just waiting. And listening. I mean, I guess technically that's her job, but sometimes I wish she'd do all the talking. The endless Tracey monologue can be exhausting.

"Do you think I should be dating my boss's roommate?" I ask her, giving up on making the couch fart.

"Do *you* think you should?"

That's the other thing I hate about Dr. Schwartzenbaum. She tends to answer my questions with questions.

"I don't know," I tell her. "I mean, I guess the answer is no, I don't think I should."

She waits.

"But I'm attracted to him. And he keeps calling me. We spent last night together—and just before I left work, he called and asked me out again for the weekend. I know I should have said no, but I said yes. I don't know what we're doing. He said it's a surprise."

Dr. Schwartzenbaum nods intently and shifts her weight in her chair, uncrossing her black-silk-pants-clad legs and re-crossing them in the opposite direction.

"Do you think I should have told him I couldn't go out with him again?"

"*Can* you go?"

"Yes."

"And you *want* to go?"

"Yes."

"Then why would you tell him you can't go?"

The question isn't rhetorical.

"I'd tell him that because nothing can come of this relationship. I'm not even over Will yet."

She nods, clearly in perfect agreement. Or is she? It's hard to tell with her. She's big on nodding, and I'm starting to think it merely means *I hear you, go on.*

She nods all the time when we're talking about Will. Naturally, we spend a lot of time talking about Will. Rather, *I* spend a lot of time talking about Will. Dr. Schwartzenbaum spends a lot of time urging me to dissect my feelings about him—which, apparently, have a lot to do with my feelings about myself. And my mother.

Who knew?

Well, Buckley knew. He warned me before I started this that therapy always comes down to how you feel about your mother, but I didn't think that applied to me. My mother is four hundred miles away.

Which is also, according to Dr. Trixie Schwartzenbaum, relevant.

"Do you think about Will when you're with this other person?" Dr. Schwartzenbaum asks now.

"No," I say quickly.

She's silent.

I think about it more carefully.

"No," I tell her again. "Not when I'm *with* him." In the biblical sense or otherwise. I admit, "But I still think about Will sometimes. How long do you think it's going to take before I'm over him?"

I wait for her to ask, *How long do* you *think it's going to take?* But she doesn't.

She says, "That depends."

More silence.

"Depends on what?"

"Do you want to be over Will?"

"Yes!"

"Are you sure?"

I *was*, but…

"Yes," I say, less forcefully, because obviously she thinks I'm not sure, so, um, maybe I'm not.

Silence.

Dammit. I hate it when she makes me feel wishy-washy.

"I *want* to be over him," I offer.

"Do you?"

"Don't I?"

"Don't ask me, Tracey, ask yourself. I wonder if you just want to be over the pain. If perhaps there's a part of you that isn't ready, yet, to let go of Will."

Okay, there's another thing I hate about Dr. Schwartzenbaum. When I try to answer *her* questions with questions, she won't let me.

Now she's waiting for a reply, sitting there in her silk suit with her legs crossed and her fingers steepled, as though she has all the time in the whole damned world.

Technically, she only has—

I check my watch—

Thirty-five more minutes.

But I guess that's enough time for me to answer the question. Which was…

Oh, yeah. She wonders if there's a part of me that isn't ready, yet, to let go of Will.

Which isn't necessarily a question. It's more like a comment.

But, apparently, she expects me to respond.

So I try.

At first, I pretend to think about whether I'm ready to let go of Will.

Then, I really *do* think about whether I'm ready to let go of Will.

I try to force myself to think about all the horrible things Will did when we were dating, but for some reason, all I can think about are the handful of nice things.

Nostalgia sweeps through me as I remember how he held

me after I slept with him for the first time, and how he took me to see *Rent* right before he left for summer stock, and how much I missed him when he left....

To my horror, tears are coming to my eyes.

I wipe them away.

They come back.

"I guess I'm not ready," I say, sniffling. "I mean...I really loved him. I don't know why, but I did. And he really hurt me. It still hurts."

"Yes."

"And as much as I try to forget all about him, I can't get over him that easily."

"No."

I pluck a tissue from a strategically placed box by the couch and blow my nose. Hard. "So does that mean I'm not ready for a new relationship?"

"What do you think?"

"If I'm not ready for a new relationship now, when *will* I be? Next month? Next year? Please tell me."

"I can't. There's no formula for something like this, Tracey."

"I know, but...I really like Jack."

"Your boss's roommate."

"Yes. Transition Boy."

"Hmm?"

"That's what my friend Kate calls Jack. She says that when you break up with somebody, you need a transitional relationship. You know—that it's too soon to fall in love with anyone for real."

"I see."

"Do *you* think that's the case?"

"Do you think you're in love with Jack?"

Dammit, I'd get more satisfying answers out of Kate. At least she gives me explicit instructions on what to do and what not to do.

Bossy, yes, but ultimately effective.

Then again, maybe not, considering I haven't exactly followed her advice.

"Of course I'm not in love with Jack," I inform Dr. Schwartzenbaum, wishing I could smoke in here. The tension is getting to me. "I just met him. I just wanted to know if it's impossible to fall in love with him—or anyone—right after a breakup. You know, like if we kept on dating."

"Nothing is impossible, Tracey. The question is, are you emotionally ready for a new relationship?"

Well, duh. She acts like she just thought of it, but that's the question *I've* been asking *her* for the last five minutes.

I pretend to scratch my chin so that I can sneak a peek at my watch. We still have thirty-two minutes to go.

I sigh and look at Dr. Trixie Schwartzenbaum. She—and her trusty prescription pad—were so helpful getting me over my panic attacks.

Too bad there isn't some kind of drug she could prescribe to heal all my other problems....

"Tracey?" she prods.

"I guess I'm not emotionally ready for a new relationship, Dr. Schwartzenbaum."

"You can call me Trixie if you'd like," she inserts.

Why won't she take the hint?

I go on. "I think maybe just I'm so afraid of being alone that I want to be with someone."

I suppose that's as good an answer as any, because she nods.

"Or maybe I am ready," I say, testing her. "Maybe the only way I can get over Will is to find someone new."

She nods again.

"But maybe I can't find somebody new until I'm over Will."

Nod.

"Which means I'm not emotionally ready for a new relationship."

Double nod.

Damn her.

Is she just going to sit here like a bobblehead while I talk myself in circles? For this, I'm paying her a hundred bucks an hour out of pocket?

I need answers.

"Do you think I'm trying to convince myself that I could fall in love with Jack because he keeps asking me out and I'm afraid to say no because I'm afraid to be alone?" I ask her.

"Does that make sense to you?"

"Well, it does sound like something I'd do. Or maybe I'm so into Jack because I know that he's supposed to be off-limits since he lives with my boss."

No reply, other than a thoughtful tilt of head.

"And what about Buckley?" I ask. "Do you think I'm attracted to him just because he's there? And he's available? And I'm lonely? Or because I know he's off-limits because he's my friend?"

"Is a friend off-limits?"

"I don't know."

"Is a boss's roommate off-limits?"

If I knew, would I freaking be asking her?

Okay, I'm starting to get the picture.

The answers I need are not going to come from Dr. Schwartzenbaum aka Trixie.

Not from Kate, either, though she's a lot more forthcoming than the shrink.

It looks like I, Tracey, need to take charge of my life. Only I can decide what's best for me—and the sooner I figure it out, the better.

11

On the fourth day of Christmas, my Secret Snowflake gave to me:

Two orchestra seats to the Radio City Music Hall Christmas Spectacular.

I am so not kidding.

On the fourth day of Christmas, Myron's Secret Snowflake gave to him:

Fudge.

It was *good* fudge.

It even had nuts in it. Pecans.

One skimpy piece cost me almost five bucks at a French chocolatier off Fifth Avenue. They wrapped it up in a little white box with a red satin bow.

The Radio City tickets, however, were close to two hundred dollars. And they were tucked into a beautiful hand-embroidered pink velvet Christmas stocking somebody hung from my bulletin board, from the empty tack that used to hold Will's headshot.

I examine them, then look around, half expecting to see a camera crew from one of those reality television prank shows. But there's nary a lurking lens to be seen, which means the gift is for real.

That does it.

Just yesterday I decided I'm going to take charge of my life, and it's time I did just that.

I've got to put a stop to this madness.

I pluck the stocking and the tickets off the board.

I am about to march down to Merry and tell her we've got ourselves a *situation* when the phone rings.

It's my line, and it's Buckley.

"You never called me back," he says.

Oops. I never did. He left messages for me at work and at home yesterday. He e-mailed, too. I didn't bother to reply.

Will called, too, and left me a message. I didn't call him back, either.

Will rarely e-mails. He claims he doesn't believe in it. He says it's an impersonal form of communication, but really, it's because he's dyslexic and has a hard time with reading and writing and is too proud to admit to being less than perfect in any way.

But enough about Will, dammit.

"I'm sorry," I tell Buckley. "I've been really busy. How are you?"

"Life pretty much sucks," he says flatly. "Sonja and I tried to patch things up Tuesday. It didn't work. We broke up again for good."

Is it just me, or wasn't the first time they broke up supposed to be for good?

I'm so not in the mood for this. I've got my own problems to worry about.

But okay, Buckley's my friend and I owe him an ear and a shoulder.

"Did you tell her you're willing to compromise about living together?" I ask him, plopping down in my desk chair, still clutching the stocking and the tickets.

"No, I didn't tell her that. Because I'm not willing. How do you compromise living with somebody?"

"I don't know…you live together during the day but not at night?" I laugh.

He doesn't.

"It's a joke, Buckley."

"Oh. Sorry." He fake-laughs.

Well, this sucks. Time for a subject change.

"You think you've got problems," I say. "My Secret Snowflake is making me feel like shit."

"Your…what?"

"Secret Snowflake. It's this thing in the office which somebody lied and told me was mandatory, only, I found out that it wasn't but I had already signed up. First, my Snowflake gives me Godivas, then a poinsettia, then a gift certificate and now two tickets to Radio City. In the orchestra. What's next? A villa in the Cayman Islands? Meanwhile, what do I buy for my Secret Snowflake? Fucking fudge. That's what."

He laughs.

"That's not a joke, Buckley."

"It struck me as funny. Sorry." He sounds completely unapologetic.

"What's funny about fudge?"

"Not just fudge. Fucking fudge. And that's not what's funny."

"Then what's funny?"

"For one thing, Secret Snowflake is funny."

"What's so amusing about it?"

He snorts. "What isn't amusing? The phrase 'Secret Snowflake' is amusing. The concept itself is pretty damned amusing, too. So is the fact that you thought it was mandatory and it wasn't. And that you actually give a damn what you're getting."

"It's not just what I'm getting, it's what I'm *giving,*" I say, irked by his mirth. "I'm *giving* crap, and I'm *getting* game-show prizes. Why the hell isn't my Snowflake sticking to the limit? Does everyone go over the limit and nobody told me? I feel cheap," I wail.

"Calm down, Trace." Buckley's laughing. Not fake-laughing, either.

"This isn't a joke, Buckley."

"Tracey, if your biggest problem in life is that your Secret Snowflake is showering you with extravagant gifts—"

"It's not my biggest problem," I protest.

"What is?"

I hesitate.

I don't want to go there. Not now.

"Never mind," I tell him. "So what are you going to do about Sonja?"

"Get over her. Want to help me drown my sorrows this weekend?"

"I, um…when, this weekend?"

"Saturday night?"

"Sorry, I've got, um, a date."

A pause.

"Oh."

Another pause.

"With that Jack guy who knows all the state capitals?"

"Yeah."

"Oh."

Long pause.

"I know all the state capitals, Tracey," Buckley says, and laughs.

We're back to the fake, forced laugh.

"Try me," Buckley says, as I try to think of something to say.

"Okay. Montana."

"Helena."

"Right!"

"Now will you go out with me on Saturday night instead?"

"Buckley—"

"Just kidding. It's okay. I just…I don't really want to sit around my apartment by myself."

"Why don't you go out with the guys?"

"Yeah. I could."

"You should."

"Okay."

"And then maybe you and I can, uh, do something on Sunday."

"Yeah?"

"Well…let me check something first. Oregon."

"Salem," is the prompt reply.

I grin. "Right again. Yeah, so…Sunday."

"It's a date."

I tell him that it is.

Except, it's not.

A date, I mean. Hanging out with Buckley on Sunday is not a *date,* date.

Mike's line is ringing.

"I've got to get that," I tell Buckley.

As I disconnect the call, I ask myself whether I wish it were a date, date.

I listen carefully for a reply, but apparently, my inner self isn't speaking to me.

I guess, when you come right down to it, despite my vow to take charge of my life, my inner self is no more useful than Dr. Schwartzenbaum.

At least I don't want to be called Trixie or charge me a hundred bucks an hour *after* insurance.

I press Mike's extension and say, "Mike Middleford's office."

"Tracey, it's me, Dianne."

"Oh, hi, Dianne. How are you?"

"Great. I'm on my way to a sale at Barneys. If you haven't finished your Christmas shopping, you should try to get over there on your lunch hour."

As if.

I'll be doing the rest of my Christmas shopping at Wal-Mart when I get to Brookside, thank you very much.

But I tell Dianne, "Sounds great. Maybe I will. You'll have to let me know if you get any great bargains."

It's a little more difficult to make pleasant chitchat with Dianne now that I know she's a one-woman axis of evil.

"In the men's department?" she asks.

At least, that's what I think she asks. She's on her cell phone and the line is crackling.

*In the men's department* doesn't make sense.

"What was that?" I ask. "I can't hear you very well."

"I said, I'll let you know if I find any bargains in the men's department."

Oh, crap. Does she think I'm going to buy something for Mike at Barneys? I was planning to get him one of those desktop executive golf games. You know, the kind that cost twenty bucks in the quick gift department at JCPenney. If there even is a JCPenney in Manhattan. Come to think of it, I've never actually seen one here.

"Yeah," Dianne says, "Mike said you and Jack are a couple now."

Gulp.

"He did?"

She laughs. "Yeah. At first I didn't believe him, because it just seemed so—"

*Crackle, crackle.*

So *what?*

*Crackle, crackle.*

I hate cell phones.

"—but he says it's true. Is it?"

"Well, I've gone out with him a few times."

She laughs again. "Sorry I called him an asshole."

That comes through loud and clear. She doesn't sound the least bit apologetic.

"Oh…uh, no problem," I say, because what else is there to say?

"Listen, is Mike there?"

"Hang on."

I go check. He's not.

"His light is on so he's in, but I don't see him anywhere," I tell Dianne.

"Oh. Well, can you check again? I really need to talk to him."

Clenching my teeth, I say, "Sure."

Like I have nothing better to do than hunt down her boyfriend every time she calls.

*Take charge of your life, Tracey.*

I put her on hold again and sit there for a few minutes, flipping through this morning's *Post*.

Then I pick up again and say, "I checked everywhere, Dianne. He must be in a meeting. I'll tell him you called."

"Okay, thanks," she says, but she doesn't sound very happy about it.

After hanging up, I push back my desk chair and head off down the hall with the Christmas stocking and the two tickets to Radio City.

They're for next Friday night, right before I leave to spend Christmas in Brookside.

Since it's on the way to the elevator, I decide to stop by Latisha's cube on my way to find Merry.

She's on the phone, but she motions for me to wait.

"Okay, baby," she says into the phone. "I will. Love you, too, baby."

She makes kissing noises, then hangs up.

"Derek?" I ask, and she nods.

"You know, you were on the rebound when you met him, Latisha."

"Huh?"

"You had just broken up with Anton after a couple of

years together. Then you met Derek, and the two of you fell head over heels, and nobody was saying you shouldn't go for it."

"Honey, *everybody* was saying we shouldn't go for it."

"I wasn't."

"You were so busy wallowing in a piss pot of self-pity after Will dumped you that you didn't say anything at all."

"I'm sorry," I say, feeling like a horrible friend, not to mention ashamed of wallowing in the piss pot.

"It's okay," she says. "I understand."

"So you're saying nobody was rooting for you and Derek when you got together?"

"Right."

"But you made it work."

She shrugs. "Well, it's only been a few months, but—"

"So you mean he could just be a Transition Boy?"

"Boy, nothing," Latisha says, with a sassy wave of her hand. "And Derek's not going anywhere, and I'm not, either."

Suddenly, I feel better about the whole Jack thing.

"What'cha got there?" Latisha asks, gesturing at my hand.

"Check this out." I hand over the stocking and the tickets.

She's all eye whites. "From Jack?"

"No. From my Secret Snowflake."

"You're bullshitting me."

"I'm not bullshitting you."

"Maybe I should'a gotten in on this Secret Snowflake thing after all. I was thinking it was all about candy canes and bubblegum, and—"

"It is!" I cut in. "I mean, it's supposed to be. But my

Snowflake is some kind of overzealous freak. What am I going to do?"

"If you don't want the tickets, give 'em to Yvonne for a bachelorette party gift. She used to be a Rockette. She can take Thor and tell him all about the old days."

Uh-oh. The bachelorette party. I almost forgot about it. It's less than a week away, and I still haven't found the stripper. They're all way too expensive for our budget.

After assuring Latisha that I've got Raphael working on the stripper situation and making plans to meet her, Brenda, and Yvonne for lunch, I head for Merry's desk.

Good Lord, her cubicle just screams *Hallelujah*. Every surface is draped with tinsel and shiny garland, and her bulletin board and computer screen are framed in blinking red and green lights.

Remember Snoopy's overdone doghouse in *A Charlie Brown Christmas?* Right. You get the picture.

Merry isn't there, so I scribble a quick note on a yellow Post-it. I keep it short and sweet—no need to alarm her by referring to the *situation*. I'll tell her in person.

*Merry, Please call me on extension 2409, Thanks, Tracey Spadolini.*

I stick the Post-it squarely on the nose of the life-sized cardboard Santa propped against the wall.

His eyes, how they twinkle.

His dimples, how...

*How they remind me of Jack.*

And my heart beats a little faster just thinking of Saturday night and the surprise date.


Thursday night, Will calls.

The cordless phone is on the table right beside me, but I

initially screen the call because I'm wrapped up in all-new Must-See TV.

I listen to him talking into my answering machine, going on and on, not because he suspects I'm here listening but because he has deep affection for the sound of his own voice, and I'm so not going to pick up—

Except that I do.

I don't know why I do and I hate that I do, but I just can't help myself.

"Tracey! You're there!"

"Yeah, I'm here." I try to sound casual, as though the sound of his voice hasn't plunged my poor empty stomach into spin cycle.

I press the mute button on the television remote and stand up restlessly, phone clutched against my ear.

"I've been trying to call you."

"You have?"

"Yeah, I left you a couple of message…"

*No, you didn't, you liar. You only left one.*

"Really?" I say innocently. "I didn't get them. Maybe my answering machine is broken."

*As broken as my heart was after you shattered it, you two-timing asshole.*

"How have you been, Trace?" His tone becomes irritatingly gentle, the way one might address a terminally ill patient.

"Great!" I say heartily, hoping he'll ask me what's so great so that I can tell him about Jack.

But, as usual, Will is utterly uninterested in any details that don't pertain directly to him.

He merely says, "That's good to hear. Listen, I was cleaning out my drawers and I found some of your stuff."

"What is it?" I ask, pacing.

"Just some clothes."

"Oh, well, they probably don't fit me anymore anyway," I say pointedly.

I hear a female voice in the background on Will's end, and he says, "Hang on a second. What?"

Muffled conversation. He's obviously got his hand over the mouthpiece.

I light a cigarette and take a deep, satisfying drag.

I wander across the room to my desk—the one Buckley and I gleefully salvaged from somebody's garbage last month. I open a drawer, push past the pile of bills that should have been paid last week, and find the envelope from the photo place.

Then I flip through the stack of Christmas party pictures until I find the close-up of me and Jack looking like a couple.

I take another drag, favorably comparing Jack to Will.

And then another drag.

And then Will's back. "Sorry, Trace."

"Was that Nerissa?" I ask, Nerissa being his female—and platonic, or so he says—roommate.

"No, it was, uh…"

"Esme," I say, jealous, even now, that she's there with him and I'm not. I wonder if she helped him clean out his drawers.

"No, actually, Esme and I broke up."

I'm so caught up in picturing Esme trying on my old fat-girl jeans—slipping her drinking-straw body into one enormous leg as she and Will share a good laugh at my expense—that it takes a moment before I actually register what he's said.

When I do, I have to stifle a gasp. "Did you say you and Esme broke up?"

"Yeah."

Okay, this breaking news about Will and Esme almost makes up for the fact that his female friend interrupted my strategic comment about my old clothes being too small.

"Unfortunately, it just didn't work out with us," he's saying.

"I'm sorry to hear that."

Yeah, sure I am. *Snicker.*

"We both have such strong personalities, there's just no way it could have lasted for very long."

Is it just me, or is he implying that I have a weak personality? Hence our three years of nonwedded nonbliss.

If Esme's out of the picture, then who's in his apartment with him? That he'd call me when he's obviously not alone grates on me. I mean, does he want me to know that he's seeing someone new already?

"So, anyway...I've got your clothes here—"

"You can just throw them away. I'm sure they don't fit," I add succinctly, determined to make my point.

"Oh, I don't know... I'd feel funny doing that without you even seeing what they are, Tracey."

I know what they are. They're plus-sized relics from my overweight and overwrought days as girlfriend of Will the Unfaithful.

Clenching my teeth, I look down again at the photo of me and Jack.

We really do look like a happy couple. Maybe I should frame it.

"Hey, I've got an idea," Will says.

I immediately kibosh the frame thing.

Transition Boys do not belong in frames. Frames are for boyfriends. Okay, and gay best friends. Transition Boys belong in envelopes in drawers.

"Tracey, why don't you come over this weekend and go through the stuff?" Will is asking.

"I can't. I've got a date."

Okay, at least I worked that in there; the next best thing to having a guy talking to *me* in the background while I'm on the phone with Will.

"You've got a date all weekend?" He sounds amused.

"It's actually two dates. With two different guys." If Buckley counts as a date. Which I've decided he does, if only for the purpose of making Will jealous. "So, yeah. I'm busy all weekend."

"Oh."

*Not so amused now, are we, Will?*

"Listen, just toss the clothes, okay?"

"Nah. I'll hang on to them until you have time to come over and get them."

"Okay," I say in the *Suit yourself* tone I learned from him.

We chat for a few minutes longer. There are no further interruptions on Will's end. Maybe his visitor went to the bathroom.

Picturing her, whoever she is, sitting on Will's toilet, fills me with envy. It isn't fair! I used to be the one sitting on that toilet.

Not that I did much when I was there. Just pee. Anything else had to wait for the privacy of my own bathroom, lest I, Tracey, stink up the bathroom of Will Almighty.

See, Will has a thing about smells.

I know. Big eye roll. I mean, who doesn't? But smells really, *really* bother Will.

To be fair, he never requested that I not take a crap in his bathroom. It was just something I did instinctively. To protect his sensitive nostrils—and preserve our relationship—I quite possibly risked permanent bowel damage by holding it in, sometimes until I was practically doubled over.

Sick, isn't it?

The thing is, I know Will must have bowels, just like anybody else. But I never witnessed any kind of reference to their movement.

Kate always said Will's problem is that he thinks his shit doesn't stink.

You know what? I honestly don't think it does.

Either that, or he *just doesn't shit.*

How scary is that?

Still clutching the photo of me and Jack, I try again to work into the conversation the facts that A) I am now thin and B) men are interested in me.

But Will either A) doesn't comprehend or B) doesn't care.

This conversation is all about Will and how busy he is. How he's been constantly auditioning. How he's back to working for Milos at Eat Drink Or Be Married. How he's staying in New York for Christmas instead of visiting his family in Des Moines.

The idea of not going home for Christmas is as incom-

prehensible to me as—well, as the idea of leaving Brookside is to my old friends who are still there.

The thing is, I may have moved away, but I would never
dream of staying away over the holidays. Where I come
from, such drastic cutting of family ties would be sacrilege.

"Aren't your parents disappointed?" I ask him.

His mom and dad are sweet, wholesome Midwestern-
ers—the last couple on earth you'd expect to spawn an ego-
driven, theatrical philanderer.

"Yeah, they're disappointed, but they'll live," he says
offhandedly.

I roll my eyes. It's been a while since I've witnessed self-
absorbed Will in action.

"I'm just not in the mood for the whole Christmas scene
this year," he says, sounding bored.

"So what are you going to do instead?"

"You mean, on the actual day?"

"Yeah."

He yawns. "I don't know. Hopefully, sleep."

*With whom?* is the first thing that comes to mind, but I
keep the question to myself, along with further commen-
tary on his plans for a solitary holiday.

I tell him I have to go.

"I'll talk to you about picking up your clothes when you
get back after the holidays, then," Will says.

"Whatever. Merry Christmas, Will."

"Uh-huh. Bye," says Ebenezer McCraw.

I hang up, trading the phone for the remote, and plop
down on the couch again.

The apartment feels tinier and emptier than usual.

Quieter, too.

But instead of raising the volume on the television again, I just stare at the screen, thinking about Will.

It's not that I want him back. I mean, now that I can see the truth about Will and our toxic relationship, I know that I'm much better off without him.

But that doesn't mean I've entirely shed the insecure part of me that equates being alone with being lonely.

Intellectually, I know I'm not supposed to jump right from one relationship into another. But, dammit, sometimes I just can't deny the longing, unhealthy or not. Some people enjoy being independent. I...

*You what, Tracey?*

*Enjoy being dependent?*

I think about my sister Mary Beth, who begged her loser husband to move back in even after he admitted to having had sex with another woman while Mary Beth was in labor with their second kid.

And about my mother, who learned how to drive back in the fifties but only took the wheel once that I can recall—and that was to drive my father to the hospital when she thought he was having a heart attack that turned out to be gas.

And about my grandmother, who serves—literally—my grandfather three home-cooked meals a day, hovering over him like a waitress, running back and forth to the fridge and stove whenever he wants a condiment or a second helping.

So maybe it's genetic?

Maybe I'm just not cut out to be a free-wheeling *Sex and the City*–type chick despite the fact that I live in the city, and lately I've actually been having sex.

Speaking of sex... I realize I'm still holding the photo of

me and Jack. I get up to put it away, but instead my feet carry me over to the window, where a few framed snapshots of my friends and family line the sill.

I pick up a four-by-six of me and Raphael, open the back of the frame and replace the picture with the one of me and Jack.

I know, I know, don't freak out. It's just an experiment, okay?

I return the picture to the windowsill and take a step back.

Ooh. We look pretty damned good together in a frame.

So damned good that I decide to leave it there. Just for tonight. Just so that I can pretend our relationship is something more than it is.

Tomorrow, I'll put Raphael back in the frame, and put Jack back into the envelope in the drawer, where he belongs.

12

Friday morning, I find the fifth and final—God willing—
Secret Snowflake gift waiting on my keyboard. It's a smallish gift-wrapped box.

Okay, small is good, I think, as I reluctantly tear away the
blue velvet bow and thick silver-foil paper.

I left Myron a small box, too. I bought him a dated New
York Jets tree ornament. It cost $9.95 plus tax at the Hall-
mark store, bringing my weeklong tally in at just under twenty
bucks. In the end, it really was impossible to stay under the
fifteen-dollar limit—not that I still don't think my Snowflake
is a candidate for Overspenders Anonymous, at the very least.

I lift the lid on the box....

*Sheer relief.*

My Snowflake also bought me a tree ornament.

I lift it out.

*Sheer disbelief.*

This ornament didn't come from a Hallmark store, and it didn't cost anywhere near $9.95.

This one is a handblown glass Christopher Radko ornament. Raphael and all his overpriced-chotchke-loving cronies are into them, so I'm fully aware that they're outrageously expensive collector's items.

With shaking hands, I set it back into the nest of cotton and stare at it.

I tell myself that I should be touched, or flattered, or honored or whatever, but I'm not any of those things. I'm just royally pissed.

*This time, you've gone too far, Snowflake.*

There's only one thing for Take-Charge Tracey to do.

I pick up the gift and march up to Merry's office in a huff.

She's at her desk, stirring a steaming cup of coffee with a candy cane. "Good morning, Tracey," she says cheerfully.

"Look at this!" I thrust the box into her hands.

"Ooh, it's beautiful. For me? You didn't have to—"

"No, it's actually for me."

"Oh." She hands it back, clearly disappointed.

Talk about uncomfortable.

I tell Merry, "It's from my Secret Snowflake."

"It's nice. It looks fragile, though. You should hang it up toward the top of your tree so that nobody bumps—"

"I don't even have a Christmas tree, Merry," I cut in shrilly.

She looks at me as though I've just told her that I eat live babies for breakfast.

"You don't have a tree? Why not? Oh!" She smiles in sudden understanding. "You're Jewish!"

"No, I'm not. I'm Catholic."

The smile evaporates.

"Merry, I don't have a tree because I, uh…"

Okay, why *don't* I have a tree?

And what the hell does this have to do with anything?

She's waiting, wearing a strained smile.

"I mean, I live alone," I tell her. "So it's just not…you know."

No. Merry doesn't know from Catholic people who live alone and don't have trees.

"I live alone, too, but…" She shrugs and looks sorrowfully at me.

We're both silent for a second.

Then I push aside a ridiculous wave of guilt and say, "Look, Merry, the thing is…my Secret Snowflake spent a fortune on me."

Her smile is even more strained. As in, *I don't get it. What's the problem?*

"This ornament had to cost sixty or seventy bucks. And the other stuff… I mean, my Snowflake has spent hundreds. Who would do this?"

"Somebody very kindhearted. Somebody very caught up in the true spirit of the season."

Uh-huh.

I was thinking somebody very psycho stalker.

"Merry, the thing is…this is making me feel very uncomfortable. I mean, the limit was fifteen dollars, and I think that if you're going to be a Secret Snowflake, you need to play by the rules."

"Tracey, I see what you're saying, but…" Merry wrings her hands.

"But it's not fair to the other Snowflakes! I mean, here I

am sticking to the limit, buying Myron measly two- and three-dollar gifts every day, and my freaking Snowflake—"

She goes from wringing her hands to slamming them over her ears in dismay. Oops. I thought I said *freaking*, but maybe I said *fucking* by accident?

"Tracey! You're not supposed to tell!"

"What?"

"You're supposed to keep your Snowflake a secret! That's why it's called a Secret Snowflake! Now I know that you have Myron!"

"I'm sorry! I thought you knew. I mean, you're in charge, so I just figured—"

"No! It's all very confidential! I have a computer system that matches up the Snowflakes. I don't peek. That would be cheating."

"Oh, well…I mean, that's really noble of you, Merry. I just didn't realize. So you don't know who chose my name?"

"No! That would be cheating," she says again, as close to bitchy as Merry is capable of sounding.

"So you can't tell me who it is?"

"No! You'll find out next week at the Secret Snowflake luncheon."

Which I was totally planning to blow off.

"You *are* coming, aren't you?" asks Merry the Mind Reader.

Another crushing wave of guilt.

"I'm not sure…."

"But don't you want to thank your Snowflake in person for all the gifts?"

Sure. That, or grab my Snowflake by the collar and ask what the fuck is their problem.

"I'll try to make it," I promise Merry.

"I really hope you do, Tracey."

"I'll really try, Merry," I snap, and stride back to my cube feeling like the Grinch, Scrooge and Will, all rolled into one.

"Great news, Tracey!" Raphael announces when he sweeps into Chin Chin that afternoon, fashionably late—and ultrafashionable, as always—for our lunch date. He's wearing some kind of powder-blue silk getup that I remember him coveting when Steven Cojacaru wore it on the *Today Show* a few weeks ago.

I stir my gin and tonic, which happens to match Raphael's outfit. I always go for the Bombay Sapphire when we're on his expense account.

"Great news, Raphael? Hmm, let me guess. You decided not to go out with Carl again after all?"

"No! Tracey! That isn't nice," he chides.

"Sorry, Raphael, but I don't feel nice today."

"What's wrong?"

He orders a Sidecar—whatever that is—and I fill him in on the latest Secret Snowflake gift.

"Ooh, is it the rocking horse ornament? I'm dying to buy that one. If you don't want to keep it, I'll be happy to take it off your hands, Tracey."

*Whoa, hands off my overpriced bauble, you* chotchke-*hoarding freak.*

"I didn't say I didn't want to keep it, Raphael."

"Oh. Then what's the problem?"

"Don't you think it's a bit odd that somebody would anonymously give me all these expensive gifts? Why would they do that?"

"I think it's a bit odd that you care. Why even stop to wonder why? Just enjoy, Tracey." He plucks the long-stemmed cherry from his Sidecar—which turns out to be a fancy drink in a sugar-crusted glass—and nibbles it delicately.

"I can't *just enjoy*, Raphael. I feel funny about it. And I feel like a cheapskate, too," I add, thinking of poor Myron and his gummy sucker.

"I'm sure you weren't the only one who stuck to the spending limit, Tracey."

"I didn't stick to the limit!" I say defensively.

"You went over? Then why are you—"

"Because I went over by five bucks, that's why. But my Secret—"

"I know, I know," he cuts in, clearly bored with *As the Secret Snowflake Turns*. "Ooooh, I forgot to tell you—guess what Carl said?"

"Fee, Fi, Fo, Fum?"

He titters. "Tracey, you're bad! No, he said that his friend Jorge is bouncing at that new club Juicebox, and he can get us in if we want to go tonight."

"Why would I want to go to a lesbian club?" I ask. Come to think of it, "Why would you want to go to a lesbian club?"

"Because it's new, and everyone wants to go," Raphael says, as if bewildered by my lack of interest. "Not just lesbians. Tracey, are you prejudiced?"

"No, Raphael, I've just got stuff to do. Like line up a stripper for the bachelorette party, which you promised you'd—"

He slaps his head. "That's the great news! Tracey, I forgot to tell you."

"Yes, you did."

"I found you a stripper."

"You did?" That *is* great news.

Raphael nods jubilantly. "Barkley says he'll do it."

"Barkley?"

"Yes, Barkley. You know—Barkley with the sexy mole?" he says in his usual *duh* tone. The tone he uses when I'm totally clueless about one of the many members of his flamboyant posse whom he swears I've met a gazillion times.

Barkley with the sexy mole, Barkley with the sexy mole…

"Oh! Terence's ex-boyfriend!" I say triumphantly.

Raphael looks horrified. "That's Bentley! And they're back together. And that isn't a mole on his face, and it sure as hell isn't sexy."

Well, gee, honest mistake, but you'd never know it by Raphael's expression.

"Sorry," I say, "I thought it was Barkley and a mole."

"No! It's some kind of disgusting growth." He shudders. "Terence says he'll break up with him again if he doesn't have it lasered off by New Year's Day. And you know what, Tracey?"

"No, what, Raphael?" I drain the rest of my drink and look around for the waiter.

"I just don't think Bentley's going to do it. It's a real shame, because he's a sweetheart when you get to know him, but who's going to bother to get past that glaring, oozing—"

"Raphael!" Time to get him back on topic. "Who's Barkley?"

Not that it matters. As long as he's affordable, willing to

strip down to a G-string or nothing at all and doesn't have an oozing growth on his face, he's hired.

Raphael tells me about Barkley: young, buff, African-American Barkley, who goes by the stage name Bodacious B.

"Bodacious B?" I wrinkle my nose. "That's so corny."

"All male strippers have stage names," declares Raphael, connoisseur of nude men.

He begins sharing the stage names of the strippers he's known—probably in the biblical sense—but luckily, the waiter shows up.

We both order the mandarin shrimp, which is my all-time favorite thing to eat at Chin Chin. I haven't had it in at least a month, and it's probably incredibly fattening, but I dig in anyway, famished after a morning of Snowflake intrigue.

As we eat, Raphael enlightens me as to why Carl is the man he's been looking for all of his life.

I only half listen, knowing Carl will be history in a matter of weeks if not days, along with all of the other men Raphael has been looking for all of his life.

My thoughts stray to Jack, who might just be the man *I've* been looking for all of *my* life, but who, if he is, has lousy timing. If only he'd come along, say, next year at this time....

Well, maybe by then I'll be emotionally healthy enough to have a lasting relationship.

By the end of our lunch, I resolve to stop thinking about why it can't last and just enjoy it while it does.

I know Jack and I weren't supposed to go out until Saturday night.

But on Friday at five-thirty, just as I'm putting on my coat, my extension rings and it's him.

My first thought is that he's calling to cancel tomorrow night's date.

"Hey, I'm really looking forward to tomorrow," he says. "How about you?"

"I am, too," I say, relieved. "What are we going to do?"

"Nice try, but it's a surprise, remember? Hey, what are you doing now?"

I hesitate.

Should I say I'm busy working? If I do, he might think he's interrupting and hang up right away.

Should I say I'm leaving? But maybe he was thinking he'd stop by my desk and say hi, and then maybe he wouldn't want to if he knew I was on my way out, and—

"Tracey?"

"I'm, um, just finishing up some stuff," I say, cursing the overanalytical and insecure Inner Tracey.

"I meant, do you have plans tonight?"

I hesitate again.

Good thing I'm not going to Juicebox with Raphael. I wouldn't want to try to explain *that* to a normal guy like Jack.

My only plan is to stop at the Key Food down the street from my apartment and get some groceries, then go home and read.

If I tell him that, will he think I'm a loser?

If I tell him I don't have any plans, will he think I'm an even bigger loser?

*Oh, for Pete's sake. Will you stop that, Tracey? Stop worrying about what he'll think of you. Just answer the question.*

*What was the question?*

*Oh, yeah. Do I have any plans tonight?*

"Not really," is how I answer it, and then I cautiously add one of my own. "Why?"

"Because I thought I had to work late to finish this plan, but it turns out they can wait until Tuesday. So I was just getting ready to leave, and I thought that if you wanted to—"

"Sure!" I say eagerly, not caring what it is that he's asking.

I'm sick of trying to figure out what I'm supposed to say and do. I'm sick of never being spontaneous.

Whatever it is that Jack is asking, I want to. Definitely. Right now. With all of my heart.

And somehow, I know I won't regret it.

Okay.

So I regret it.

I made a little mistake.

All right, a huge mofo of a mistake.

Maybe, if I weren't so caught up in the exhilaration of an impromptu date with Jack last night, I'd have remembered…

But I didn't remember. I forgot.

How could I have forgotten?

Things were perfect. We went out for sushi, saw the new Adam Sandler movie, which was hilarious and, afterward, had a couple of glasses of pinot noir at a wine bar off Second Avenue.

From there, it was a straight shot downtown in a cab to my apartment. My idea, not his. I think after what happened with Mike the other morning, he knew better than to ask me back to his place.

But I didn't hesitate to invite him back here. I was still in my carefree, spontaneous mood.

When we got to my apartment, I never even made it over to the lamp to turn it on before Jack grabbed me and kissed me. We fell into my bed, made passionate love and slept in each other's arms.

No problem there.

Woke up, made love again.

No problem there, either.

We talked a little afterward, lying there with his arms around me and my head on his chest.

I told him about the Secret Snowflake gifts, and he agreed that it was bizarre. He also hinted that he wanted to go with me to Radio City next Friday night—at least, I thought he was hinting—so I worked up the courage to ask him.

"I'd love to," he said. "But I might have to go to Atlanta on business on Thursday overnight, and I don't know what time I'm flying back Friday. If I'm around, I'd love to go. Can I let you know?"

I told him of course he could.

Then, feeling even bolder, I asked him why he came over to me in the first place at the Christmas party that night.

"You want to know the real reason?"

Uh-oh.

Maybe I didn't.

But I told him that I did, and added that I hoped he wasn't going to tell me that he did it on a dare or something.

"A dare?" he asked, looking confused.

Yes, a dare.

You know, like when the class cutup dares the football quarterback to ask the ugly fat girl to the prom. And she's all thrilled and says yes, and her parents buy her a dress and on prom night she sits there and sits there and he never shows because he's at the prom with his real date, the head cheerleader.

And then—not in real life but if it's one of those movies I wasn't allowed to see until college because my parents took NC 17 very seriously—the ugly fat girl grows up and becomes thin and beautiful and she goes on a bloody rampage and kills the head cheerleader, the football quarterback and the class cutup, even though he's a nice guy now and is in love with her but doesn't know her real identity....

You never saw those movies?

Well, in case Jack didn't either, I didn't tell him any of that.

Besides, he didn't know about my past life as an overweight, insecure high-school girl, and I wasn't about to enlighten him.

So I just waited, praying it hadn't been a dare.

"It wasn't a dare," Jack told me, and I exhaled the breath I hadn't realized I'd been holding.

"Okay, then why did you come up to me?" I asked him.

"Promise you won't be insulted?"

Gee, this gets better every second.

"Promise," I lied, and resumed holding my breath.

"Right before we met, I was standing there at the party talking to my assistant, Maggie, who doesn't know how to mind her own business and always has to analyze me and my personal life, and she told me that my problem with women is that I always go for the wrong type."

Hmm, interesting. I'd have rubbed my goatee if I had one. I didn't realize Jack had a problem with women.

"And I asked her what type she meant," Jack went on,

"and she looked around for a minute and then she pointed at you. There you were, wearing that short, low-cut dress, and when I saw you, I made a beeline over there, partly because I wanted to spite Maggie for being such a pain in the ass. But once we started talking, I realized you weren't the way I thought you'd be."

"What way?"

"You know...kind of...easy."

Still not insulted.

Not really.

"Maggie's so surprised that you turned out to be this nice, wholesome person instead of a slut."

Okay, now I'm insulted.

*Mental Note: Burn red Christmas party dress.*

"Didn't you think it was slutty of me to sleep with you on the second date?" I asked Jack.

"Nah. And, anyway, I like sluts, remember?" he said, and we laughed.

That was when it happened.

I was facing him and the kitchenette over his shoulder.

He was facing me and the window over my shoulder, and I was admiring the way the winter sun brought out golden highlights in his wavy brown hair.

In fact, I was so focused on his hair that I didn't even notice the look on his face until he said, "Is that *us*?"

It didn't make sense. Is that us? Is that us? What the hell was he talking about? He could have been speaking in a foreign language for all that meant to me....

Then...

Flicker of realization.

Oh, God.

Oh, no.

No, please…

It was like a slow-motion movie scene from there on in.

I saw Jack's expression go from puzzled to stunned to horrified.

I turned my head to follow his gaze.

I saw what he was looking at….

And *kerplunk*.

The bottom abruptly dropped out of our perfect morning-after.

Because there, on the windowsill…

Oh my God, it's so horrible I can't even say it….

Was—is—a picture of us.

Me and him.

In a frame.

*Is that us?*

Now it makes sense.

*Yes.*

*Yes, it is.*

*That is us.*

And so here I am, speechless, still staring at the picture because I can't bear to look at him.

Why the hell did I have to go out with him last night?

Why wasn't I content to have a Saturday-night date and leave well enough alone?

And why, if I did feel compelled to go out with him on the spur of the moment, did I have to invite him back here?

So much for carefree, spontaneous Tracey.

At the moment, I'd much prefer to be uptight, insecure Tracey, alone in my apartment with newly bought groceries in the cupboards and the snapshot back in the drawer where it belongs, blissfully looking forward to tonight's surprise date with Jack.

Now I think it's safe to assume that there will be no more dates with Jack, surprise or otherwise.

No guy in his right mind would continue to see someone who gets him to pose with her looking like a couple five minutes after they meet, and then frames the picture. I mean, I might as well have worn a wedding gown to Tequila Murray's on our first date.

Fighting the overwhelming urge to flee—and only because I don't want him to get a glimpse of my naked ass on my way out—I sneak a peek at Jack.

The good news: He doesn't see me.

The bad news: He doesn't see me because he's too busy looking around the apartment like he's wondering what else I've got stashed here.

A mock-up engagement announcement for the *New York Times*?

Stationery printed with the name Tracey Spadolini Candell?

Wouldn't it be great if this weren't really happening?

Maybe it isn't.

Maybe I'm not even awake yet and it's just a blood-chilling nightmare.

It's certainly the kind of thing I'd dream.

Once, when I was dating Will, I dreamed that I was costarring with him in an all-nude version of *Hello, Dolly!* on Broadway, only, when I got onstage Will was there in his Horace Vandergelder three-piece suit, and the rest of the cast was also fully costumed, and I was standing there in nothing but a sweeping turn-of-the-century hat with a feather in it.

When I woke up, my face was burning hot, just like it is now.

Okay, so this has to be a dream, too.

I squeeze my eyes shut and count to three....

Then to five...

I make it ten for good measure, and open my eyes.

Jack's still here, and he's still wearing that dazed expression, only now he's looking at me.

He doesn't say anything, so of course I have to.

"I'm sorry," I blurt.

It's the first thing that comes to mind.

Well, after, *You must think I'm some desperate stalker chick.*

On the off chance that he doesn't, I don't say it.

But he must.

Think that I'm a desperate stalker chick, that is.

It's written all over his face.

He doesn't respond to my apology, just lies there looking blank, so I take a deep breath and try again.

"A friend of mine was over the other night and she was, uh, she stuck that picture in the frame as a joke."

Oh, please. I couldn't have come up with anything better than that?

No. I couldn't. I mean, go ahead. *You* try to come up with a good reason why someone you barely know would be smiling in a frame in your apartment.

The mythical prank-playing friend is my story, and I'm sticking to it. *Ad nauseum.*

"She's a big practical joker," I rattle on.

No reaction from Jack.

"April Fools' Day is her favorite holiday."

Somebody stop me!

"Last April Fools' Day, she filled my sugar bowl with salt. But I don't use sugar much, so I didn't find out till July." Nervous laugh.

Jack laughs, too. But barely.

I can tell by his expression that he doesn't believe any of this.

I want so badly to shut up.

I want so badly to tell him the truth....

But the truth is so goddamned embarrassing, I think I'd rather play Dolly Levi in the nude.

Instead, conscious of the cold sweat breaking out under my bangs, I settle for another, "I'm sorry. I know you must think it's pretty odd, but my friend…"

"It's okay," he says at last, casting another dubious glance at the framed photo. "It's a good picture."

"You think?" I force a smile.

I can feel a panic attack coming on. Oh, Lord.

"Yeah." He smiles back.

It's not his usual wholehearted, dimple-baring grin, but it's not an *I'm not laughing with you, I'm laughing at you* smirk, either.

The panic attack subsides before it can become full-blown. At least, for now. Which is good, because I hardly look my best while hyperventilating into a paper bag.

Still looking and sounding awkward, Jack asks if I feel like going out to breakfast.

Naturally, I tell him I can't. I say I have to go to a spinning class. Which is a joke because I have no idea what spinning even is. I just know that Kate does it early on Saturday mornings, and that it has nothing to do with wool, which is what I first thought.

Jack doesn't look like he minds not going to breakfast with me.

In fact, it's almost like he can't get out of here fast enough, telling me he'll call me later about tonight.

The minute the door closes behind him, I burst into tears, knowing I've scared him away.

After I put the picture of me and Jack back in the drawer and the one of me and Raphael back in the frame, I spend the day reading my book when I'm not drifting around my apartment, waiting for the phone to ring and for Jack to tell me he can't make it tonight after all.

When he doesn't, I call him instead.

"I'm so sorry," I tell him. "I think I'm coming down with some sort of stomach thing, Jack. I'm really queasy and I haven't been able to eat anything all day."

That's true, actually. But it's not a stomach thing. It's a humiliation thing.

"That's okay," Jack says.

Is it my imagination, or does he sound relieved?

Well, duh. Of course he sounds relieved.

He probably spent the day trying to figure out how to let me down easily, because he's a nice guy.

"So…I'll see you at work on Monday, then," Jack says.

"Sure."

"I hope you feel better soon."

I hang up, thinking, *So do I.*

On Sunday morning, I go to church at St. Fabian's again.

I know I'm supposed to be listening to the sermon—I mean, that's the purpose of being here, right?

But I spend the whole time reliving the moment when Jack saw himself in a picture frame in my apartment.

Well, not the *whole* time.

I spend part of the time rewinding to Thursday night and the phone call from Will, whose fault, I have concluded, this whole mess really is.

If Will hadn't called, I wouldn't have felt lonely enough to take out the picture of Jack and fantasize about our relationship. I wouldn't have put the picture in a frame to see how we looked as an official couple. I wouldn't have left it there overnight…or forgotten to take it out. Jack wouldn't have seen it.

Blaming Will feels good.

Well, as good as anything can feel on this miserable Sunday morning when I'd much rather be in bed asleep.

I can't stop yawning. Have I ever been this exhausted in my whole life? Not just physically exhausted. Emotionally exhausted.

I mean, misery and humiliation take a lot out of a gal.

Ironically, the organist plays "Joy to the World" as mass ends.

Yeah, right.

No joy in the world of Tracey, I think, stepping out into the cold, gray, rainy morning. That's right. Rain. Again.

Back home in Brookside, December is snowy, transforming the small and somewhat dingy town into the proverbial Currier and Ives print.

Here in Manhattan, it never snows.

Oh, wait, it *did* snow. It snowed the night Jack and I were at the Rockefeller Center tree.

Yeah, it snowed, but it didn't stick, I think gloomily, trudging along Eighth Street.

Nothing ever sticks.

Snow.

Relationships.

I scowl.

Well, at least my pissy mood is a perfect match for Buckley's. He called me just before I left to remind me that we're hanging out later.

He sounded depressed about Sonja and said he'd meet me at our favorite dive bar later.

We can cry on each other's shoulders about love gone wrong.

Gee. I can hardly wait.

★ ★ ★

"I made it!" I shout gleefully. "Did you see that? I made it!"

"I saw it. You did!" Buckley slaps me a high five and I jump around a bit to celebrate sinking the second-to-last ball into the corner pocket, just the way I called the shot.

I've never been very good at pool, but we've been playing for two hours straight and tonight I'm on fire.

"Okay, that striped ball over there into that pocket over there," I tell Buckley as I line up the next—and last—shot.

"Are you sure? Not the corner pocket?"

"Nope. That pocket," I insist, pointing.

He shrugs.

I squint. Aim. Shoot.

The ball goes right into the pocket I predicted.

With a squeal, I break into a happy little dance across the empty barroom floor, using my pool cue as a prop. You know, like a cane. Like in *A Chorus Line.*

"What are you doing?" Buckley asks, laughing.

"I beat you again. I won. So I'm dancing," I say in an *Isn't-it-obvious?* tone.

"You look like you're having a blast," Buckley says dryly.

I *am* having a blast.

I know I said I thought tonight would be a bust, but the whole time we've been playing pool and drinking beers and cracking jokes, neither of us has even mentioned Sonja or Will or Jack.

Maybe it's the beer. Maybe it's my sudden pool ace status. Or maybe it's just being with Buckley.

In any case, I'm feeling lighthearted for a change.

Humming "One," I sway a little too much to the left and almost fall over.

"Oops."

Buckley laughs and reaches out to steady me.

I pull on his hand. "Come on, Buckley, do a kick line with me. Let's be *A Chorus Line*."

He protests, but I drag him around until he joins in, and we're having a good old time dancing around the almost empty pool room.

Until I do an overexuberant move and swing the cue stick into his hand.

Actually, it would have been something far more vulnerable than his hand, but he saw the stick coming and used his hand to protect himself.

"Ow!" he howls, doubling over.

"Sorry," I say, feeling too giddy to mean it.

"That thing is dangerous." He snatches it out of my hand.

"Hey! That's my cane."

"Why do you need a cane?"

"You know…" I hum a few more bars of "One."

You know, *Dut-da-da-dut-da-da-dut-da-dadadadada-dut-da-da-dut-da-da-daaahhh….*

Buckley the Broadway Musically Challenged still doesn't get it.

"Why do you need a cane?" he repeats.

"Didn't the dancers use canes in *A Chorus Line?*"

"I don't know. I never saw it," Buckley says.

"I didn't either." I stop dancing, stricken by inspiration. "We should see it!"

"*A Chorus Line?* Didn't it close years ago?"

"I don't know. Let's find out."

"How?"

"We'll ask someone."

"Who?"

I look around the bar.

The bartender is busy on the phone in the corner, and the only other patrons are a couple of unshaven, red-faced, unkempt career drunks sitting on stools watching television. They look like they've been here every night for the last forty or fifty years.

"Excuse me," I call to them. "Does anybody know if *A Chorus Line* is still playing on Broadway?"

I guess nobody knows, because nobody even turns around.

"Yoo-hoo!" I call. "Men at the bar!"

One guy barely swivels in his stool and grunts, "Yeah?"

"Do you know anything about *A Chorus Line?*"

"Nope. And I don't want to, either."

He swivels back.

"Yeah, well, you could all use a little culture," I mutter, scowling. "Don't you think they could all use a little culture, Buckley?"

"Yeah, let's clean them up and take them to the Met."

"Seriously?"

"Are you out of your mind?" Buckley laughs. "You're drunk, Tracey."

"I am not," I protest lamely, then say, "So are you."

"Yeah," he agrees, "I am feeling a little trashed."

We both laugh.

Then we lean against the pool table, side by side. I'm a little winded from all that dancing.

"Want to go get something to eat?" Buckley asks, checking his watch. "It's late. We never got dinner."

"No. I want a cigarette."

"No smoking." He points to the sign.

"Well, then I want to go see *A Chorus Line.*"

"Why? What's up with you and this sudden fascination with *A Chorus Line?*"

"I don't know. I just miss seeing shows. I used to see them all the time when…"

"When you were with Will," he finishes for me when I trail off.

I didn't mean to go there.

But now that I'm there….

"Yeah. When I was with Will, I saw all the shows he was in, and all the shows his friends were in and a lot of other stuff, too. But I never saw *A Chorus Line.* And now I might never get to," I add, feeling desolate.

"Does it matter?"

"Yes."

I don't know why it matters, but suddenly it does. A lot. So much that I have a lump in my throat.

"I really miss Will, Buckley."

"You're drunk, Trace," Buckley says again. Only, this time he doesn't sound amused. He sounds sad.

"I know. I am drunk. So are you."

"I know. And I miss Sonja."

"I know you do. And I miss Jack."

"I know you—wait a minute. Jack? State Capital Guy Jack? You just went out with him last night."

"No, I didn't. I was supposed to, but…" I quickly—and mostly without slurring—explain to Buckley about the photo and Jack fleeing my apartment.

To my utter irritation, Buckley is amused again.

"It's not funny," I say, jabbing him with my elbow.

"I think it is. I'm trying to picture myself going out with somebody twice and then—"

"Three times," I amend. "Four, if you count the Christmas party."

"Still—four times, and you find yourself in a frame in some girl's apartment?" He laughs. Hard.

"I hate you," I say darkly.

"I'm sorry. It's just funny."

"Not to me. I really liked him, Buckley."

He stops laughing. "I know you did. And I'm sorry." This time, he sounds like he means it.

He also sounds so…*something*. Something that I can't put my finger on.

"You know," he says seriously, "you said yourself that this guy Jack was just supposed to be Transformer Man, so it's not like—"

"Transition Boy," I correct him, pulling myself up so that I'm sitting on the edge of the pool table. "He was Transition Boy."

"Right. Transistor Boy." He shrugs and sits beside me. "I thought you figured you'd only go out with him a few times and then it would be over, anyway."

"I did think that."

"But…?"

I stare down at the Marc Jacobs shoes Raphael bought for me on one of our splurges. They're a half size too big and they give me blisters on my heels, but they look great with these jeans.

Buckley prods, "You did think that, but…?"

"But I really liked Jack," I admit. Hell, might as well put it all right out there. "And I'm sick of being alone."

"Yeah." He touches my hand. "That sucks. But, Tracey, I'm kind of glad Jack blew you off."

"He didn't blow me off, really," I protest before I realize what he's said.

I look up at him in surprise. "What do you mean, you're glad, Buckley?"

"I can't believe I'm saying this, but I was jealous."

"Jealous?" I gape at nice, sweet, cute Buckley. My good friend Buckley. The one who now—like me—is available.

"Yeah." He looks sheepish. "Lately I've been wondering if we—"

"Don't say it!"

"Say what?"

"Say what I think you're going to say. About us. Because if you say it—"

"What? That lately I've been wanting to kiss you again?"

I wince.

Okay, it's an exhilarated *Buckley-wants-to-kiss-me-again!* kind of wince.

"You said it," I say with as much dismay as I can muster. "I told you not to say it."

"I couldn't help it. I'm drunk."

"That's no excuse. We've been drunk together before, plenty of times, since that time you kissed me. Which you never should have done in the first place."

"I thought we were out on a date."

"Yeah, but I didn't think that. And I had a boyfriend."

"You don't now."

I realize that he's gone from patting my hand in sympathy to holding my hand.

"True…"

My head is spinning. My hand feels snug and secure clasped in his.

"But this isn't a date, Buckley," I remind him.

"It feels like one."

He's right. It does. I try to focus intently on his face, to envision him as good, old, platonic Buckley.

But I can't. Suddenly, he's this guy I want to kiss.

And he's staring right back at me, into my eyes, like he wants to do just that.

How can he want to kiss me?

He's seen me at my worst. He's seen me throw up; he's seen me with my face broken out and with no makeup; scariest of all, he's seen me in a bathing suit before I lost all of my weight.

Uh-oh. He's leaning in.

"Buckley…"

"Let's try it, Trace," he says. "Just once."

"We already tried it once."

"That was six months ago. And you were in love with Will. It doesn't count."

"Count? Count as what?"

"You know, as…a test."

I pretend I have no idea what he means. In truth, I know exactly what he's saying.

As he elaborates, I find myself staring at his full lips, and my stomach gets all quivery.

"If we kiss and we both feel nothing, we won't have to wonder anymore," he tells me. "And if we kiss and we both feel something…"

"We won't have to wonder either?"

"Exactly," he says, squeezing my hand.

Yeah. And what if we kiss and one of us feels something and the other one feels nothing? What if the one who feels something is me and the one who feels nothing is Buckley?

Then I'll have been rejected by two guys in the space of a single weekend, which has to be some kind of world record. Three guys, if you count Will and expand the time frame.

Then again, Jack hasn't officially rejected me…yet.

And what if Buckley is the one who feels something and I'm the one who feels nothing?

"I'm going to do it now," Buckley says, jarring me out of what-iffy-ness.

"Okay. Go ahead…." I close my eyes.

Nothing.

I wet my lips nervously.

Still nothing.

I open my eyes.

Buckley's face is, like, two inches away.

"I can't do it," he says. "I want to, but I don't want to ruin—"

Take-Charge Tracey cuts him off by grabbing his head, pulling him closer and kissing him. Brazen, I know. But I can't help it. I wouldn't be able to stand it if we got this far and I didn't find out….

That kissing Buckley six months later isn't like kissing a friend at all.

That I'm attracted to him.

That my heart is pounding and it isn't impossible to imagine taking things further than this.

When we pull apart, my eyes snap open and I have a moment of dread. What if Buckley is wearing a distasteful expression and it's clear that he wasn't as into the kiss as he seemed?

Enough with the what–ifs, already. Sheesh.

His expression isn't distasteful. But it is uncharacteristically anxious.

"Was that okay?" he asks.

"Yeah," I tell him, smiling. "Very okay."

He looks relieved. "I thought so, too. I'm glad you did it. I thought it might ruin our friendship."

"It didn't," I say. "Right?"

"Right," he agrees with a grin.

I find myself looking for his dimples before I remember that he's not Jack.

We sit there on the edge of the pool table, side by side, swinging our legs.

"Want to play another game of pool?" he asks.

"Maybe. Do you?"

"Maybe. Do you want another beer?"

"Maybe in a minute."

"Okay."

We sit there in companionable silence.

Then Buckley asks, "So now what?"

"Hmm?"

"What happens next?"

"I don't know," I say, not sure if he's referring to the next five minutes or the grand scheme of our relationship.

"Maybe we should try a real date," Buckley suggests.

Grand scheme of relationship, I conclude.

"A real date would be fine," I tell him.

"Great. What should we do?"

"We could go see *A Chorus Line*."

"I really think that closed a few years ago, Trace."

"Then we could go see the Radio City Christmas Spectacular," I tell him, remembering. "I've got two tickets to see it on Friday night."

Technically, I already asked Jack, but there's no way he's going to go after what happened Saturday morning. I'm sure he'll say he'll be stuck in Atlanta Friday night. Or maybe even all weekend, just to be sure I won't try and corner him into another date.

"That would be fun," Buckley says. "I haven't seen it since I was a kid."

"I've never seen it."

We smile at each other.

Look, I want to see the Radio City show with Buckley. Really, I do.

It's just…

I still feel a little pang of regret at the thought of Jack.

Okay, a huge pang that's more of a stabbing *pain,* really, when I think about how I'll never know what the surprise was, and, even worse, how we'll never have a chance to see where things might have gone with us just because I made one stupid, stupid mistake.

I mean, kissing Buckley was great.

But kissing Jack was great, too.

With Jack, there was more…

Mystery.

Less…

History.

Not in a bad way. It's just…different.

Buckley and I have already been through so much together. We know each other's favorite foods and favorite authors, biggest fears and worst pet peeves, our quirks and faults and goals. In fact, sometimes it seems that the only thing I don't know about Buckley is what he's like in bed.

Not that I haven't imagined it.

And not that I don't want to find out....

At least, I might want to.

But not yet. Certainly not tonight. And with my track record...

"I think we should both go home," I tell Buckley.

His grin fades. "Oh."

"Not because you kissed me, or anything—"

"Um, Trace? *You* kissed *me*."

"Oh, right. Whatever. The kiss isn't why. It's just...I'm tired and it's late and we both have to work tomorrow morning. And if we stay here for another game of pool and another beer—"

"And another kiss—"

"Exactly—who knows what will happen? It might be something we'll both regret in the morning."

"And it might not be."

"Right. But, Buckley, I'm just too exhausted to find out tonight. Okay?"

"Sure. It's fine."

"Really?"

"Really. No big deal."

I can tell he means it.

There's something really nice about being with somebody you know so well.

Outside, we walk two blocks over to Broadway. My feet are killing me in these shoes. I'd give anything for Band-Aids for my heels.

Band-Aids make me think of Jack. He wanted to give me a Band-Aid for my sore knee after I fell the other morning in his hallway.

You know, it's definitely better if Jack and I stop seeing each other, if only because that way, I won't have to worry about glimpsing Mike in his underpants again. Maybe, in time, I'll even get the hideous image out of my head.

"Are you okay, Tracey?" Buckley asks.

"I'm fine," I say quickly. "I'm really glad about the kiss. Really."

"I didn't mean that. I mean…you're limping."

Oops. "I'm fine," I say again. "My shoes just hurt."

He puts his arm around my shoulders. Which doesn't help me walk at all, and doesn't lessen the pain or anything, but still, it's a sweet gesture.

The sidewalk and street are shiny from the rain, but it's stopped at last. The temperature feels a little warmer than it was earlier, and mist hangs heavy in the glow of passing headlights and the streetlights across the way in Madison Square Park.

There are twinkly white Christmas lights and poinsettias in store windows.

Oh, yeah. It's Christmastime.

Again, I think of Jack. I think of kissing him by the Rockefeller Center tree in the falling snow.

Buckley hails a cab for me and opens the door for me to get in. He's always been a gentleman, but now it strikes me as a romantic gesture, like the arm around my shoulder and the hand-holding in the bar.

He would be an attentive boyfriend.

"Night, Trace," he says, and bends to kiss me on the forehead before closing the door.

I smile and wave.

Then the cab lurches and I'm careening down the avenue toward home.

I reach for the seat belt. The buckle feels sticky.

Why is everything in New York so filthy? I fasten it anyway and wipe my hand on my jeans.

By the time I turn to take one last look at Buckley through the rear window, I can't spot him anywhere.

Oh, well.

I settle back against the seat and smile contentedly.

Buckley kissed me at last.

Wow.

Okay, *I* kissed *him*.

Still wow.

And I get the feeling that if I'd wanted it to happen again, it could have.

And it still can, considering that we have a date—a real date—on Friday.

Talk about complicated.

And exhausting.

I lean my head back against the seat, too weary to stress about the many grimy heads that may have touched it before mine.

I close my eyes and remember how Buckley's lips felt against mine.

Then I stifle a huge yawn and rub my aching neck muscles, longing to crawl into bed.

Five more minutes, and I'll be there. Alone—and grateful for that, for a change.

I've spent the last six months nursing a secret crush on Buckley, wondering what it would be like if he were my boyfriend.

Now that it's not such a far-fetched possibility, I'm starting to think it's not such a good idea to rush into things.

After all, Buckley has been there for me since June.

He's not going anywhere, and neither am I.

Except home for Christmas, which just might give me the rest—if not the perspective—that I need.

Jack called.

Oh my God.

He left me a message.

Oh my *God!*

"Hi, Tracey. It's me, Jack. I hope you're feeling better. Give me a call if you feel like it. I'm home. It's Sunday. Maybe you're out, or just...sick? I hope you're not still sick. Feel better. Okay, 'bye."

Standing there, staring at the answering machine as the tape whirs and rewinds, automatically erasing, I am stunned.

He sounded so...*normal.* Sincere.

Not at all like somebody skittishly trying to avoid a desperate woman who apparently considers him her boyfriend.

Is it possible that I didn't screw things up with him after all?

Is it possible that we're still...seeing each other?

But what about Buckley?

Talk about lousy timing. Why did he have to choose tonight to kiss me?

*Um, hello? You kissed him, remember?*

*Shut up with that already,* I scold my inner self. Buckley was

the one who brought it up. And he was *about* to do it. I just
took the bull by the…

What is it that you take the bull by?

The balls?

Or is it the horns?

Do bulls even have horns?

They definitely have balls.

So, apparently, do I. I mean, I grabbed Buckley and kissed
him. So it's as much my fault as it is his.

Thanks to me and my balls, Buckley and I have a date
Friday night to see the Rockettes.

But what if Jack wasn't traumatized from seeing that picture of himself in my apartment?

What if he'll be back from Atlanta on time and he wants
to see the Rockettes, too?

Too bad there isn't a way to go with both of them.

If I were a zany sitcom heroine, I'd buy another set of tickets and I'd take both Jack and Buckley to the show. But I
wouldn't tell them, because zany sitcom heroines are big on
secret capers.

I'd meet both guys there and I'd spend the night running
back and forth between the two of them, pretending to be
going to the ladies' room and back to the usher for another
program and outside for a cigarette.…

For a moment, I wonder if it could actually work.

Then I remind myself that I am *not* a zany sitcom heroine.

I am a real-life chick with a knack for sabotaging her own
love life.

Why did I have to ask Buckley to the show?

Why did I have to ask Jack?

It's all my Secret Snowflake's fault for giving me the tickets in the first place, I think grimly. My Secret Snowflake's fault, and of course Will's fault, because everything wrong in my life is Will's fault.

I look again at the phone.

Should I call Jack back?

Probably.

But I don't.

I'm too tired to think clearly, let alone carry on a rational conversation.

I crawl into bed.

My last thought, as I drift into a deep sleep, is that I'll probably dream about Jack. Or Buckley. Or maybe Jack and Buckley in a *ménage à trois.*

But I don't.

I dream that I'm starring in an all-nude version of *A Chorus Line* on Broadway. The drunks from the bar are playing the other dancers, and Will is playing one, too. It's opening night and the audience is packed and I'm all pumped up to go on.

Only, when I make my entrance—you guessed it.

The other dancers—Will and the drunks—are all fully costumed.

And there I am, wearing only a top hat, wondering why I didn't learn my lesson in *Hello, Dolly!*

Wondering why I never learn my lesson, ever.

14

Monday morning, I wake up convinced that I dreamed the answering machine message from Jack.

I try to check the machine, but of course the message has been erased.

Why didn't I keep it as evidence?

Now I can't call him back, because if I do and he didn't really call, I'll look like even more of an idiot than I already do to him, if that's even possible.

But if he didn't really call me and I don't call him back, it'll seem like I'm blowing him off.

Well, maybe he'll call again.

Or maybe he never will.

Maybe we'll meet some day as senior citizens, and we'll put it all together and rekindle the flame.

You know, like those people you read about in Dear Abby—the World War II vets and the girls they left behind.

The ones who never got together because one of them never got a letter the other sent, so their hearts were broken and they went off and married other people....

You've never heard about those people?

Well, it happens all the time. Trust me.

And it could happen to me and Jack, all because I might have imagined his phone call....

But then again, I might not have.

When I limp to my desk—my heels are now oozing blisters beneath the Band-Aids that keep peeling off—I half expect to find a Secret Snowflake gift waiting.

Mercifully, there's nothing.

The poinsettia is still there, drooping a little. Guess I need to water it. Or maybe it needs light or something. Maybe I should bring it home with me, since there aren't any windows anywhere near my cube.

I lift it off the desk, and several of the pink-and-white leaves promptly drop off, drifting to the floor.

Oops.

I quickly plunk it back onto the desk.

More leaves fall off.

It seems to be dying a slow death. How depressing.

I check my voice mail, hoping Jack might have left me a message.

Nothing.

I check my e-mail.

Nothing there, either.

Talk about depressing.

I bet I imagined that answering machine message.

I scroll through a long, boring e-mail from Kate about her long, boring weekend with Billy. She wants to know if

I want to meet her for lunch today since she has to return something to Saks and it's in the neighborhood. I write back that I'll meet her at Sephora, which is also in the neighborhood. I might as well spend my Secret Snowflake gift certificate.

Then I scroll through one of those chain-letter prayer things from my sister-in-law, Sara, who's too superstitious not to forward every single one she receives.

This one says that if you send it to everyone you know, something fabulous will happen within seven days. If you don't, something tragic will happen. It goes on to talk about all the people who won the lottery or were miraculously cured of cancer after forwarding the chain letter, and all the ones who were hit by a bus when they didn't.

I almost delete it.

I usually do.

But then my superstitious Sicilian gene takes hold, and I decide not to tempt fate. So I forward the chain e-mail. Not to everyone I know—just to Kate, Raphael and Buckley. Just to be safe.

I'm about to stand up when I notice that I've got mail again.

I click on the inbox…

Lo and behold, there's an e-mail from Jack!

Okay, that's freaky.

It's not like I really believed the chain-letter thing, but…

I close my eyes, count to three, open them again.

The e-mail is still there. Definitely not my imagination. And definitely from Jcandell, in-house, Blaire Barnett.

I check the date and time. It was sent one minute ago.

*Hi, Tracey. Hope you're feeling better. If you're here and reading this, you must be. Talk to you soon. Jack.*

"Hi, Chief. What's so funny?"

I look up from the screen to see Mike standing there, watching me. I realize I'm wearing a huge grin.

"Nothing," I tell him, too thrilled about the e-mail to remember to be embarrassed about falling down naked in front of him last week. "It's just some joke my sister-in-law sent me."

"What is it?" he asks, like he's all geared up for a good laugh.

"Oops, sorry, I just deleted it," I lie. "How was your weekend?"

"Busy. Dianne and I went skiing up in Vermont. Sorry to hear you were sick. Jack was disappointed about Saturday night. He had everything all set."

"He did?" I wonder what that means.

"Yeah, and he didn't want to waste all those groceries...."

Groceries?

"So he made the stuff anyway, last night. It was great."

"Stuff?"

"Yeah, the stuff he was going to cook for you. Something French—I can't pronounce it."

"He was going to cook for me?"

"You didn't know?"

"No."

That was the surprise. Oh my God. How freaking sweet. No guy has ever cooked for me.

Well, except Will, who thinks he's a good cook but who only used low-fat ingredients in whatever he made me, which I took as an insulting hint.

I bet Jack uses real butter and cream. French recipes always call for butter and cream.

"I didn't even know that he knew how to cook," I tell Mike.

"You didn't? I thought—"

"He said he had a surprise for me."

"Uh-oh. Then I just ruined it. Don't tell him, okay?"

"I won't," I promise. "I just can't believe he knows how to cook."

"Yeah, he told me he wanted to be a chef, but his father talked him out of it. Said he'd make more money in advertising, like he did."

"Jack's father?"

"Yeah."

"He's rich?"

"Yeah. He was a big creative director twenty or thirty years ago. He made a fortune, and then there was a big buyout in the eighties and he sold his share and retired young. He's a real bastard."

"Why?"

"He pushed Jack into advertising. He said he wouldn't pay for culinary school, only for an MBA. Then, when Jack graduated, he said he was through supporting him, and he wouldn't even help him get an interview. He said he did it on his own and he expected Jack to do it without his help. He wasn't thrilled when Jack landed in the media department."

"Why?" I ask. "Because it's low-paying and not the 'glam' part of the business?"

Mike shakes his head. "Don't tell Jack I told you his father's a bastard. You'll see for yourself when you meet him. And his mother's a snob, too."

I can't help feeling a little jolt of excitement at Mike's assumption that I'll be meeting Jack's parents.

"Wow. I had no idea he came from money," I tell Mike.

Not that it matters. I mean, I was into Jack when I thought he was a poor, starving media planner with a dumpy apartment.

In fact, he *is* a poor, starving media planner with a dumpy apartment.

"Yeah," Mike says, "you wouldn't think somebody from his background would be living in Brooklyn with me, would you? Maybe I shouldn't have said anything to you. Maybe he didn't want you to know."

"It's okay," I say quickly. "I won't tell him. Anyway, he did mention that his parents live up in Bedford and he has cousins in Scarsdale. He said they were stuffy."

He just failed to tell me that his parents apparently are, too.

Oh, well, who cares about that?

I can deal with stuffy in-laws as long as they're up in the suburbs and Jack and I are—

*Hold it right there, missy. What the hell are you thinking?*

Oops.

Even if Jack has forgiven me for framing us together, and even if he still wants to go out with me...

That doesn't change the fact that I'm not anywhere near ready for a relationship. I mean, if I were, I wouldn't be going around kissing Buckley.

*Going around? Come on, Tracey, it was one kiss.*

On long, luscious, lip-smacker of a kiss.

*Mental Note: One errant kiss does not a floozy make.*

And anyway, I only kissed Buckley because I thought I'd lost Jack.

Okay, and also because I've always been attracted to Buckley.

If I were ready for a real relationship, I'd be able to focus on one person.

Plus, I wouldn't still be hung up on Will.

Not hung up in the sense that I want him back, but hung up in the sense that I still think about him a lot, and I care about what he thinks of me.

And even though I mostly hate him, there's a tiny part of me that might still love him. Just a little. Just the nice part of him…which he keeps so well hidden that it's usually pretty easy to forget that part of him even exists.

My sister Mary Beth told me last summer that you don't just get over somebody you used to love by turning off your feelings for him. It's not that easy. No matter how badly somebody treats you, you have to fall out of love, just like you fell into it. And you have to *want* to fall out of love.

Mary Beth didn't want to. She couldn't let go.

Watching her take her cheating husband back was enough to make me swear I'd never give Will another chance.

Not that he even wanted one.

Anyway, I know in my heart—and definitely in my head—that it's truly over between us.

It's just that he keeps popping up in my life, damn him, and every time he does, it's not just a reminder of the good times I had with him, but also of how hard it is to be alone.

I want to be in love again, dammit.

Not with Will.

With Jack.

Or maybe with Buckley.

Or maybe just with *someone*.

I want to be a couple.

*You want it so badly that you're willing to plunge in head over blistered, oozing heels with whoever comes along and pays the slightest bit of attention to you,* accuses Inner Tracey.

I haven't even given myself a chance to be single for a while. I haven't even explored the dating world yet. I can't throw myself into a relationship with Jack or Buckley or anyone else until I've learned to be on my own first.

"Are you still with us there, Chief?"

I look up at Mike, realizing I must have a glazed-over expression on my face. "Nothing. I'm just tired. I guess I need some caffeine. I better go get coffee. I'm down a quart."

He laughs like that's the funniest thing he's ever heard.

I leave him and head for the kitchen, where I find Brenda waiting for the coffee to brew.

"How was your weekend?" I ask her.

"Sucky. Paulie and I had a fight. Don't ever get married," she says darkly.

Okay.

"How about your weekend?" she asks me.

I fill her in on Friday night with Jack and Saturday morning's fiasco.

She doesn't laugh the way Buckley did. She just pats my shoulders and tells me she totally understands how humiliating it must have been.

"It was," I say. "But he still called me last night, if you can believe that."

"What did he say?"

"He left a message. I was out with Buckley. Oh, yeah, and Buckley kissed me," I add.

Brenda's eyes bulge. "He did?"

"Well, no. I kissed him, actually. But it was his idea."

"I knew the two of you were going to hook up sooner or later!" Brenda says. "You're perfect for each other."

"What about Jack?"

She shrugs. "He's nice, too. But you've known Buckley longer. I can't see you getting serious about somebody you just met after what you went through with Will. At least you know Buckley is trustworthy."

"Jack seems trustworthy, too."

"Yeah, but Buckley is just so…wholesome."

"So is Jack," I tell her. To illustrate my point, I tell her how he was late for our first date because he was busy escorting a gaggle of little old ladies to Grand Central and carrying a disabled person and his wheelchair down the subway stairs.

"And you believe that?" Brenda asks.

"Of course I believe it."

She shakes her head.

"What? You think he could make up a story like that?"

"It doesn't matter what I think, Tracey. You're not going to listen to me anyway."

Actually, it does matter what she thinks. I don't trust my own judgment anymore.

And I can tell she doesn't think I should be so into Jack.

But I'm not in the mood to be convinced, so I change the subject.

"Is everything set for the bachelorette party Wednesday night?"

"Yeah. I told Latisha about Bodacious B and she was psyched. She said he sounds hot."

"Why does she think that?"

Brenda shrugs. "I guess just because his name is Bodacious

B. And anyway, Raphael found him, right? He's a hot-guy magnet."

"Who are we talking about? Raphael?" Yvonne asks, coming into the kitchen.

"How'd you guess?"

"He's the only hot-guy magnet I know," she says, then adds with a wink, "besides me, that is."

"Are you excited about marrying Thor?" I ask her.

"Honey, if anybody's excited, it's Thor," she informs me with her enviable supreme Yvonne confidence.

"I thought it was just a green-card marriage," Brenda says.

Yvonne waves her manicure airily. "Whatever. He gets the green card, and I won't kick him out of my bed, that's for sure."

I grin.

So does Brenda.

Yvonne pours a cup of coffee and leaves the room.

"I hope I'm like her when I'm that age," I tell Brenda.

"Yeah, me, too. Except for the wedding to the Swedish pen pal part. I plan to be married to Paulie forever."

"Yeah, I hope I'm long married by the time I'm Yvonne's age, too."

"To Buckley?" Brenda asks with a grin.

I give a noncommittal shrug. "Maybe."

"You're thinking Jack," she accuses.

"I am not!" I protest. "And anyway, what do you have against Jack?"

"I don't have anything against him. I just don't think you should rush into anything."

"Last week you told me how cute he was and that I should go out with him. And you just now finished saying I should marry Buckley."

"I didn't say that. Not exactly. And anyway, with Buckley, it wouldn't be rushing. You've known him forever."

"Just since last spring."

"Well, it seems like forever. And it is, compared to Jack. I just don't want to see you get hurt again, Tracey. You're still getting over what Will did to you."

"I won't get hurt again."

Not by Jack, or anyone else. My guard is up, no matter what my friends think.

"Be careful, Tracey."

"I will, Bren. I promise."


I limp over to Fifth to meet Kate at noon. As we browse through Sephora, she pretty much echoes Brenda's big "be careful" speech, much to my irritation. The way my friends are acting, you'd think I can't take care of myself.

Finally, just to shut her up and get out of the store, I buy some elaborate herbal concoction whose ingredients sound more like a recipe than a lotion. It comes in a tiny tube and costs ten bucks more than the gift certificate. I'm now officially broke until payday tomorrow and I haven't even paid this month's bills yet. Just one more thing for which I can blame my Secret Snowflake.

I'm in Saks waiting for Kate to exchange an outrageously expensive and ugly scarf she bought Billy for Christmas—for one that's even more outrageously expensive and ugly—when I could swear I spot Will over by the leather gloves.

My heart skips a beat, as always.

Then the man in question turns his head, and I see that he's about twenty years older than Will is. So old, in fact, that his hair is salt-and-pepper at the temples. He's got a double chin, too.

"What do you think?" Kate asks, showing me the ugliest and most outrageously expensive scarf of all.

"He'll love it," I say, turning away from old, fat non-Will, insanely jealous of Kate for having a boyfriend to shop for.

"You think?" She runs her finger along the gold cashmere fringe. "Because he's so fussy, and if I buy it for him, he'll wear it to make me feel good, but he won't want to."

"Come on, Kate, who wouldn't love that scarf?"

I lie because I know that's what she wants to hear, and because, in a mean-spirited way, I want Billy, who is strictly standard issue L.L.Bean meets Brooks Brothers former frat boy, to have to wear the god-awful thing.

Kate smiles and has it gift-wrapped, and by the time Billy's present is ready, it's too late for us to have lunch. Which is fine, because I'm too poor for that, anyway.

I scrape together enough pocket change to grab a yogurt from the deli on the way back up to the office.

I've had two spoonfuls when Jack—like his e-mail this morning—suddenly materializes out of nowhere.

"Hi," he says, in full showstopper dimple mode, his broad shoulders practically filling the doorway to my cubicle.

"Hi, yourself."

Cheesy, I know, but I can't help feeling a little breathless. His familiar, soapy-minty Jack scent wafts in the air. It's all I can do not to close my eyes and inhale like some bizarre stoner taking a hit.

"You look like you feel better," he comments.

"I do. Much."

"Good. In that case, want to go out with me tonight?"

"Tonight? I, uh…sure."

"Really? Great. I was disappointed about Saturday night."

"You were?"

He steps all the way into my cube and leans against a filing cabinet. "Yeah."

"Even after…"

*Shut up, Tracey. Leave it alone. No need to bring it up.*

"Even after the whole picture-frame thing?" I hear myself asking. Because, you know, I have to destroy all that is good and positive in my world.

I fully expect Jack's smile to fade, but instead the dimples deepen.

"Yeah, that was pretty crazy," he says. "For a second there when I saw the picture, I thought…"

He trails off.

"You thought…" I hum the *Twilight Zone* music.

He laughs. "Yeah, that's pretty much what I thought. But then you told me about your friend, and—"

What the hell is he talking about? What friend?

"I mean, I have friends who do stuff like that," he says.

"You do?" I'm clueless.

"Yeah, my friend Danny is always pulling pranks on people."

D'oh! Right. Naturally, he's talking about the prank-pulling friend who supposedly put the picture of me and Jack in the frame.

I almost feel bad all over again about lying.

Then again, he obviously bought it, so what the hell?

Besides, he asked me out again, and if I tell him the truth, he'll decide I really am some kind of nut job.

"I'm glad you're over it," I tell him. "I mean, it would freak me out if I saw myself framed in some guy's apartment, too, after only a week or two of going out."

"Yeah, frames shouldn't come into play until at least a month into a relationship," he says, so deadpan it takes me a second to realize he's teasing.

"You think?"

"Don't you?"

"I was thinking more like six weeks," I say with a flirtatious flop of my hair. "Or even two months. Two months, and you're definitely in the frame stage."

"That long?"

"Well, maybe six weeks," I amend. "In special cases."

"Or a month," he says, "in really special cases."

"Maybe."

We smile at each other some more.

It feels great to be back to normal with Jack.

Not that we've been together long enough to even *have* a "normal."

But maybe we can.

I know I shouldn't be thinking like this, but maybe, in a few weeks, I'll be able to take that picture of us out of the drawer and put it back into the frame after all.

Monday night after work, Jack takes me out to dinner at a cozy Italian restaurant in the East Fifties, right off Second Avenue. There's a piano bar and we hang out until late, drinking cappuccinos and singing along to Christmas carols. It's really fun. I love that Jack just loves to sing, even though he stinks at it.

Then we go back to my apartment. I don't even remember whose idea it was, and it doesn't seem to matter.

Tuesday morning, we ride the train to work together.

It feels strange walking through the lobby with Jack, and getting into the elevator with him. For a change, there's no wait, and for a change, it's empty when it arrives.

"What if somebody sees us?" I whisper to him as he presses the buttons for my floor and for his.

"Who cares?" he whispers back.

The doors slide closed.

He kisses me.

He's still kissing me when the doors open again on my floor, but he's right. Who cares?

Buckley calls me that morning.

"Are we still okay about Sunday night?" he asks.

"Of course," I say, trying to stifle a little twitch of guilt. "Why wouldn't we be?"

"Because you didn't call me yesterday."

"You didn't call me, either."

"I was waiting to see if you called me."

"Well, so was I."

That, and I was out sleeping with Jack.

But Buckley doesn't have to know that.

"Want to have lunch today?" he asks.

"I can't. I have to go shopping with Latisha and Brenda for X-rated bachelorette party gifts for Yvonne. We're going to some porn shop in the Village."

"Really?" He sounds intrigued. "Are you going to pick me up a pair of edible undies while you're there?"

"Buckley! That's disgusting!"

"Just kidding, Trace." He laughs. "About the underwear, anyway. Sounds sticky. But if you see something while you're browsing that you think I might like…"

"One set of handcuffs and a whip, coming right up," I promise.

"Great. We can try them out Friday night, after the show."

Thud.

My stomach just landed on the floor by my desk in the litter of newly dropped poinsettia petals.

I forgot all about Friday night.

Jack didn't even mention it.

Well, maybe he forgot.

Obviously, Buckley didn't forget.

"I was just kidding about the handcuffs, Buckley," I say nervously.

"What about the whip?"

"Oh, uh…"

He chuckles. "Relax, Tracey, I was kidding, too."

"Good. Because I, uh…"

"You're not into S&M?"

"No!" I pause. "Are you?"

See, this is one of the few things I don't know about my good friend Buckley. I mean, Sonja was pretty moody, and sometimes I thought he took a lot of shit from her. For all I know, that could have been only the tip of the iceberg. He could be into the whole dominatrix thing.

I have only one thing to say about that.

Ew.

"Of course I'm not into S&M," Buckley says. "You know I have a low threshold for pain."

Okay, that's true. Relief washes over me. Buckley freaks out over stuff like going to the dentist and stubbing his toe.

"So I'm not going to see you till Friday?" he asks.

"I guess not. Tomorrow I've got Yvonne's bachelorette party, and Thursday is laundry night with Raphael. We could have lunch—"

"Never mind. I'm working from home again this week, and I'm on a deadline. Friday's fine."

"Good."

He gives an odd little laugh. "This is weird, isn't it?"

"What?"

"You know…"

I do know, but I can't admit it. "What?"

"It's just…things aren't different, but in a way, they are."

"You think?" I ask, like I'm surprised.

But I'm not. And he's right. The kiss changed everything.

Now he isn't Buckley, the friend in whom I confide everything.

He's Buckley, the potential boyfriend.

"I guess I'll see you on Friday," he says.

"I guess you will," I agree, praying that Jack will get stuck in Atlanta—or that he forgot all about my inviting him to the show.

Jack didn't forget about the show.

He e-mails me first thing Wednesday morning with his trip itinerary from the travel department. *Look, my flight lands before five, so I can go to Radio City with you,* he writes, and tags on one of those little smiley face icons. You know, :-)

I write back, *Great news! I'm so glad! :-)*

Meanwhile, I'm totally thinking :-o

Now what?

Jack asks if we can go out tonight for dinner after work.

I'm almost glad I have to tell him no because of Yvonne's party.

He stops by my desk just before five o'clock.

"I wanted to say 'bye. I'm flying out first thing in the morning."

"Oh…I'll miss you," I tell him.

He leans over and kisses me. "Be good while I'm gone."

Be good while he's gone?

What the hell kind of thing is that to say?

I mean, it's not like we're married.

It's not like I'm not allowed to see somebody else if I feel like it.

It's not like—

"I hear that Bodacious B is hot stuff," he adds with a grin.

Oh.

"I'll try to keep my hands off of him," I say.

"If the party gets over early and you want to stop by on your way home…"

"You're in Brooklyn," I point out. "Not exactly on my way home."

He shrugs. "I'll be up late, so if you change your mind…"

I smile. "Thanks."

"Otherwise, I'll see you on Friday night. I'll call you when I land."

"Great."

With that, he's gone.

I'm still sitting there stressing about Friday night and which guy I'm going to blow off when Latisha sticks her head in a few minutes later.

"Brenda's waiting by the elevator. Ready to go?" she asks.

"All set." I stand and turn off my desk lamp.

"What about the chocolate penises?"

"Oops, forgot them." I reach into my drawer for the bag containing the party favors.

"Are you okay?" Latisha asks, peering at me.

"Yeah. It's just…"

"Jack?"

"How'd you know?"

"Brenda said you really like him."

"I do, but—"

"Take it one step at a time, Tracey," Latisha advises. "Don't go rushing into anything."

"I thought you were the one who said I should go for it with Jack."

"No, I didn't. I said be careful."

"No, you didn't. You said he had tight buns."

"Yvonne said that."

"Well, you agreed. Plus, you said not to listen to people who warn me not to fall for him. You said you and Derek didn't listen, either."

"Did I?" She shrugs. "Well, you and me are different, Tracey. You're younger. You're more…what's that word?"

"Vulnerable?"

"No…"

"Sensitive?"

"Nope…"

She ponders it as we walk toward the elevator bank.

My thoughts stray to Jack, and how sweet it was for him to come down to say goodbye. I find myself wondering how late the party is going to go tonight. If it does end early, maybe I really will go over to see him.

*But what about Mike?* Inner Tracey protests. *He'll be there.*

*And what about Buckley?*

*For God's sake,* I tell the annoying inner Tracey, *don't you ever just shut the fuck up?*

"Naive," Latisha says abruptly in a loud, lightbulb-going-off voice. "That's it. You're naive."

"Naive? Me?" I force a laugh, aware that everybody in the vicinity is eavesdropping. "That's ridiculous. I'm not the least bit naive. I'm about as naive as…as…"

Dammit. I can't think of a single soul who's suitably un-naive, so I just say again, "I'm not naive."

"Sure you are. You go around all starry-eyed, thinking some guy is going to come along and sweep you off your feet. You're just waiting for it to happen." Latisha waves her finger in my face. "And honey, it ain't like that. No guy is going to save you."

"Save me from what?" I ask, royally pissed off at her know-it-all attitude.

"Save you from yourself," she says. "From being alone."

I want to lash out at her….

But I can't.

Because when you come right down to it, isn't she telling me the same thing I've been trying to tell myself all along?

Maybe she's right.

Maybe I am naive.

Then again…

What if I'm not? What if Latisha—and everybody else I know—is too jaded? What if I prove them all wrong and marry my Prince Charming and live happily ever after?

I mean, fairy-tale endings have to happen to somebody.

Why not me?

# 15

When we get to the bar where we're having Yvonne's party, the table is all set up in the small back room. We invited twenty of Yvonne's closest friends.

Brenda, Latisha and I have about five minutes to put a chocolate penis at every place and blow up the balloons— also shaped like penises. The porn shop had a very limited inventory. It was penises or boobs, and we figured penises would be apropos for all the guests, except Yvonne's lesbian friend Char.

Soon the guests—including the guest of honor—trickle in. In no time at all, everyone is doing flaming rum shots and telling raunchy jokes.

"What time is Bodacious B supposed to get here?" Brenda whispers to me, about an hour into the party.

I check my watch. Uh-oh.

"Fifteen minutes ago," I tell her.

"Maybe you should go call Raphael."

"Good idea."

I'm on my way to do just that when I spot a short, balding, bespectacled guy hovering in the doorway. He's wearing a suit and tie and carrying a briefcase, obviously some displaced office drone, probably stood up by a blind date.

"There's a private party in here," I tell him politely.

He looks nervous. Pale, too. He's almost as white as his rumpled dress shirt.

"Is this the bachelorette party?" he asks.

I eye him warily. Okay, how does he know that?

"Yes," I say slowly, thrown by the *the*, "it's *a* bachelorette party, but…"

Then it hits me.

*Mental Note: Kill Raphael.*

"You're not…"

*Nah.* He can't be. He's the furthest thing from buff-and-black—not to mention bodacious—that I've ever seen.

But he's just standing there. Why is he just standing there, with that expectant look on his face?

He *can't* be. Can he?

I clear my throat and try again. "Are you Bodacious B?"

"No."

Sheer relief.

"I'm Steve. Bodacious B is my roommate."

He's Steve. Thank God, thank God, thank God he's Steve.

Then again…

"Where's Bodacious B?" I ask Steve.

"He, um, got called out of town on business, so—"

"Called out of town on business?" I cut in. "What kind of business? He's a stripper."

"Okay, the thing is, um, not really."

"He's not really a stripper?" I swear Raphael is so a dead man.

"No, I mean he really is a stripper. But he didn't really get called out of town on business. He just told me to say that, but, I, uh, guess I'm not a good liar."

*No, you suck at it.*

"So where is he?" I ask through clenched teeth.

"He's in jail."

He's in jail. That's swell.

"For what?" I ask, like it matters.

"Soliciting," he says, like I should've known. "He needs me to go bail him out, but I'm short on cash, so…"

I wait.

"So, what?" I ask finally.

So he wants a loan? Because he's definitely come to the wrong place for that. Between this party and Christmas, yesterday's paycheck is spoken for, and anyway, I don't even know Bodacious B, and I'm not about to put up bail for him. The nerve of some people….

"So I'm going to do the job," Steve says logically, "and then I'll use the money to get him out."

"The job?" I echo. It takes a minute to sink in. "You mean, *this* job?"

"Right."

"You're going to *strip*?"

"Yeah. I, uh, do it all the time."

He's right. He's a horrible liar. His neck is all blotchy above his tie.

The last thing I want is to see more of his blotchy skin, but he's a determined little bugger.

"My stage name is, um, Sexual Steve."

"Sexual Steve?"

This can't be happening.

"Look," he says apologetically, "I know you're thinking I'm no Bodacious B. But that's partly because of how I'm dressed. I had to come straight from the office…"

I look him up and down. Somehow, I find it hard to believe that there's a hunka hunka burning lurve under that Gentlemen's Wearhouse suit and polyester-blend button-down.

"Just let me do this," he pleads. "I promise I won't let you down."

Poor guy. I can see the sheen of sweat on his balding head. How can I hurt his feelings? I'll have to let him down easily.

"Listen," I say, "Steve…"

Or should I call him *Sexual?*

"I'll give you ladies a really hot show." He's almost pleading now. "Honest."

I doubt that. I really do.

Because he couldn't be hot if you poured rum over him and lit him on fire, and because only little boys who are lying say *Honest.*

But it's either Sexual Steve or nothing, and I promised everyone full frontal male nudity, so I sigh and say, "Fine. Do your stuff."

"Okay. Thanks. Listen, you wouldn't happen to have a boom box with you, would you?"

"Um, no. I don't usually carry one. Sorry."

He looks around at the roomful of chatting, drinking women.

"They don't carry boom boxes either," I tell him.

"Are you sure?"

"Positive."

"Okay, I'll just wing it without music. Which one is the bride?"

I point to Yvonne, who's standing under a No Smoking sign puffing away on a menthol.

"That old broad is the *bride*?"

Yeah, and the ugly little weasel with the paunch is the stripper.

Some party, isn't it?

As Sexual Steve goes to stash his briefcase under a chair, I can't help hoping maybe I'm wrong about him. Maybe he will give us a really hot show.

Uh-huh.

As I was just telling Latisha, I'm not naive.

Oh, noooo.

"Hey, who's the creepy little dude in the glasses?" Brenda asks, sidling up to me.

"Him? He's Sexual Steve," I say nonchalantly. "He's pinch-hitting for Bodacious B."

She sputters and chokes on her drink.

"Tracey…" she says when she can speak again.

"I know. I'm sorry. Bodacious B is in jail. What else can we do?"

Brenda goes into full Joisey-girl mode. "We can kick the little motherfucker out of here on his scrawny lily-white ass, that's what we can—oh shit, look. He's starting."

The room has fallen eerily silent, punctuated only by the throbbing bass from the barroom jukebox next door. Sexual Steve has removed his glasses and is standing there blinking. There's a red slash across the bridge of his nose from the glasses.

He gives a hollow-sounding, warbling, "Hellooooo, ladies!" and starts unfastening his tie.

Unfortunately, the knot seems to be stuck, and his hands are shaking like crazy. After much fumbling and a few curses, he finally unfastens his collar buttons and pulls it over his head.

"Dear God, no," Latisha says under her breath as Sexual Steve sashays over to Yvonne, swinging the tie around like a cowboy with a lasso.

I hear her mutter, "What the fuck?"

Sexual Steve loops his tie over her head like a noose, snagging it on her sprayed pink bouffant on its way down.

"Get the hell away from me right now before I step on you," Yvonne barks, patting her showgirl hair back into place.

He scuttles back to the front of the room.

Watching Sexual Steve strip is like sitting in the dentist's chair waiting for a root canal.

You can go for the novocaine—or in this case, a couple of flaming shots—but it doesn't fully numb the pain. You know what's coming, you wince, you close your eyes, you squirm, and you try your damnedest to avoid the inevitable, but in the end, you just can't.

It's utterly excruciating and it drags on, and on, and on, and all you can think is, *I'm actually paying to be subjected to this?*

I look around at the others as Sexual fumbles with the plastic white buttons on his dress shirt. They're mesmerized.

Not in a good way.

He struts around the room, removing one piece of clothing after another, bumping and grinding and shoving his crotch in front of a few of us like he's expecting tips, moving on when we recoil in horror.

The best thing about a root canal is that when it's over, nobody is naked.

The worst thing about Sexual Steve stripping is that when it's over, Sexual Steve is naked.

A moment ago, I thought nothing could be more heinous than him gyrating, doughy and blotchy, in his tighty whities, but I was wrong.

"Well, *hello*. Check it out. Looks like Sexual Steve is turned on," Latisha murmurs.

"At least somebody is," Brenda grumbles.

Looking smug, Sexual Steve takes a bow.

There's a reluctant smattering of applause. Actually, it only comes from me. The others are too busy being repelled.

"Thanks, Steve, that was, uh, great." I shove his bail money into his hand and start to hustle him out.

"I need to get my clothes," he reminds me, settling his glasses on his face once again.

Oh. Right. His clothes. Thank God for those.

I expect him to grab his stuff and slink out of here, but a miraculous transformation seems to have taken place. Gone is the cowering nerd of yore.

Sexual Steve has been liberated, proudly embracing his nudity. He flaunts his manhood like a flag-bearing honor guard, sauntering around the room collecting his clothes, stopping to make conversation here and there, apparently oblivious to the guests' blatant aversion.

Finally, he makes his exit.

For a moment, dead silence falls over the room.

Then Yvonne's friend Tammy swallows hard and says, "I feel queasy."

"Maybe it's all the rum," I suggest.

"Yeah, or maybe it's revolting Sexual Steve and his disgusting penis," Brenda snaps.

"If I hadn't sworn off men ten years ago, that would've done it for me," Char the lesbian announces.

"I think that just *did* do it for me," Yvonne says, fanning herself with her cigarette pack.

"Flaming rum shot, anyone?" I offer.

Tammy is still clutching her middle. "Maybe just some ginger ale."

The party breaks up pretty quickly after that.

In fact, it's barely nine o'clock when I let myself into my apartment. Much earlier than I expected to be home. I'll have time to clean the bathroom, which desperately needs it, pay all my bills that have been piling up and maybe even do a little reading before bed.

Or...

*You could call Jack.*

Nah. He didn't really mean it when he said that. And anyway, I've got a lot to do before I go away, so...

The message light on my answering machine is blinking.

"Hi, Trace. It's me, Jack. Just calling to say I hope you had fun tonight, and if it's not too late when you get back, give me a call. I'm here."

I smile.

Then I dial.

An hour later, dirty toilet and bills be damned, Jack and I are sprawled on the couch in his living room. We're eating Chinese food out of cartons and channel surfing, when a key turns in the lock.

"That's Mike," Jack says when I look at him in panic.

"I thought you said he'd be out late tonight."

"It is late, for Mike." Jack laughs. "Don't worry. It's no big deal that you're here."

"Are you sure?" I ask, because I'm right back into the whole awkward dating my boss's roommate thing. I set aside my chopsticks, the moo shu pork suddenly churning in my stomach.

"Positive. Mike loves you."

Two seconds later, Mike, who supposedly loves me, steps over the threshold with a woman I recognize as Dianne.

"Hi!" Mike says, looking surprised. "I thought you had a bachelorette party tonight, Chief."

"I did. It just, um, ended early."

"Stripper problems," Jack puts in. "Trust me, you don't want to know. Want some Chinese?"

"No, thanks," Mike says. "We just ate."

"I'm Dianne," Dianne announces, stepping toward me and sticking her hand out. "Since nobody's making introductions."

She shoots a snotty glance at both Jack and Mike.

"I was just about to," Mike says, suddenly nervous. "Dianne, this is Tracey."

"Hi," I say, smiling. She does seem a little Hilton Sisterish, but I'll give her the benefit of the doubt.

"I figured out who she was, Mike," she says. "Nice to meet you in person."

"You, too."

Suddenly I feel underdressed in my jeans and long-sleeved

T-shirt and socks. Granted, I'm just sitting on the couch, and she probably hasn't changed since work. But I didn't look anywhere near that put-together at work today, either.

Dianne is wearing a navy-and-green plaid wool suit that sounds ugly but looks great, and she has on sheer navy hose and navy pumps that match perfectly. Her gold jewelry is real. I know this because Jack told me; he said she picks it out and Mike buys it for her. I also happen to know that his credit cards are almost maxed out and he's always broke because he spends every penny of his salary on Dianne.

"So I guess you got over that breakup, huh, Tracey?" she asks.

"Um, yeah."

"That's great." She smiles. "I mean, just a few weeks ago you were heartbroken, and now look. You have Jack."

"Yeah." I can't look at him. I don't want to see his reaction to the fact that I "have" him. A lot of guys don't want to be "had." Doesn't Dianne know that?

"What are you two doing for Christmas?" Dianne asks, all friendly.

*Who two?*

She's looking at me.

*We two?* As in, me and Jack?

She can't be serious. Does she actually assume we're spending the holidays together?

"I'm going upstate to visit my parents," I tell her.

Jack remains silent, other than crunching some Chinese noodles.

"Is Jack going with you?" Dianne wants to know.

I look at Mike. He's busy hanging up his coat.

I look at Jack.

He smiles pleasantly, crunching some more noodles.

"No," I tell Dianne. "He, uh…"

What the hell am I supposed to say? I don't even know what he's doing for Christmas. Should I ask him to come home with me?

My parents would freak out. They think Christmas is for family. *Only* family. The year before Sara and Joey got engaged, they didn't even want him to bring her to my grandmother's for our Christmas Eve fish dinner. I can't show up with some guy from New York I've been dating for two weeks.

Jack saves me by saying, "I'm going skiing with my family in Colorado over Christmas, Dianne. I could have sworn I told you that."

"Did you? I guess I forgot." She yawns. "Well, good night, everyone. Come on, Mike."

He trails after her obediently.

"I told you," Jack says, as soon as they leave the room. "She's a—"

"Shh!"

He shrugs and grabs another handful of noodles.

Only when I hear the door close down the hall do I say, still in a whisper, "She's not that bad."

"She's a bitch on wheels."

"I didn't think she seemed bitchy. She was making conversation."

"She was being nosy. Why does she care what you're doing for Christmas? Every time I bring somebody home, she puts them through the third degree."

Okay, I know I'm not the first girl he's had in his apartment, but I don't really appreciate feeling like one in a constant parade.

Jack sees my expression and adds hastily, "Not that I bring people home much. Not lately, anyway."

"Because of Dianne?"

"No. Because it's been a while since I met somebody I wanted to spend much time with," he says, putting his arm around me.

He pulls me close and kisses me.

Then he says, "So you told me you went through a breakup, but you didn't mention that you were really heartbroken."

"Aren't breakups always heartbreaking?" I ask.

"Not necessarily." He shrugs. "My last few weren't."

"Were you the dumper, or the dumpee?"

"The dumper."

"Right. Only the dumpee gets their heart broken."

"I take it you were the dumpee."

I make a face. "Yeah. Can we talk about something else?"

"How about if we don't talk at all?" he asks, and leans over to kiss me again.

The next morning, I get up extra early to take a shower while Jack packs for his business trip. I fully intend to be out of here before Mike and Dianne get up.

I packed a bag before I came last night, so this time, I have my own toothbrush, underwear and two towels I brought along just in case.

There's a knock on the bathroom door as I'm combing through my wet hair.

"Yeah?" I ask in a hushed tone, assuming it's Jack.

It's not. It's Dianne, and she sounds aggravated.

"Can you hurry up in there? I have an early meeting, and I've been waiting for ten minutes."

"Oh! I'm really sorry. I'll be right out."

"Thanks."

I listen for her footsteps to retreat back down the hall, but they don't.

Which means she's standing there, waiting for me to come out.

Which means she wants me out now.

I had planned to get dressed first, to avoid a replay of last week's disaster. But I don't want to piss her off even further by making her wait, so I hurriedly grab my stuff, wrap one of my towels securely around my body and the other around my hair, and open the door.

Sure enough, Dianne is standing there, practically tapping her foot.

"Good morning," I say sweetly.

"Good morning," she says tartly.

"It's all yours."

"Thanks."

I tread cautiously down the hall toward Jack's room.

"Oh, and Tracey," she calls after me.

"Yeah?"

"Not to be a pain or anything, but you should really only use one towel when you take a shower here. In case you haven't noticed, these guys are short on towels and they don't do laundry very often."

I open my mouth to tell her they're my own towels, but the bathroom door has already closed behind her with a click.

Bitch, I think.

Jack is taking a car service to JFK, so I'll have to ride to midtown myself today—unless I want to hang out and wait for Mike and Dianne.

Which I don't.

"I'll see you tomorrow night," Jack tells me. "I'll call you as soon as I land. If I get in on time, we can get dinner before the show."

Right. The show.

Tell him.

"Sounds perfect." That's what I tell him.

After all, I invited him first.

And I really want to take him.

The thing with Buckley was…well, it was just an experiment. Not that I'm not attracted to him, and not that I want to hurt him….

Crap.

I don't want to hurt him.

But I don't want to hurt Jack, either.

And most of all, I don't want to hurt me.

As I stand there shivering in the icy morning air, watching Jack wave out the back window of a black Town Car as it pulls away, I realize that I've got a big decision to make in the next twenty-four hours.

No matter which way I go, a great guy is going to get hurt.

Thank God I have my weekly appointment with Dr. Trixie Schwartzenbaum after work. I know she won't tell me what I should do, but maybe it'll help to talk to somebody—even if she doesn't talk back, damn her.


"Good morning, Tracey," Merry says, sticking her head into my cube an hour later. "Did you bring your dish to pass?"

"Dish to pass?" I look up from my fat-free muffin, which is dry and flavorless—unless you count the chemical aftertaste—as fat-free muffins always seem to be.

"For the potluck."

*Welcome to Kansas, Dorothy.*

"What potluck, Merry?"

"The Secret Snowflake luncheon at noon," Merry says. "Did you forget?"

"That's today? I thought it was tomorrow."

"We had to change it because the Creatives needed the tenth-floor conference room and there was nothing else available. But the caterer wanted to charge extra to make it a day earlier so we decided to make it a potluck instead. I wrote it all in the e-mail."

"I didn't get it."

"So you didn't bring something to pass?" She looks around my office like she expects to see a covered dish peering out from under a stack of folders.

"I don't usually bring casseroles to work just for the hell of it, Merry."

"Oh, it doesn't have to be a casserole. I'm not bringing a casserole."

"What are you bringing?"

"I made a goose and a *bûche de Noël*."

Part of me would love to know where the hell one finds a goose in postmillennial Manhattan and what the hell a *bûche de Noël* even *is*, but another part of me just wants Merry to get the fuck out of my cube.

That's the part that snarls, "Well, I can't make it to the potluck today."

The nicer part of me adds, "Sorry."

"But…it's mandatory."

"No, it isn't, Merry."

"Yes, it is, Tracey."

"Let me guess. There's a list of Secret Snowflake bylaws, but somebody forgot to e-mail that to me, too?"

"You really don't have to get all snippy."

Yes, I really do.

Because I'm not in the mood for any of this. I've got two tickets to Radio City tomorrow night and two dates, and if that isn't more important than a potluck luncheon, I don't know what is.

I glare at Merry, hoping she'll get the hint and leave.

She doesn't.

I glare harder and send her a telepathic message.

*Just back out of the cube slowly and nobody gets hurt, see?*

She doesn't get that, either.

"Tracey, you really have to come to the luncheon," she says. "It's—"

"If you say mandatory one more time," I say, wagging my finger in her face like a wise-ass street punk, missing only a bandanna, a switchblade and a vocabulary dotted with Yo's, "I'm going to…"

What *am* I going to do?

I'd like to smush my fat-free muffin into her face, at the very least. But I've never been in a girl fight in my life, and I can't start now.

For one thing, it's a safe bet that beating up a co-worker is grounds for termination.

For another, it would probably get back to Jack, and something tells me wise-ass street punks aren't his type.

"Hey, Chief, what's going on?"

I look up to see Mike looming in the doorway behind Merry.

It's hard to believe that I once thought the *Chief* thing was cute. Now I think if I hear that one more time, I'll have to smush my fat-free muffin in Mike's face, too.

"Is everything okay?" he asks, looking from me to Merry.

"Mike, please tell her that there's no such thing as a mandatory Secret Snowflake luncheon," I say.

Mike blinks. "The Secret Snowflake luncheon isn't mandatory?"

"It is," Merry says.

"Yeah, just like the Secret Snowflake thing was mandatory."

"It *is*," she repeats.

"Then why am I the only one in my whole department who was suckered into doing it?"

"I did it, too," Mike says.

Oh.

Well, clearly, Merry and her committee prey on new employees who don't know any better.

"I thought it was mandatory, too," Mike says.

"It is," Merry says for the third time. This time, she adds, "In a way."

Mike and I exchange a glance.

"I can't go to the luncheon today," I inform Merry again.

"Then I guess you'll never find out who your Secret Snowflake is," she says primly, folding her arms.

She doesn't say *So There,* but she might as well.

I don't roll my eyes, either, but I might as well.

"It's probably better that way," I tell her, "because if I found out who my Snowflake is, I'd probably just want to ask her why the hell she spent all that money on me. I'd tell her how shitty it made me feel, getting gifts that cost at least ten times what I was spending on my own Snowflake every—"

That's when I catch the expression on Mike's face.

And in that terrible instant, my Secret Snowflake's identity becomes crystal-clear.


The day started off badly, and it goes rapidly downhill after the Secret Snowflake hullabaloo.

Merry beat a hasty retreat out of my office, and I wished Mike would follow her, but he didn't.

Instead he stayed to apologize—repeatedly—for showering me with extravagant gifts.

He told me that it was all Dianne's idea. Apparently, she felt sorry for me because I didn't have a boyfriend this Christmas.

She was the one who suggested that Mike pass along some of the gifts he gets from magazines and television stations.

It turns out everything he gave me—with the exception of the Sephora Gift Certificate, which he bought at Dianne's suggestion—was regifted. Even the tickets to Radio City were comps from one of the TV networks.

"I'm sorry, Chief," Mike said about a thousand times. "I was trying to do something nice for you. I didn't realize you were upset by it."

"It's okay, Mike," I said every time he told me he was sorry.

But the whole thing has left me with a bad taste in my mouth, and it isn't from synthetic muffin.

Just when I was getting over the whole tighty-whitie/naked fall, this put a whole fresh strain on my relationship with Mike.

I don't blame him if he thinks I'm an ungrateful wench.

Who in her right mind would be offended by a pile of expensive presents?

Never mind that Mike didn't pay for most of them...and that he only gave them to me because he and Dianne decided I was pathetic.

I should have accepted graciously and kept my mouth shut.

Well, I should do a lot of things.

Except the thing I *shouldn't* do.

Which I have an uncanny knack for doing.

Like inviting Buckley to see the Rockettes with me tomorrow night after I had already invited Jack.

I'm starting to suspect that I need to uninvite him ASAP.

Which *him,* you wonder?

I wonder the same thing.

I have Jack's travel itinerary, and I can call him at the hotel tonight if I want.

Or I can call Buckley at home.

But which guy should I uninvite?

I think I know.

But I need to run it by somebody first. Namely, my shrink.

Unfortunately, on Thursday afternoon, Dr. Trixie Schwartzenbaum's office calls to cancel my appointment. It seems she's taken a spill on an icy sidewalk and fractured her wrist.

Okay, there goes my plan to run the potential blow-off by Dr. Trixie Schwartzenbaum.

Since I don't trust my own judgment, and since I'm avoiding all of my work friends today due to the stripper disaster, and since I already know that Kate will automatically say I should choose Buckley over Jack, I'm left with only one person to turn to for advice.

God help me.

My laundry's already in the spin cycle and One-Sock Sally's taken up three dryers by the time Raphael breezes into the Laundromat with a sack full of laundry over his shoulder and a wicker basket in his hand.

Inside the basket, on a nest of white linen napkins, are a silver cocktail shaker and two glasses.

"No martinis for me," I tell him, holding up my Rolling Rock. "I can't afford to get trashed tonight. I've got a major decision to make."

I wait for him to ask what the decision involves, but he's too busy folding the linen cocktail napkins, setting up the glasses and saying, "These aren't martinis, Tracey. They're Brandy Alexanders, in honor of the boy I met last night at Oh, Boy. Guess what his name was?"

"Um, Joe?"

"No! Tracey, it was Alexander," he says, oblivious to my sarcasm.

"What happened to Carl?"

"He has a boyfriend," he says with an easy-come, easy-go wave. "Alexander is beautiful. Blond, like Carl. Tall, too. But not as meaty."

Eeew.

Speaking of meaty...

"If that's how it works, I should be drinking Sexual Steve Slammers today," I tell Raphael.

"Ooh, sounds yummy. What's in them?"

I smack him in the arm and snap, "They're not a real drink, Raphael, and it's a miracle I'm not a Juicebox convert after what I witnessed last night."

I fill him in on the whole sordid Sexual Steve tale.

Unlike Jack, he's sympathetic and horrified. No self-respecting gay male would be the least bit amused by the thought of a less-than-perfect physique being flaunted in a public forum.

Raphael shudders profusely, then apologies profusely. He also offers to make it up to me—by sending the newly sprung Bodacious B over to my place for a private lap dance.

"No, thank you," I say politely, because God only knows where Bodacious B's "lap" has been.

"Anyway, listen, Raphael, I have a huge problem and it's really been bothering me. I need you to tell me what I should do."

"Electrolysis," he says promptly, rattling the silver cocktail shaker above his head with both hands. "I've been hoping you'd ask."

*"What?"*

"Aren't we talking about your upper lip, Tracey?"

"No, we're not talking about my upper lip!"

My hand goes right to my recently—but apparently not recently enough—waxed mustache, courtesy of my Mediterranean heritage.

"Oh." Visibly troubled, Raphael pours himself a drink. "Are you sure you don't want one, Tracey?"

"I'm positive." I snatch the shaker from him and try to glimpse my reflection in its silvery surface.

*Mental Note: Price electrolysis while home for Christmas; will be cheaper in Brookside than Manhattan.*

"So if we're not talking about your upper lip, Tracey, what are we talking about?"

I plunk the cocktail shaker down on the table next to the laundry he's beginning to sort. "I need to run something by you, Raphael. It's about Jack. And Buckley."

"Delicious," Raphael pronounces, sipping his foamy white drink and closing his eyes in ecstasy. "Not as delicious as Alexander himself, but—"

"Raphael, please!"

"Sorry. I'm listening," he says in his best, soothing Frasier Crane voice.

So I tell him. About Jack, and about Buckley, and about the kisses and the dates and the tickets.

And as I talk, it becomes clear to me which guy I have to uninvite.

Good thing, because Raphael the lush is no more help than Dr. Trixie Schwartzenbaum.

By the time I'm done sorting things out aloud, he's done sorting his laundry, and half in the bag.

Raphael. Not the laundry.

"How much booze is in those Brandy Alexanders, Raphael?" I ask, plucking a wayward pair of red velour socks out of his pile of whites.

"I don't know. Do you think too much? I couldn't remember which was the jigger and which was the shot. Want to try some?"

"No, thanks."

I need to be clearheaded for the grim task ahead.

He answers on the third ring.

"Tracey!" he says. "I was just thinking about you."

"What are you doing?" I ask.

He sounds breathless. "Crunches," he tells me, and my lusty brain instantly downloads an image of his washboard abs.

Then I quickly shove it out of my head. I don't dare think of how attracted I am to him when I'm about to tell him I can't see him again.

Nor do I dare ask him why he thought of me while he was doing crunches, since he has to have noticed that my abs are not the least bit washboardy.

"Listen, I have to talk to you," I say, determined to stay on task, here.

"Uh-oh. Sounds serious."

"It is. I feel really bad, but…" I take a deep breath.

"You're going to tell me we can't go out tomorrow night, aren't you?"

Caught off guard, I sputter, "Why…who…what makes you think that?"

"I've been blown off enough times to recognize the tone."

"I'm sorry," I say, and to my horror, I start to cry.

"It's okay," he says. "I understand."

"You do?"

"Yeah. I don't think either of us is in the right place for this right now."

"You're a great guy," I tell him, meaning it with all my heart.

"I know I am. But not for you," he says.

"Right." I sniffle.

"Have fun with State Capital guy," Buckley says.

And, shoving aside a wistful little pang for what might have been, I promise him that I will.

16

The Saturday-morning flight from LaGuardia to Buffalo is oversold, and I have to admit, there's a moment when I actually consider giving up my seat.

Visions of Christmas in Manhattan with Jack dance through my head....

But only momentarily.

Because Jack won't be here for Christmas, remember? He'll be in Aspen, where his family has rented the same house every Christmas since he was ten.

So if I don't get home to Brookside, I'll be stuck here in New York for a solitary Christmas, and who, besides Will McCraw, who is his own favorite companion, wants that?

Certainly not me.

I slink down in my seat and I don't volunteer to get bumped.

Apparently, nobody else on the plane is interested in a

solitary Will McCraw Christmas because they don't volunteer to get bumped, either.

Which leads to involuntary bumping.

Which can get ugly, especially at Christmastime, and quickly does. It's like a *Survivor* tribal council featuring, in the Jeff Probst role, a fake-smiling, fake-blond flight attendant with fake boobs, pretty much manhandling those who have been voted off.

Finally, those of us who make the cut find ourselves in the air for the "short ride over to Buffalo," as the pilot puts it when he comes on the intercom. Pilots always make it sound so easy, like they're driving the carpool around the corner to school.

Meanwhile, there's snow. Snow and turbulence.

Such bad turbulence that I have my first full-blown panic attack in ages.

My chest is constricting, I can't breathe and I'm certain death is imminent.

The man on my right is calmly reading his *New York Times,* with its headlines about holiday travelers as terrorist targets.

The old lady on my left is clutching her rosary beads and muttering about Jesus, no doubt convinced she's about to meet Him in person.

I try to distract myself, first by reading the Caleb Carr novel Buckley lent me last summer and I never had a chance to read, then, when I can't get into nineteenth-century forensics, by replaying last night.

It helps a little.

Okay, it helps a lot.

Especially when I relive the part where I saw Jack striding toward me along Sixth Avenue as I stood in front of Radio City waiting for him, and he saw me, and his face lit up and his pace quickened.

In that moment, I knew I'd made the right choice, choosing him over Buckley.

No matter what anybody says. I really like Jack, and Jack really likes me, and I'm sick of overanalyzing our relationship.

Last night was wonderful.

So wonderful that if this plane freaking crashes, I'm going to be pissed as hell—if one can be pissed as hell in the Great Hereafter.

But the plane doesn't crash and my panic attack subsides and the next thing I know, I'm walking through the gate and into my sister Mary Beth's arms.

"Thanks for driving in and picking me up," I tell her when we're done hugging.

"Are you kidding? No problem. I stopped at Toys "R" Us on the way here, and I got all my Santa shopping done in an hour. The place was a zoo, but I was so happy to be out on my own that I didn't care."

"Where are the boys?"

"Home with Vinnie."

I guess she can tell by my expression what I think of him, because her round face becomes earnest and she says, "Things are going great with him, Tracey. Really. He's changed."

"I hope so, Mary Beth. For your sake. And for the boys', too."

"He has. Really!"

I wonder who she's trying to convince.

As we walk downstairs to the baggage claim, she fills me in on marriage counselling and tells me how happy my nephews are to have their dad living under their roof again.

I try to act enthused, but it isn't easy.

"All I'm doing is talking about myself," Mary Beth says as we stand by the idle luggage carousel. "What about you?"

I open my mouth to tell her about Jack, but before I can, she frowns and says, "You look skinny."

"Thanks."

"It wasn't a compliment."

I shrug off the classic Spadolini bluntness. "It was a compliment to me."

Mary Beth shakes her head, looking me up and down.

I'm carrying my down parka and wearing a black turtleneck, black jeans and black boots.

"Don't you eat anything anymore?" she asks.

"Of course I eat. Jut not as much as I used to." And not as much as she does, by the look of it.

I immediately feel guilty for noticing that she seems to have gained weight since I last saw her, at Thanksgiving.

But I can't help it. I know I'm being catty, but she's being judgmental, too.

And anyway, how can I miss the fact that the buttons on her red cardigan sweater are gaping at the boobs? The sweater is a hand-me-down from me, and it fit perfectly when I gave it to her last month.

It's pretty clear that my sister is rapidly becoming a clone of our mother, who is a clone of *her* mother.

Nor can I help thinking that there, but for the grace of God—and a huge spaghetti dinner every single Sunday for the rest of my life—go I.

"You know, men don't like scrawny women," my sister informs me.

I wonder where she heard that? Probably from my mother. Certainly not from Vinnie, who nags Mary Beth about her weight every time she puts something into her mouth.

"I'm not scrawny," I tell her.

"Yes, you are. You just can't see it. I've read about that happening. Your body image is distorted when you look in the mirror."

"That's what happens to anorexics, Mary Beth. I'm not anorexic."

She shrugs.

Luckily the baggage carousel beeps twice and lurches into motion, curtailing the conversation.

I step closer, keeping an eye on the heap of dark-colored bags rumbling our way. I tied a bright red ribbon to the handle of mine so that it would stand out.

So, it appears, did everybody else on my flight.

Finally I've got the right bag in hand, and Mary Beth and I are stepping outside.

The cold air hits me with a swirl of snowflakes. I shiver violently and zip my coat.

Mary Beth doesn't even flinch, and she left her coat in the car.

"It's Lake Effect," she says, trudging through the blizzard, jangling her keys. "We're getting a foot today and two feet tomorrow."

Snow.

Aspen.

Jack.

Funny how everything segues back to him in my newly obsessed brain.

I open my mouth to tell my sister that I met somebody, but she's talking again, telling me about the tool set she ordered for Vinnie for Christmas from the *Craftsman Tool Hour* on QVC.

Oh, well, it can wait.

Two days later, I still haven't told anybody about Jack.

At this point, I figure I might as well keep the news to myself.

My sister is wrapped up in Vinnie and the kids; my brothers won't give a shit; my parents won't be happy to hear that I've met a great guy unless he's from Brookside, is still living in Brookside, and has pledged never to leave Brookside.

The only person in whom I'd be tempted to confide is my sister-in-law Sara, but she's got a horrible case of the flu and has been home in bed ever since my plane landed.

This afternoon, as yet another—or perhaps one long, continuous—Lake Effect snowstorm rages outside, my mother, Mary Beth and I are in the kitchen working on the *cucidati*.

In case you were wondering—and I can't imagine that you weren't—*cucidati* are Italian fig cookies, kind of like trapezoid-shaped homemade Fig Newtons. They're a family tradition, as much a part of Christmas as the bright-colored strings of big oval bulbs my father staple-guns to the porch roof every December.

By the time I hit junior high, I wished we could have tiny

white lights like the Gilberts down the street, just as I wished we could get regular cutout Christmas sugar cookies from the bakery at Tops Market like the Gilberts down the street.

Of course, my mother turns up her nose at store-bought cookies and says they taste like sawdust. Personally, I think *cucidati* taste like poop wrapped in pastry, but I wouldn't tell her that.

The Gilberts never heard of *cucidati* until they moved to Brookside from the Midwest and met us. I know this because one December, when I was around eight, my mother sent me over there with a plateful to welcome them to the neighborhood.

Yes, this was back in the days when you sent a little girl to the new neighbors' house without worrying that they might be serial-killer pedophiles.

So there I was, all buck teeth and pigtails, offering the plate to WASPy Mrs. Gilbert, who peered under the foil and said politely, "They're...very nice. What are they?"

And even after I told her, she still didn't know.

Since moving away from Brookside, I've met plenty of people who've never heard of *cucidati*. In fact, I don't think I've ever met anybody who *has*.

Certainly none of my new friends would agree to spend two whole days in a steaming kitchen making twenty dozen of them, which is a three-man job. Rather, three women— because in the Spadolini family, the men don't cross the kitchen threshold unless it's time to eat.

Not that I mind making the *cucidati* this time. It's kind of cozy, and I'm feeling nostalgic, rolling out the dough as my nephews drive their Matchbox cars around the linoleum under the table the way my brothers used to do, and the Ray

Conniff singers croon "Silver Bells" from the stereo in the next room.

My life in Manhattan seems a world away, almost as though it belongs to somebody else.

"You're rolling too thick," my mother says, peering over my shoulder. She takes the rolling pin from me and expertly rolls out a patch. "See? Thin. Like this."

I try it. The dough crumbles.

"Here, let me try." My mother does it again.

Perfect.

I try again.

"Well, that's the way the *cucidato* crumbles," I say, when it falls apart.

My mother, who takes her Christmas baking very seriously, doesn't even crack a smile.

Switching to a flattery tactic, I tell her, "Maybe when I'm your age, Ma, I'll be able to do it as well as you can."

Yeah, like I have any intention of killing myself every Christmas to make a truckload of cookies nobody likes.

"When I was your age, I was doing it as well as I do now," she tells me. Then she shrugs. "Of course, I was married already and I had Mary Beth."

"I was married when I was Tracey's age, too," my sister observes from her sentry point by the huge tub of figs.

"That's right, you were," my mother agrees. "Speaking of getting married, Bruce Cardolini just got engaged to Angie Nardone. They're getting married on Valentine's Day."

"Angie Nardone? She's only nineteen," I say in disbelief.

"She'll be twenty next month," my mother tells me.

"Oh, well, then, that changes everything," I say sarcastically.

I keep forgetting we're in Brookside, land of child brides and twenty-five-year-old spinsters.

"We'll all be invited to the wedding," my mother says. "Bruce asked for your address after mass last week, Tracey."

"That's nice, but...I don't know if I can make it."

"Maybe you'll get to bring a date," Mary Beth says, as though that's the only reason I'd consider not flying home to Buffalo again in two months.

I realize that both my mother and my sister are looking at me as though they feel sorry for me.

I want to tell them that I'm leading a very fulfilling single life in the city.

So why do I blurt, "I met someone" instead?

They look blank.

Vinnie Jr. drives a miniature Harley over my sock-clad foot as I clarify, "I met a guy. A really nice guy."

"Are you getting married?" my mother asks, crossing herself.

"Is he weird like that Will was?" my sister asks.

Why did I have to go and say anything?

Too late to take it back, so I muster all my patience to say, "No, he's not weird, and I've only known him a few weeks so we're not getting married, but I really, really like him."

"Where's he from?"

"Westchester."

My sister, the home-shopping-channel addict, lights up with recognition. "That's QVC headquarters. In Pennsylvania, right?"

"No, not West Chester, Pennsylvania. Westchester County, New York. Right near the city."

"He's from the city?" My mother looks disappointed.

"No." I swallow a sigh. "He's from *near* the city."

"Where are his people from?" she wants to know, as she rolls out more dough on the flour-dusted vinyl poinsettia-covered tablecloth.

"His people? He's not an emperor, Ma," I say lightly.

She doesn't laugh.

"Tracey, you know what she means," my sister says.

She's right. I do. And that's why I'm feeling pissy. His ethnic heritage shouldn't matter to my family.

"I don't know where his people are from, Ma. His last name is Candell."

"That's not Italian."

"How do you know? Maybe it was Candellini or Candello, and the guy at Ellis Island shortened it."

My mother brightens. "Maybe."

"Or maybe it was Candellinski," I say, "or Candellowitz, or O'Candell or—"

"Maybe his mother's people are Italian," my mother decides. "Who was she from home?"

Translation from Spadolini Speak: *What was her maiden name?*

"I don't know who she was from home, Ma," I say as she checks the thickness of the dough, then keeps rolling. "I've never even met her or Jack's father."

"His name is Jack?"

"Yeah."

"Short for John?"

"I guess."

"You don't know?"

"No."

"Oh," my mother says with a tight-lipped little shrug.

"What *do* you know about him?" my sister asks as my nephew drives the mini Harley up my jeans leg making brrm, brrm noises.

"I know that he's bighearted, and smart and he, uh…"

*Mental Note: Do not mention state capital thing. They won't appreciate it.*

*Addendum to above: Do not mention vast Candell wealth. Re-member how Ma always bad-mouthed the Carringtons back when she was watching all those* Dynasty *reruns.*

"He what?" Mary Beth prods.

"He cooks." There.

*They can't criticize that. They cook, too.*

"He cooks?"

*Sure, they can criticize it. They can criticize anything.*

My mother frowns, deft hands working the rolling pin. "What, he's a chef?"

"No, he works in advertising, but—"

"You mean he cooks for *fun?*" my sister asks. "Like a hobby?"

"Yeah."

Clearly this, to the two of them, is as newfangled a con-cept as all-white holiday lights and store-bought Christmas cookies.

"He was going to surprise me by cooking dinner for me last week," I say.

"Why didn't he?" Mary Beth wants to know.

"Because I got sick."

"That's because you don't eat," my mother comments darkly.

Shit.

Before she gets on a you're wasting away to nothing roll,

I say brightly, "Jack went to Atlanta on business this week and he brought back peach jam for me."

"He sounds like a smooth operator," is my mother's response.

A smooth operator?

Yes, of course. How could I have forgotten that smooth operators frequently use Southern preserves to lure unsuspecting women to their lairs?

"Be careful, Tracey," warns my sister, devoted wife of Vinnie the Philanderer. "I'd hate to see you go jumping into something so fast."

"I'm not jumping into anything, Mary Beth."

"You just said you were thinking about marrying him."

"I did not. Ma said that."

"I didn't say that," my mother denies.

"Yes, you did, Ma. I said I met someone and you said, Are you getting married?"

My mother just shrugs.

My sisters says, "Tracey, you don't have good judgment when it comes to men."

Flabbergasting.

I say, "But—"

"Just don't let him break your heart," my mother says ominously.

"I won't, Ma," I say, because what else is there to say?

On Christmas Eve, Sara tells us that she doesn't have the flu after all; she's pregnant.

My mother and Mary Beth and my brother Danny's wife, Michaela, crowd around her, giving advice and asking questions and sharing morning-sickness stories.

I stand apart, feeling left out, longing for…

Something.

To be a part of the married mommy club?

Or to flee?

I don't know. I just have this unsettled feeling. Sara was my ally in the family, and now she's one of *them*. And here I am, single Tracey, living in New York, hopelessly hung up on a "smooth operator" who seems too good to be true and probably is.

At six on the dot, we go as a group to my grandmother's for seven different kinds of fish and *strufoli,* which are a heap of little honey-drizzled balls of dough covered in red and green sprinkles. Later we go, again as a group, to midnight mass, and then back home through the snow to drink wine and eat the sausage that has been simmering in the Crock-Pot since dusk.

There was a time when I could dig into sausage with peppers and onions at two in the morning, then climb into bed and sleep soundly till noon.

Those days are as over as my size-fourteen jeans.

I think about Angie Nardone getting married, and about Sara having a baby, and I feel like crying.

I don't want to be them….

Really, I don't.

But sometimes, it's kind of lonely being single.

Okay, excruciatingly lonely. I want to be in love. I want to belong to somebody. I want it so badly that…

*That you're not willing to wait for Mr. Right to come along? That you're trying to convince yourself that it can work out with Jack?*

Everybody knows that things that seem too good to be true really are too good to be true.

Which means, of course, that Jack will never call me again.

There's always Buckley....

No. There isn't.

He was great about the whole Radio City thing, but I know his feelings must be hurt. There's no way he's ever going to make a move on me again now, and I can't do it, either. Not after I blew him off once. It just wouldn't be fair to jump into his arms every time I'm lonely. Or horny. Our friendship is too important to me, and I get the feeling that Buckley and I are meant to be platonic. Period.

After a restless night and the worst case of heartburn I've ever had, I wake to the smell of bacon frying and the sound of my mother calling, "Tracey! Phone's for you."

Yawning, I fumble into my robe and go into my parents' room. Unlike the cluttery rest of the house, the master bedroom room is spartan: just a double—rather than queen-size—bed, a bureau with mass cards stuck into the mirror, and white-painted walls that are bare aside from a framed wedding picture and the obligatory plaster crucifix.

I sit on their neatly made chenille bedspread and reach for the telephone—blue, with a curly cord—that's on their bedside table.

I'm certain it must be Kate, who promised to call me from Alabama the second she gets engaged, *if* she gets engaged.

But it isn't Kate.

"Merry Christmas," a familiar male voice greets me.

My still-burning heart flops around excitedly. "Jack! Merry Christmas."

I can hear clattering pans and running water in the background. For a second, I think it's coming from Jack's end of the line.

Then I distinctly hear my mother say, "I don't know if it's him. I just said it was a man. She's not a teenager anymore. I feel funny asking his name."

Oh, crap.

"Hang on a second," I tell Jack sweetly. I hold the receiver against my robe and holler, "Ma! Hang up the phone! I got it!"

I put it back to my ear just in time to hear a clatter, and then silence.

"That's better," I say.

"Your mother sounded suspicious when I asked for you," Jack informs me.

"That's because she thinks you're a smooth operator."

"What?"

"Never mind. How's Aspen?"

"Snowy. How's Brookside?"

"Snowier, I bet," I say, glancing out the window to see a Christmas morning wonderland.

"I miss you," Jack says.

"I miss you, too."

"I was thinking I wished I had bought you a Christmas present."

Wow.

Smooth operator or not, too good to be true or not, I'm in love.

"You gave me that jam," I point out.

"Not jam," he says. "I mean a good present."

"You don't have to—"

"I know, but I wish that I had."

I smile.

"Yeah, me, too. I mean, I got all those presents for Myron…I could've picked up a little something for you. A football lollypop or something."

He laughs. "For the record, I'm a Giants fan."

"I'll remember that."

We chat for a few minutes more and make plans to see each other as soon as we're both back in New York.

I hang up, smiling, thinking that he did give me a Christmas present—and it was the best one I've ever received.

# 17

Back in Manhattan, the next few weeks pass in a happy blur.

Kate is planning her June wedding to Billy, who didn't give her a ring for Christmas but gave her one at midnight on New Year's Eve. She called me at my parents' house first thing the next morning to share the news. I was miserably hungover from too much cheap white Zinfandel at the annual Most Precious Mother church hall bash, but I think I managed to sound thrilled when Kate asked me to be her maid of honor.

Buckley and Sonja are giving it another go-round. She took back her living-together ultimatum, and he actually told me, over a game of pool last week, that he might consider living with her now that he doesn't feel so cornered.

Mike seems to have gotten over the whole Secret Snowflake thing. He even teases me about it now.

Merry doesn't, though. Whenever I see her in the elevator or cafeteria, she turns the other way. I doubt she'll ever speak to me again.

Raphael, as usual, has a new hairstyle, a new wardrobe and a new boyfriend. This time, it's Terence, who broke up with Bentley, who refused to laser before the first of the year. I guess he likes his hideous oozing growth better than he likes Terence, which works out well for everyone, particularly Raphael.

Yvonne is back from her honeymoon, and I have to say marriage agrees with our blushing bride. Okay, granted, the only thing that's truly blushing about her is her hair, but she's definitely softened a bit.

Brenda and Paulie are trying to get pregnant; Latisha and Derek are, too. I asked Latisha if she'd consider getting married first—or ever—and she shrugged and said she doubts it. I'd give anything to be as self-sufficient as she is.

Speaking of self-sufficiency—rather, my lack of it—Will keeps calling. He's left me at least five messages about the clothes he's holding hostage in his apartment.

I don't want to see—or even speak to—him until I've run it by Dr. Schwartzenbaum, who won't be available for at least another week. I guess I'm worried that seeing Will after all this time might undo all the progress I've made in getting over him.

And I really am getting over him.

Mostly because Raphael isn't the only one who has a new boyfriend.

Yup, Jack and I are a couple.

We've spent almost every night together since the beginning of January, mostly at his place.

The problem with my place is that I forgot to pay my bills

before I went away, and they shut off the cable. I spent so much on Christmas presents at Wal-Mart that when I got back, I was only able to pay the necessary ones like Con Ed and the telephone. It'll take me at least until the end of the month to be able to afford cable again.

So, since Jack and I both like to hang out and watch television at night, we've been spending most of our time in Brooklyn. Which is fine, even if Mike's around—unless Dianne is, too.

I can see now why she gets on Jack's nerves. When she's not being fake-nice, or talking to Mike in this annoying little-girl baby talk, she makes these nasty little digs. Mostly at Mike, but often at Jack and sometimes at me, too.

Like, she'll tell me how lucky I am that I can "dress down" for the office when I'm standing there in my best outfit.

Or she'll tell me I remind her of someone and she can never remember who, and then Mike will suggest flattering would-be doppelgängers like Sandra Bullock or Parker Posey, and Dianne will say "No!" in an *Are you high?* tone and I'm left paranoid that she thinks I look like Carnie Wilson pre–stomach-stapling surgery, even though I know that I don't.

I'm getting kind of sick of her.

Jack's been trying to cook that dinner for me for the past two weekends, and both times Dianne put a wrench in our plans.

The first time, she accidentally broke the oven dial off the stove and it took almost a week for the landlord to get it fixed.

Then Jack brought all the groceries once again and we

were all set for our romantic dinner, but Dianne got some horrible stomach bug and instead of going skiing with Mike or going home to her mother, spent the weekend lying on the couch while he waited on her.

Naturally, Mike, Jack and I all caught the bug, too. I spent twenty-four hours in the bathroom, half the time not sure if I should sit or kneel, cursing Dianne all the while.

"Why don't you just move?" I ask Jack one night when we've barricaded ourselves in his room so we don't have to play Trivial Pursuit with Mike and Dianne, the self-proclaimed champion of all board games.

"I'd love to, but if I move, I'm moving into Manhattan, and I can't afford to live alone," he says.

By now he's told me all about his parents' money, and how his father refuses to help support him. It's pretty much the way Mike said it is, but Jack doesn't seem to mind. He figures his dad just wants him to make it on his own, the way he did.

"Well, then, why don't you get a different roommate?"

He shrugs. "Most guys I know aren't interested in a roommate unless it's a girlfriend."

"You could answer one of those roommate-finder ads."

"Nah. I don't want to live with a stranger."

"You'd rather live with Dianne? Did you know she called you an asshole behind your back before I even knew you existed?"

He laughs. "She's called me one plenty of times to my face, too. I just keep thinking maybe Mike'll come to his senses and dump her." He pulls me close and kisses me, then says, "Why don't you and I move in together?"

My stomach flip-flops.

He's kidding, right?

I open my eyes.

It's hard to tell.

But he must be. We've only known each other six weeks.

"You're kidding, right?" I say.

He hesitates, then says, "Yeah, just kidding."

I'd be lying if I said I'm not disappointed.

But that's ridiculous.

I mean, people don't move in together after a few weeks.

Well, Billy and Kate did.

And now they're getting married.

But Buckley and Sonja broke up over moving in together after six *months*.

And Will wouldn't live with me after three *years*.

So, yeah, of course Jack is kidding.

Except that he's not.

I know this because he suddenly says, "I was lying, Tracey. I wasn't kidding."

I stare at him.

I have to feign ignorance in case I'm wrong about what he wasn't kidding about. I say, "Huh?"

But my heart is pounding.

"About living together. I wasn't kidding. My lease is up in April."

"But…it's January."

"It's almost February."

"So April is…it's two months away. Who knows what could happen in two months?"

"You mean, what if we're not together?"

I nod. The thought of us together is still so new that I actually tingle when I hear him acknowledge that we're a couple.

"We will be," he says, oozing confidence.

"How do you know?"

He kisses me. More tingles.

"Tracey, I've never felt this way about anybody else."

Tingles and goose bumps.

And my mother's voice, ominous.

*Smooth operator. Beware.*

"And you told me you've never felt this way, either," he goes on.

Did I say that?

Oh, yeah. I guess I did. In a moment of unbridled passion. I assumed he wasn't paying much attention. Geez, talk about multitasking.

"I don't want to scare you off," he goes on, "but I'm just thinking that if we're still together in a few months, there's no reason why we shouldn't try living together. You're here or I'm at your apartment every night as it is. Plus, we're both broke. It would be cheaper to live together and split everything."

He does have a point.

Still…scare *me* off?

*I'm* usually the one who's scaring people off. *I'm* usually the one who's craving a commitment from somebody who's frantically scrambling toward the Exit sign.

Suddenly, it's like I just don't know how to *be* in this kind of relationship. I don't know what to do, and I'm afraid of how I feel.

Because how I feel is…reckless. I feel like I want to say, "What the hell? Let's do it."

But I can't throw caution to the wind.

I can't, because Inner Tracey won't let me.

She keeps screaming at me to be careful. She keeps telling me that I'm so desperate to not be alone that I'm latching on to the first guy to come along since Will.

"Just think about it, okay?" Jack says over Inner Tracey's shrill admonishment.

I *am* thinking about it.

I'm thinking I should tell him he's crazy, and I'd be crazy, too, if I said yes.

"Will you, Tracey?"

"Sure," I tell him. "I'll think about it."

"You'd look great in the teal one, too," Kate says, grabbing a dress off the rack and adding it to the armload of pastel gowns she's holding.

We're in Kleinfeld, a vast bridal salon in Brooklyn. I hear it's a loony bin on weekends and during their famous annual sales, but the place is pleasantly empty on this slushy Monday morning in late January. Kate convinced me to call in sick, and Jack promised he won't tell Mike that I'm not.

He left for a business trip to Seattle early this morning. Jack, not Mike. I miss him already. He won't be back until Friday night.

"I look washed-out in teal," I tell Kate. "I think the red would be best on me. Or black."

"My maid of honor can't wear black," Kate informs me.

"People do it all the time."

"Yeah, in New York. We're getting married down South, remember? In June. And there are eight other bridesmaids, who are expecting pink dresses. Or lavender. I can't put them in black."

"Then what about red?"

Kate makes a face. "Try the teal, Tracey. Please? For me?"

"Okay."

We head toward the dressing rooms. Naturally, Kate the Control-Freak Bride is coming in with me.

Which I suppose is only fair, since she's buying my dress for me, since she's rich and she knows that I'm not and that I have to somehow scrape together plane fare to Alabama for the wedding in June.

She already bought her dress from a salon in Mobile. She's flying down every month between now and June for fittings.

"I'm so stressed out, Trace," she says, as we step into the dressing room and the saleswoman closes the door behind us. "Don't ever let anybody tell you six months is enough time to plan a long-distance wedding. It might as well be six weeks."

"Speaking of six weeks," I say, stepping out of my jeans, "Jack wants to move in together."

"Here, try this one first." Kate passes me the hanger holding the teal dress. Then, "What did you say?"

"I said, Jack wants to move in together."

"Is he crazy?"

"Of course he's not crazy," I say, even though I've secretly been wondering the same thing.

"Yes, he is, and so are you if you do it." Kate's twang is more pronounced, the way it always is when she's telling me what I should do.

And even though I've basically told myself exactly what she just said, I retort, "That's not fair, Kate. I didn't say you were crazy when you moved in with Billy."

"That was different. Billy and I moved in together for different reasons than you would be, Tracey."

"How do you know that? What are my reasons?" I pull the dress over my head. The full skirt swishes down over my bare, white, goose-bumpy legs.

"There's just one big reason, and it's that you don't want to be alone," she says, zipping the dress up the back for me.

Ouch. That's true, and it's almost as painful as my reflection in the teal dress.

I may have lost a ton of weight, but every ounce that still clings to my belly, hips and thighs is highlighted by slippery teal satin.

I grimace at myself in the mirror, and I ask, "Well, who *does* want to be alone?"

"I shouldn't have put it that way. I meant, you think you *can't* be alone. You haven't even given it a try."

"So, like, what? I'm just supposed to spend a year hibernating in my apartment before I'm allowed to date?"

"Of course not. You should date. I'm the one who told you to go out with Jack in the first place, when you didn't want to. Remember?"

"Yeah. So why are you changing your tune now, Kate?"

"Because it's too soon for you to jump into a permanent relationship, Tracey." She stands beside me, looking serene and beautiful in her creamy white sweater and trim khaki pants, her pale blond hair pulled back in a simple ponytail.

Next to her, I look like the jolly teal giant.

Our eyes meet in the mirror.

"I can't wear this, Kate," I say.

"No," she agrees. "You can't. It looks awful."

So do all the others, when I try them on. The pastels are bad; the metallics are worse.

The saleslady returns to see how we're doing.

"None of these are my color," I tell her.

"No, they aren't," she agrees. "How about red? With your dark hair and those big brown eyes, you'd be gorgeous in a red dress."

I don't dare look at Kate.

"No red," she says firmly.

Yes, but I'd be gorgeous in a red dress.

I was wearing one the night I met Jack.

He came over to me for all the wrong reasons.

But maybe—just maybe, no matter what anybody says—he stuck around for all the right ones.

After what happened with Kate, I wasn't going to tell Brenda, Yvonne or Latisha about Jack wanting us to move in together.

They might be over the Sexual Steve thing, but they're not over thinking that I rushed into the relationship with my boss's roommate. Lately, I tend to downplay to them the fact that I'm still seeing Jack.

Still, a few days after Kate tells me I'm crazy to consider moving in with him, I find myself spilling the whole story over a margarita lunch with the girls from work. I can't help it. I need advice, and if you can't turn to Dr. Trixie Schwartzenbaum…who can you turn to?

Your friends, that's who. They might not tell you what you want to hear, but at this point, I'm not sure what I want to hear.

"Don't do it, Tracey," Yvonne says promptly, in her raspy voice.

Okay, maybe that's what I don't want to hear, because disappointment crashes through me at her words.

"Why not, Yvonne?"

"Why tie yourself down at your age? You have plenty of time for that. Stay single as long as you can."

Coming from somebody who didn't get married until years after she got her AARP card, this doesn't strike me as particularly sound advice.

"But I really love being with him," I say, just for the sake of argument.

And okay, just because it's true.

"You can be with him and still have your own place," Latisha points out.

"But we're together all the time anyway. Would you believe that my cable got turned off weeks ago and I haven't even missed it?"

They don't look convinced. Of anything.

"Plus, I can tell that he really cares about me," I add.

"Well, if he cares that much," Brenda says dubiously, "why doesn't he just propose?"

Easy for her to say. The only thing that kept Paulie from proposing right after they met was that he was too young for a driver's license so he could go to the mall to buy the ring. They were a couple in junior high and engaged not long after high school. In her world, like in Brookside, that's the norm.

"It's too soon for us to even think about getting married, Bren," I tell her. "It's only been six weeks."

"Exactly. It's only been six weeks. I hate to see you jumping in headfirst with another guy so soon, now that you're finally rid of that asshole Will," Latisha tells me. "You should be living it up."

"Can't I live it up while I'm living with Jack?" I protest.

"We have fun together. He treats me really well. He even cooks for me."

"He does?" Yvonne raises an eyebrow. "What does he cook?"

"Fancy stuff. Well, he's going to. Saturday night. Mike and Dianne are going skiing, finally. Jack's making me a special dinner."

"Is that when you're supposed to tell him whether you're going to move in with him?" Brenda asks.

I shake my head. "He said to take my time and think about it."

But I already know what I should do.

Kate is right.

My work friends are right.

Inner Tracey is right.

I should say no.


"Of course you should say no," Buckley tells me that night, over coffee at the Barnes & Noble superstore near his apartment.

"Not because I'm jealous or anything," he adds quickly. "Just…it's way too soon."

"That's what I thought. I mean, think," I amend. "That's what I *think*."

He looks up doubtfully from his coffee cup. "Are you sure?"

"No," I admit. "I'm not sure. Every time I think it's ridiculous to even consider moving in with somebody I haven't even been dating for two months, I see him and I get all…"

"Smitten?" asks Buckley the copywriter.

I smile. "Yeah. *Smitten*'s a good word for it." A good

G-rated one, anyway. "And then I start thinking maybe I should just go with my gut for a change, instead of analyzing everything to death."

"And your gut is telling you to do it?"

"Yeah."

He shrugs and remains silent, toying with the edge of the white plastic bag full of books he just bought.

"What's the worst that can happen?" I ask him. "Wait, you don't have to tell me. I know. I'll get my heart broken again, just like with Will. But Jack is different, Buckley."

"It sounds like he is, but... Tracey, when you used to talk about Will back when we first met, he sounded like a great guy, too. You had your blinders on."

"I know I did."

"Maybe you still do."

"Maybe."

"Ask yourself why he wants to move in together so soon."

"Because he's ready to take our relationship to the next level?"

"Or because he hates his roommate's girlfriend and he hates living in Brooklyn and he can't find a new roommate?"

I scowl.

"I'm just quoting him, and what you told me," Buckley says with a shrug.

"I know you are. But that's just...circumstantial evidence. Those things might be true, but they don't mean that he doesn't care about me, too. Maybe he's just ready for a commitment at this stage in his life. And maybe he's head over heels in love with me. Did you ever think of that?"

"For your sake, Tracey, I really hope that's the case."

Yeah. So do I.

★ ★ ★

By Thursday night, I still haven't made up my mind about Jack.

I so want to believe that he's my Prince Charming....

I so want to believe that we're both ready for a live-in relationship....

But I'm not convinced of anything. Not after listening to what my friends had to say about it.

I mean, they know me better than I know myself, right? They knew that Will was wrong for me. If I had listened to them, I'd have broken up with him long before he did it for me.

What if I don't listen to them this time, and I get rejected again?

*Yeah, but what if you take a chance, and you don't get rejected again?*

*Mental Note: There goes Inner Tracey trying to be all take-charge again. Beware. She thinks she knows what she's doing, but she's the one who made you kiss Buckley.*

Then again...

If I hadn't kissed Buckley, I'd still be wondering what it would be like. I'd still be wondering if he could be my Mr. Right.

Now I've got that out of my system, and I know that he isn't Mr. Right, and I'm free to focus on Jack.

Or not.

Lugging two weeks' worth of laundry, I meet Raphael at the Laundromat. I blew off suds and suds last week because Jack invited me to a launch party for a new entertainment magazine.

Not that Raphael minded, since he was busy with Terence anyway. According to him, they're in love.

I give it two weeks.

One, if Raphael sets foot in Oh, Boy sooner than that.

He's waiting for me, this time with a six-pack.

"What happened to the cocktail shaker?" I ask, plopping my heavy sack of laundry onto the floor.

"All that hard liquor isn't good for me, Tracey," he says earnestly, handing me a Molson. "Terence said it's like poison in my system."

"What does Terence say about beer?" I ask, sipping, then sorting.

"He says it's healthier than hard liquor, but you have to watch the carbs. He's teaching me about nutrition. I'm really striving for a healthy lifestyle now. Oh, and, Tracey, he said we should only use scent-free detergent from now on, because the other kind can cause a rash."

"Does Terence have something to say about everything?"

"Almost everything. He graduated summa cum laude. Oh, and he's psychic."

I fight the urge to roll my eyes, and wonder what the paranormal and preachy Terence would have to say about my moving in with Jack. Or not.

I decide not to bring it up with Raphael.

And then, of course, I do.

I can't seem to help it. He's the only one of my friends who hasn't yet weighed in with an opinion.

Plus, Jack is constantly on my mind. I miss him like crazy, even though he calls me every morning and every night from Seattle.

Out of nowhere, as I'm adding detergent to my darks, I blurt it out. "I'm thinking of living with Jack."

For a second, Raphael doesn't seem to hear me. He's busy sending One-Sock Sally the evil eye, which she ignores, as usual.

Then he looks at me and shrieks, "Tracey! What did you just say?"

"I'm thinking of living with Jack."

"That's what I thought you just said! Tracey, you can't do that. You've only known him for a few weeks."

"A few months. And you've moved in with people after a few days, Raphael. In fact, I think you've moved in with one-night stands."

It never ceases to amaze me how hypocritical my friends can be. Especially Raphael the Healthy Lifestyle Striver, now opening his second beer in five minutes and lighting a new cigarette from the one in his hand.

"True, but we're not talking about me, we're talking about you, Tracey," he says. "I worry about you."

"That's sweet, Raphael, but don't. I can take care of myself. Really."

"Not if you're thinking of moving in with some guy you just met, you can't. Why would you want to tie yourself down now that you're finally free?"

"Because I hate being free," I say, feeling ornery. "I like being tied down. And I like—" maybe even *love* "—Jack."

"So? You don't have to move in with him. What's wrong with just being his girlfriend?"

"Nothing's wrong with that," I admit. "But…"

"So? Be his girlfriend. Keep your own place. Then, when you break up, nobody has to move anywhere."

"Maybe we won't break up, Raphael. Ever think about that?"

He shrugs. "Everybody breaks up."

"No, they don't. Some people get married."

He shrugs. "Same thing."

"It is *not* the same thing. Marriage is forever. Not everybody gets divorced."

"No, not everybody does," he agrees. "But did you ever see a married couple who was head over heels in love?"

"Plenty of times."

"Name one."

I think of my parents. My siblings and their spouses. Brenda and Paulie.

Okay, they're all still together, and most of them are still pretty happy.

But head over heels in love?

"You're so cynical, Raphael," I tell him. "I think it's sad."

"I think it's realistic."

He puts his arms around me and looks into my face, dead serious for a change. So serious that it scares me.

"I just don't want to see this guy hurt you, Tracey. Because you're a great girl, and you deserve the best."

I swallow hard over a sudden lump in my throat.

"Thanks, Raphael."

He's right, I think, as I stand with a cartload of wet laundry waiting for a dryer.

They're all right.

It's too soon for a commitment like that.

I can't do it.

I have to tell Jack.

Saturday night, I think, watching One-Sock Sally's black knee-high rotating behind the glass circle. I'll tell him Saturday night, when he cooks me dinner.

# 18

Jack calls me first thing Saturday morning.

First thing for him, that is, since he's still on West Coast time. I've been up for a few hours, but I haven't gotten out of bed yet. Not having television has given me a lot more time to read. And think. I've been lying here with my Caleb Carr book and trying to convince myself that not moving in with Jack is the right thing to do.

"Hey, you. I'm back," he croons as I clutch the phone against my ear. "Did you miss me?"

"Definitely," I tell him. "How was your flight?"

"Long," he says, "and late. I didn't land until after midnight. I wanted to call you, but I figured you might be sleeping. Or out."

"I was sleeping," I lie.

In reality, I was tossing and turning, wondering what Jack will say when I tell him I can't live with him.

What if he breaks up with me?

*If he does, then you're better off without him,* Inner Tracey informs me.

Easy for her to say.

I'm the one who would have to face the loneliness and heartache. I've noticed that she tends to keep a low profile when the going gets tough.

"What are you doing today?" Jack asks.

"Reading. What are you doing?"

"Shopping. You didn't forget about dinner tonight, did you?"

"Nope." I smile, envisioning the two of us at the tiny table in his kitchen, clinking champagne glasses over candlelight.

"Listen, about tonight…"

Oh, no. Please, God, no. Don't let him cancel. I've been looking forward to this all week. For weeks, in fact. And every time I think it's going to happen, something goes wrong.

*Mental Note: If he's calling to cancel, it's a sign.*

"What about tonight?" I ask nervously, crossing my fingers in my lap.

If he blows me off, it's definitely a sign that this just wasn't meant to be. None of it. Not just living together, but me and Jack in general.

"Just that…you don't mind if we, um, watch the Giants game, too, do you?"

My romantic vision of the two of us in his kitchen evaporates, but so, thank God, does the clammy fear that fate has thrown a wrench in our relationship.

"No," I say, "I, uh, don't mind. I mean, I like football."

Yeah, I like it the way I like church. I know other people are really into it, and I can't help feeling like I should
be, too, so I make an effort.

"I wouldn't care if it weren't the playoffs," he says. "If they
win, they're in the Super Bowl, so…"

"It's fine." I'm trying to sound upbeat. "I'm a Giants fan,
too."

"I thought you said you were a Bills fan."

"Only until they're out of the playoffs." Which, unfortunately, is earlier and earlier every season. "When the Bills are
out, I switch to the Giants. After all, I live in New York now.
They're my hometown team."

Even if they do play in Jersey.

We hang up, and I go back to my book, relieved.

I've read only three pages when the phone rings again.

"Hello?"

"Tracey! You're there!"

"Oh. Hi, Will."

I should have screened the call. He's the last person I feel
like talking to.

"I've been trying to reach you since Christmas," he says.
"How long did you stay up at your parents'?"

"Almost two weeks."

"Oh." Pause. "Then you've been back for a while."

"Yeah."

"Didn't you get my messages?"

"I did, but…I've been busy. I kept meaning to call you
back. Sorry."

"It's okay. So how are you? How was Christmas?"

My ears prick up. Will's asking how I am? And he's ask-ing about Christmas? Usually, he just launches into a long-winded monologue about himself.

*Mental Note: New attitude is evidence that playing hard to get works with Will.*

Not that I'm playing hard to get. But it's too bad I didn't think of it back when we were together. Things might have been different.

Not that I wish we were still together, or anything.

"I'm good. And Christmas was nice," I say. "How was yours?"

"Relaxing. I needed it."

"Yeah. Well, that's good."

"What are you doing tonight?" he asks.

What should I tell him? If I say I have a date, it might sound too casual. Jack is more than a date, and I want Will to know I have a boyfriend now.

In fact, I almost wish I were going to move in with Jack, just so that I could tell Will about it.

It's not that I haven't fallen out of love with him, because I just realized that I finally must have.

I mean, my heart didn't jump when I heard his voice, and it's been weeks since I thought I saw him on the street.

But it's only human to want Will to want me, right? Even though I no longer want him?

"Tracey? Are you busy tonight?"

"Actually, I am," I tell him. "I've been seeing someone for a while now, and…we have plans."

"Oh." He sounds disappointed. "I still have your stuff. I thought maybe you could come over and get it."

"Yeah, well…you can throw it all away, Will. Really. I wish you would. I don't want it."

*And I don't want you.*

Damn, it feels good to think that and mean it.

"Are you sure you want to throw it all away, Tracey?"

He's talking about the clothes.

"I'm positive, Will," I say.

And I am.

About the clothes, and about everything else.

Jack calls me back an hour later.

"Hi," he says.

Right away, I notice that he sounds funny. Not funny, *ha ha.* Funny, *I'm about to piss you off or hurt your feelings or make you cry or all of the above.*

Trust me.

After three years with Will, I know the tone.

"What's up, Jack?" I ask, trying not to sound like an anxious mother who's just opened her door to a police officer in the middle of the night. "Is everything all right?"

"Everything's great," he says, and I can tell immediately that everything most certainly is not great.

"In fact," he goes on, "my friend Ben just called me…"

He trails off.

Oh, crap.

This is so painful. I have to nudge him along.

"Is he the one you met in college? The one who's a media supervisor over at OMD?" I ask, quite the aficionado in all things Jack-related.

"Yeah, that's him." He sounds surprised. "Good memory, Tracey."

"Did something happen to Ben?"

And what does Ben have to do with me?

And why couldn't it wait until I see Jack tonight, whatever it is?

"No, Ben's fine. Great, in fact. He just scored four tickets to the Giants playoff game at the Meadowlands tonight. Can you believe it?"

"No, I can't."

*Code Red. Code Red.*

*Home-cooked dinner has been aborted.*

*Repeat: Home-cooked dinner has been aborted.*

"Yeah, the seats aren't great," Jack says over the sirens in my brain, "but who cares? It's the Giants in postseason."

*You must calm down, Tracey.*

*This is not a sign.*

*If he were cancelling the date, that would be a sign.*

*So he'll cook you dinner another time. You'll go to the football game with some other couple—does Ben have a girlfriend?—and you'll snuggle together under the stars. It'll be fun. At least you'll be together.*

"That's great, Jack," I say, but my voice sounds hollow. "What time is the game?"

"Not till tonight, but actually, I've got to leave soon.

We're driving, and Ben wants to stop off at the mall to ex-change something."

*I've* got to leave soon?

*I've* got to leave soon?

I'm so stunned that I can't find my voice.

I'm not going to the football game?

*We're* not going to the football game?

*He's* going to the football game?

With Ben, and…

And who?

"Tracey? Are you still there?"

"Yeah. I'm still here. Who's going?" I ask, trying to sound casual.

"Oh, just some of the guys. Otherwise, I would have brought you along. But they weren't my tickets, and Ben… well, he wanted it to be just the guys."

"Oh."

Breathe.

Swallow.

Speak.

"So who's going?" I ask, because it seems important.

"You know…."

*No, Jack, I fucking don't know, you fucking asshole.*

"Ben," he says again.

"Yeah. You said Ben."

"And Tommy. Did I ever tell you about Tommy?"

"The one who works at Goldman Sachs."

"Right. You're great with details, Tracey."

"Thanks," I say shortly. "Who else?"

I need names, here. I need to know who I should hate forever for taking Jack away from me on our home-cooked dinner night.

"Just Pat," he says.

"Which one's Pat? The one who still lives at home with his parents?"

"Uh, yeah...that's Pat, but he's not the one," Jack says. "And he's technically living in the mother-in-law apartment above his parents' garage now that his grandmother went into a home, so..."

Is it my imagination, or is he hemming and hawing?

"So who's *this* Pat?" I practically spit into the phone.

"Pat is, uh, actually Patty. She used to work at Blaire Barnett, too. But I call her Pat sometimes, so..."

*She.*

*Her.*

Pat is Patty. Pat is a woman.

And he wasn't going to let on, the bastard. He was going to let me think Patty was Pat, one of the guys.

"I thought you said just the guys were going to the game," I say, stung.

How could he do this to me?

"It is...mostly. Patty's like one of the guys. She's a bigger Giants fan than the three of us put together. Plus, she's the only one who's got a car. We need her to drive."

"Oh."

My throat aches from trying not to burst into tears.

My friends were right.

He is a jerk.

Okay, they didn't say he was a jerk.

*I'm* saying it.

"Tracey, are you okay?"

'No," I say, "I'm not."

"You're mad about the game?"

"Yes, I'm mad about the game. We haven't seen each other in a week. I missed you so much—"

"I know," he says. "I missed you, too."

"Yeah, right. Then how could you do this to me?"

"Look, I'm sorry. I just…when Ben called about the tickets, I got excited. I guess I just didn't think you'd mind. You were so great about it when I asked you before if I could watch it tonight, so I figured—"

"You figured wrong, Jack. I can't believe you'd just blow me off like this. I mean, the least you could have done is invited me to go, too."

"I told you, it's a guy thing."

"What about Patty?"

"She's just like a guy," he says, sounding bewildered.

"Yeah, I'll bet."

"Are you jealous of *Patty?*" He sounds incredulous.

And I sound like a screaming shrew.

"No, I'm not jealous of Patty. I'm not jealous of anyone. I'm just…I'm pissed off at you. I thought you were different. I didn't think you were a selfish asshole like…like…"

*Like Will.*

"Well, I guess you were wrong, huh?" he asks coldly.

No more Mr. Nice Guy.

"I guess I was. Good thing I found out now, before…"

*But you weren't going to move in with him anyway, remember?*
*You were going to tell him no, remember?*

Shaken, I say, "Have fun at the game."

"Yeah," he says curtly. "Believe me, I will."

I slam the phone down without a goodbye.

It takes almost an hour for the tears to subside.

When they finally do, I'm left with eyes that feel freshly poached and a throbbing head that might as well have been repeatedly squeezed between subway doors.

I make my way to the bathroom, where I splash cold water on my red, blotchy face, and I tell my reflection, "You're an idiot. A complete and total *naive* idiot."

How could I have fooled myself into thinking Jack was a great guy?

*Because you wanted so badly for him to be The One, that's how.*

Yeah, and he put on a good act, between the talk about moving in together and the cooking and the...the peach jam.

Oh, Lord, my mother was right.

He really is a smooth operator.

How did she see it from four hundred miles and two generations away, and I didn't see it when it was right in front of my face?

Yeah, well, I didn't see it last time, either.

With Will.

When will I learn not to listen to my heart, but to my friends and family instead? Clearly, they know what's best for me.

And clearly, it isn't Jack.

I feel tears welling up in my eyes again.

I can't believe it.

He seemed so genuine, I think, sniffling.

I reach for a tissue, but the box on the back of the toilet tank is empty and has been for a couple of weeks now. I've been so busy with Jack that I haven't bothered to buy more.

I blow my nose on a wad of toilet paper.

The roll is just about empty, and I'm all out of that, too.

Is that the most depressing thing you've ever heard? That I was supposed to be at Jack's place having a romantic dinner, but, instead, I'm going to be out buying toilet paper?

And I can't even lose myself in mindless TV during the long, lonely weekend that stretches—

The phone rings.

Startled, I glance at it.

*It's Jack.*

Terence isn't the only one who's psychic.

I'm as certain that it's him as I've ever been about anything before in my life.

He's calling to tell me he made a mistake.

He's going to say that he wants me to go to the game with him.

Or, wait, no! He's going to say that he's so sorry, and he gave his ticket away and he's cooking dinner for me at his place after all.

I stare at the phone as it rings again.

Okay, if it's Jack, and he says that, it's a sign.

It's a sign that we're meant to be together.

I take a deep breath, cross myself for good measure and pick up the receiver.

"Tracey?"

It's not Jack.

It's not a sign.

I deflate. "Hi, Will."

"I was just thinking—I have to be in the Village later this afternoon to pick up some sheet music from my voice teacher. Why don't I just drop off your clothes then?"

Why doesn't he just drop off my clothes then?

Because I told him to throw them away, that's why not.

Why doesn't he get the hint?

"Will—"

Wait a minute.

There's no reason Will shouldn't come over here to drop off my clothes.

No reason at all.

What am I so afraid of?

It's just Will.

It's just clothes.

"Come on, Tracey, I'll be right in the neighborhood," he says. "I know you said you're busy, but I thought that wasn't until later."

He wants me, I realize. He wants me because he can't have me. The tables have turned. Now *he's* the one who's jealous and cajoling, and *I'm* the one who's elusive and evasive.

It should feel good, but it doesn't. Nothing could possibly feel good right now.

He asks again, "So can I stop over?"

Hatred reels through me. Hatred toward Jack for cancel-ing our plans, hatred toward Will for all the hurtful things he ever did to me.

But I hate myself most of all.

And I know Will doesn't want to come over here because of the clothes I left in his apartment.

I know it, and he knows it, too.

I open my mouth to tell him to go to hell.

Instead, I tell him to come on over to my place.

And anyway, at the moment, that's kind of the same thing.

I spend the next hour rushing around cleaning my apart-ment, and the hour after that taking a shower, putting on makeup, fixing my hair, getting dressed.

I might be sick to my stomach and heartbroken over Jack, but on the outside, I've never looked better.

Now there's nothing to do but sit here and wait. Will won't be here for another forty-five minutes.

I pace over to the window and look out.

The late-afternoon sky hangs low with storm clouds. Good. Maybe it'll rain on Jack at the Meadowlands. Or maybe it'll snow.

Snow would be better, because snow might remind him of me and that night at Rockefeller Center.

No, it won't.

That was fake. He wasn't feeling anything then, so why would he remember? It was all a part of his Nice Guy act.

There's that damned lump again, rising in my throat.

Because the thing is…

It didn't *feel* fake.

Nothing about him felt fake.

When I look back over the last six weeks with Jack, I try to find evidence that he's a selfish jerk, but there isn't any.

There's nothing but—

The intercom by my door buzzes.

Startled, I look at the clock.

Will is early. Way too early.

Oh, well, it's not like I have anything else to do, besides sit here and wallow in self-pity.

I stand up and go over to the panel by the door to buzz him in.

I take one last look in the mirror as I wait for him to climb up four flights of stairs.

I'm wearing a red dress.

Not the one from the party. That's too fancy.

This is a red sweater-dress, one that hugs my curves. The deep shade of crimson makes my hair look darker and my eyes look bigger.

When Will sees me in this dress, he's going to want me.

But…

But I don't want him.

Not anymore.

The truth washes over me like a refreshing wave on a stifling day, taking my breath away.

I don't want him.

I'm not going to do this.

I'm going to tell Will what I should have told him long ago: To get the hell out.

Out of my apartment, out of my life.

I'd rather be alone....

And you know what?

I've always *been* alone.

How's that for a bombshell revelation?

I was more alone than ever when I had Will.

And you know what else?

I never "had" Will. If I had listened to my heart when I was with him, I would have realized that.

I'd have understood that what I felt for Will wasn't love.

It was infatuation.

Love is...

Love is...

Okay, I don't know what love is. But I definitely know what it isn't.

There's a knock on the door.

I steel myself and reach out to open it.

*Jack.*

"Dianne's right," he says. "I am an asshole."

I just stare at him.

He's wearing a down jacket, and under it, a Giants jersey and jeans. He's holding a brown paper bag in one arm, with leafy greens sticking out the top. In the other arm is the biggest bouquet of red roses I've ever seen.

"These are for you," he says, thrusting them into my hands.

"But..."

He can't afford them. They must have cost him a month's worth of utility bills.

"So are these," he says, holding up the grocery bag. "But they're heavy, so I won't hand them over. Your stove works, right? And you have pots and pans?"

I nod. My heart is pounding; my thoughts are racing. I just stand there clutching the roses, staring at him.

This is the sign, I think.

The sign I was looking for.

The sign that it's meant to be.

Jack looks down at the floor, then back at me.

"I'm sorry," he says quietly. "Really, really, really sorry. I don't know what the hell got into me. I just...I really wanted to go to that game, and I'm not used to stopping to think about anybody else's feelings first. I know it makes me sound like an insensitive clod, but...that's what I am."

"No," I say, and swallow hard. "You aren't."

"Yes, I am. But I'm going to try really hard not to be, from now on."

"But...what about the game tonight?"

He shrugs. "We got as far as the other side of the Lincoln Tunnel before I came to my senses. So I got out of the car and I walked until I found a bus stop, and when the bus came, I took it back to Manhattan. I would've been here sooner, but it was running on a Saturday schedule. So was the subway. Plus I had to stop at the florist and the grocery store."

"For me," I murmur. "You did all that for me."

"Yeah," he says. "I'd do anything for you, Tracey."

"Even give up the Giants? Because my cable is still turned off, so if you stay—"

"I know. I can't see the game. It's fine."

"It is?"

He shrugs. "I'll catch them in the Super Bowl."

"They might not make it."

"I might never have another chance with you. Will you forgive me?"

Remember how I vowed to stop listening to my heart?

Remember how I concluded that I don't know what's best for me?

Well, I was wrong.

It's time to start trusting Tracey.

It's time to start taking chances.

It's time to start doing what I want to do, and the hell with what everybody else wants me to do.

And what I want to do is…

Take a chance on Jack.

He's not perfect. Nobody's perfect. Not Jack. Not me. And not our relationship.

But it's what I want. I don't have to try being alone.

Been there, done that.

Time to move on.

So I tell Jack, "Yes. I forgive you."

He steps into my apartment, sets down the groceries and opens his arms.

I close the door and step into them.

We kiss for a long time.

When we're done kissing—at least for now—he says, "I

have something else for you," and he reaches into the pocket of his coat.

He pulls out a flat, rectangular gift-wrapped package and hands it to me.

"What is it?" I ask.

"A present. Something that you need."

I tear off the wrapping with trembling fingers.

"A picture frame," I say, a bit puzzled. "It's...it's really nice."

"Yeah," he says, dimples deepening.

And then it dawns on me.

"It's for the picture of us!" I tell him, and he grins and hugs me.

For a split second, I'm elated. And then I remember.

Twinge of guilt.

Shred of doubt.

"Jack," I say, because I have to. Because it wouldn't be fair if I didn't. "There's something I have to tell you."

"What is it?" He pulls back to look down at me, concern in his eyes. "Is something wrong?"

"I lied," I say.

"About what?"

I take a deep breath.

"Remember the morning you saw the picture of us in the frame? And I told you that one of my friends put it there as a prank?"

"There was no friend. You did it yourself."

Stunned, I ask, "How did you know?"

He tilts his head. "I just figured."

"But...I thought you believed me. You said—"

"I didn't want to embarrass you. I knew you were mortified."

"And it didn't scare you off? Knowing that I'd done something like that? Knowing that I wanted you to be my boyfriend so badly I framed a picture of us?"

"Maybe it scared me for a split second," he admits.

Then he says, "Okay, for a little longer than that, since we're being totally honest here. But then I realized I missed you. And that maybe I wanted you to be my girlfriend. And I still do. I still mean what I said about living together, Tracey."

"You still want to do it?"

He nods. "Do you?"

Yes.

I do.

But just to be safe, I say, "Can I think about it for a few months?"

"Sure. My lease isn't up until April."

"Okay."

We smile at each other.

A lot can happen in a few months.

A lot just did.

As if to punctuate the realization, the door buzzes.

Jack asks, "Are you expecting somebody?"

So Will actually showed. Imagine that.

"No," I tell Jack. "I wasn't expecting anybody."

"So do you still have that picture?" Jack asks.

I nod.

"Where is it?"

"It's in the drawer."

The door buzzes again.

Jack asks, "Do you want to check and see who that is?"

"I'm sure it's not for me. Ignore it."

He shrugs. "Okay. So...do you want to get the picture out of the drawer?"

I do want to, and I do get it.

He puts it into the frame and carries it over to the windowsill.

The door buzzes again.

I smile, watching as Jack gently but firmly moves aside the other pictures—the ones of Raphael, and Kate, and my work friends and my family.

He puts the picture of the two of us right in the center.

"There," he says. "How does that look?"

*Like it's right where it belongs,* my heart tells me.

And this time...

I listen.

On sale in March from Red Dress Ink...

# Fat Chance

## by Deborah Blumenthal

*Fat Chance* is the story of plus-size Maggie, also known as America's Anti-Diet Sweetheart, who is perfectly happy with who she is and the life she leads. Until she gets a call from Hollywood's most enticing bachelor, Mike Taylor. Bursting with wit, insight and heart, this delicious novel reaches beyond the story of Maggie O'Leary to every woman who has tried to find fulfillment. *Fat Chance* is a lusciously guilt-free pleasure that is good to the last page!

*"Fat Chance* is a modern Cinderella story... and great fun!"
—Susan Issacs, author of *Long Time No See*

**RED DRESS INK**
TM

Visit us at www.reddressink.com                    RDI03041-TR

Also available in March from
the author of *Guilty Feet*...

# Spitting Feathers
by Kelly Harte

Tao Tandy has escaped her suburban life and
boring fiancé to live rent-free in an exclusive
London mansion—in exchange for...baby-sitting
a parrot (ah, life is too easy). And her luck doesn't
end there, because Tao then lands a job with a
gorgeous TV celebrity. But there's a catch—there
always is—while Tao starts off jumping for joy,
she soon finds herself spitting feathers!

RED
DRESS
INK
TM

Visit us at www.reddressink.com
RDI03042-TR

Available in March from
the author of *Carrie Pilby*...

# Starting from Square Two

by Caren Lissner

Twenty-nine-year-old Gert Healy thought she
would never have to return to the craziness of the
dating world. Would never have to worry about
what to wear and what to say and whether she
was pretty enough. But the death of her husband
two years earlier has forced her to clad up in
miniskirts and leather jackets and brave it...again.
But does Gert have it in her to fight through the
singles crowds in search of a second miracle?

It's back to square one on everything. Well, actually, she's done it all before. Square two, then.

"Debut author Caren Lissner deftly delivers
a novel that is funny, sarcastic and
thought-provoking. (4 stars)"
—*Romantic Times* on *Carrie Pilby*

**RED
DRESS
INK**
™

Visit us at www.reddressink.com

RDI03043-TR

# Who was Tracey Spadolini before she was *Slightly Settled?*

## Pick up a copy of *Slightly Single* by Wendy Markham and find out.

## Praise for *Slightly Single*

Another "undeniably fun journey for the reader."
—*Booklist*

**RED DRESS INK**
™

Visit us at www.reddressink.com

RDI0102R-TR

# Are you getting it at least twice a month?

## Here's how: Try RED DRESS INK books on for size & receive two FREE gifts!

### Here's what you'll get:

### Engaging Men *by Lynda Curnyn*

Angie DiFranco is on the age-old quest to get her man to pop the question. But she's about to discover the truth behind the old adage: be careful what you wish for....

### Cosmopolitan Virtual Makeover CD

Yours free! With a retail value of $29.99, this interactive CD lets you explore a whole new you, using a variety of hairstyles and makeup to create new looks.

## YES! Send my FREE book and FREE Makeover CD.
### There's no risk and no purchase required—ever!

Please send me my FREE book and gift and bill me just 99¢ for shipping and handling. I may keep the books and CD and return the shipping statement marked "cancel." If I do not cancel, about a month later I will receive 2 additional books at the low price of just $11.00 each in the U.S. or $13.56 each in Canada, a savings of over 15% off the cover price (plus 50¢ shipping and handling per book*). I understand that accepting the free book and CD places me under no obligation ever to buy any books. I can always return a shipment and cancel at any time. Even if I never buy another book from Red Dress Ink, the free book and CD are mine to keep forever.

- - - - - - - - - - - - - - - - - - - - - - - - - - - - - - - - - - - - - - - - - - - -

160 HDN DU9D    360 HDN DU9E

Name (PLEASE PRINT)

Address                                                          Apt. #

City                    State/Prov.                    Zip/Postal Code

In the U.S. mail to:
3010 Walden Ave., P.O. Box 1867, Buffalo, NY 14240-1867

In Canada mail to:
P.O. Box 609, Fort Erie, ON L2A 5X3

## Order online at www.TryRDI.com/free

RED DRESS INK ™

RDI03-TR

On sale in September from Red Dress Ink

# Lucy's Launderette

## Betsy Burke

Ever had the feeling that your life is spinning
out of control? Lucy has! Despite her degree in
fine arts, she is working as a professional gofer
for an intolerable art gallery owner, her
free-spirited grandfather has just passed away,
leaving behind his pregnant girlfriend, and she is
the only sane member in her eccentric family.
Read LUCY'S LAUNDERETTE to find out what
finally puts Lucy back on the road to happiness.

**RED**
**DRESS**
**I N K**
™

Visit us at www.reddressink.com                    RDI09031-TR